Annika Rose

Annika Rose

a novel

Cheri Johnson

Red Hen Press | *Pasadena, CA*

Book design by Mark E. Cull

Library of Congress Cataloging-in-Publication Data

Names: Johnson, C. M. (Cheri M.), author.
Title: Annika Rose: a novel / Cheri Johnson.
Description: First edition. | Pasadena, CA: Red Hen Press, 2024.
Identifiers: LCCN 2023040165 (print) | LCCN 2023040166 (ebook) | ISBN
  9781636281209 (paperback) | ISBN 9781636281216 (ebook)
Subjects: LCGFT: Bildungsromans. | Novels.
Classification: LCC PS3610.O32367 A84 2024 (print) | LCC PS3610.O32367
  (ebook) | DDC 813/.6—dc23/eng/20231013
LC record available at https://lccn.loc.gov/2023040165
LC ebook record available at https://lccn.loc.gov/2023040166

The National Endowment for the Arts, the Los Angeles County Arts Commission, the Ahmanson Foundation, the Dwight Stuart Youth Fund, the Max Factor Family Foundation, the Pasadena Tournament of Roses Foundation, the Pasadena Arts & Culture Commission and the City of Pasadena Cultural Affairs Division, the City of Los Angeles Department of Cultural Affairs, the Audrey & Sydney Irmas Charitable Foundation, the Meta & George Rosenberg Foundation, the Albert and Elaine Borchard Foundation, the Adams Family Foundation, Amazon Literary Partnership, the Sam Francis Foundation, and the Mara W. Breech Foundation partially support Red Hen Press.

First Edition
Published by Red Hen Press
www.redhen.org
Printed in Canada

ACKNOWLEDGMENTS

I'm grateful to the Minnesota State Arts Board and the Metropolitan Regional Arts Council for supporting the writing of this book. Thanks are also due to the many organizations that have supported my work over the years: the McKnight Foundation, the Bush Foundation, Yaddo, the Fine Arts Work Center in Provincetown, and the Knight Foundation.

Many people offered valuable insights on this project. Thanks to Amanda Rea, Steven Polansky, Will Bush, Charlie Conley, Amanda Coplin, Julie Johnson, Kerry Berg, Jeff Lambert, Carolyn Johnson, Joseph Laizure, Kevin Fenton, Salvatore Scibona, Sari Fordham, Bryan Bradford, Bob Cowgill, Doug Green, Steve McClure, Tom Boyle, Michael Walsh, Michael Hinken, Emily Graff, Sarah Bowlin, Siân Griffiths, Neal Karlen, Katy Nishimoto, Jennifer Thompson, and Eric Struve. I'm probably missing someone. If I am, please let me know so I can buy you a drink.

My deepest thanks to everyone at Red Hen for your careful attention to this book and to Melanie Conroy-Goldman for choosing it.

Thank you to Ted Schneider and Jennifer Erickson for your expertise on all things forest-related. And to Kerry Berg, my first writing partner. The world changed when I met you!

I'm grateful to my family for always being willing to trade stories that helped sharpen my memories about everything from hoof clippings to porcupines. I have that rare type of family filled with people who are endlessly curious, creative, and full of love and boundless enthusiasm for one another's projects and interests. I know how lucky I am to have all of you. Just to name a few: my mother Carolyn, Tami & Julie, Uncle Al & Aunt Robyn, Jamie & Alie, Uncle Ted & Aunt Lisa, Aunt Carol & Uncle John, Abbie & Alex, Kim & Joe, Penny & Dan, Aunt Gene, Cheri & Bruce, Kristina & Doug, and Gretchen, Steve & Louisa. Dad,

Grandpa Del, and Grandma Betty: your voices and knowledge fill these pages. I miss you dearly.

Thank you to my teachers and mentors at Lake of the Woods School, Augsburg University, the Hollins University MA in Creative Writing and English program, the Loft Mentor Series, and the University of Minnesota MFA in Creative Writing program, for teaching me not only how to write, but how to think and read deeply.

To my friends who always believed in my work and never let me forget it and inspired me with your own work, I owe you everything.

Thank you to Eric Struve, for always encouraging me to take risks and supporting me when I do.

Bob Schneck, without your timely phone call, this book might never have happened. I am grateful to you!

For my mother and my father

I

CHAPTER 1

In the weeks following her high-school graduation, Annika Rogers waited for a moment of elation and relief that did not come; and in the last week of June, she suffered a long, lonely, quiet morning, when even the dry rasp of the gelding's tail against the wood of his stall startled her and made her skin creep.

She struck out walking on the gravel road. She turned from County 4 onto 66 and saw a girl in front of the Blocks' old house, flagging her down.

Annika stood on the road for a minute chewing her thumb. The girl was a stranger, and her sudden appearance against the flat green and gold landscape was as startling as if someone had barged in on Annika when she was in the bathroom.

The girl beckoned more intensely. Annika stayed still. A terrible thought had dawned on her. Someone standing in front of the Blocks' house meant that most likely someone had also been inside and had seen what was in there.

Annika stared at the girl. The girl stopped waving and stared back. Finally, inaction became unbearable and Annika turned into the dirt driveway. When she was almost to the house, the girl called out, "Hi there, have you seen a gray cat?"

Annika shook her head. No. She had not seen any gray cat. She had seen a few other cats of various colors, picking their way distastefully out of the wet ditch. She didn't say any of this out loud.

She came haltingly the rest of the way down the drive. The girl resumed clanking a spoon in an empty tuna can, watching Annika uneasily. She was big, fleshy, striking-looking, about Annika's age, almost eighteen. "I'm Tina," she said, and added pointedly that she was moving into the Blocks' house with her husband. He had just gone out back, so . . .

Annika cleared her throat and introduced herself, pointing to the country blue single-wide where she lived with her father, a half mile south on County Road 4.

Tina relaxed then. "Okay," she said. "I was starting to think that maybe . . ."

She explained that several things had happened on her new place in the last ten minutes. She had lost track of her cat, right after she discovered something strange.

A jolt went through Annika's heart. She sneaked a look at a first-floor window of the house, impossible to see in as it reflected the bright summer light.

In the driveway was a van, behind it a pickup. Annika hadn't seen a vehicle at the Blocks' place for over a year, though that didn't mean that all that time there had been no one in the house.

"Oh," she said, losing her breath, "what was it?"

"What was it?" Tina said. "It's a cat?"

"What you found in the house?" Annika said.

Tina cocked her head; she said she thought she'd heard a meow. She dropped the can and spoon on the grass and began to sift carefully through piles of junk dotting the yard. Scraps of old siding, cinder blocks. Under the refuse, the grass was flat and yellow.

Annika spotted the cat's eyes glinting in the shadows under the wooden front steps and Tina went down on her knees to coax it out. Afterward, she rose again to her full height—and she was tall for a woman. Perhaps so as not to dazzle the short and spindly Annika too much, Tina stood squatly, her feet apart like a duck, her hands in the back pockets of her shorts. The gray cat—Tina introduced it as Charlie—dragged its tail over her long bare legs.

When Tina asked, in a gentle tone intended for a child, what grade she was in school, Annika corrected her with a grimace. Then Tina studied her, unembarrassed. Annika felt, as she often had, that she must be awfully funny-looking. Small, too small, and with her blazing yellow-crimson hair.

Tina was very pretty, her hair long and almost exactly the attractive red-brown color of a summer deer.

Had turning into the driveway been a mistake? They might be headed for an awkward moment if Annika couldn't hold it together and keep her mouth shut.

Originally, she'd been heading for the Blocks' pasture. She felt the loss of that easy, peaceful afternoon, the sweet, nutty smell of field grasses, the rigor of digging for rocks amongst the tough roots, each clunk in her leather bag.

And yet, at the same time . . .

Tina peered again around the yard, before turning back to Annika. "I don't know where Jesse got to. Do you want to come into the house and see the funny thing I found in there?"

Annika stared at her. A pucker formed between her eyes. It appeared there so often it was already leaving a wrinkle.

"All right, for a minute," she said.

She had been in the Blocks' house, a tattered but roomy old frontier building, once or twice when that family still lived here, and many times since. She had begun breaking into the house over a year ago. Today, as always, it was as dusty as a barn, the walls largely unfinished, the light dim and watery, some of the windows covered in drooping swells of plastic nearly opaque with dirt. The kitchen held the odor of mildew and an undefinable animal smell.

Annika trotted ahead to find the living room emptied of everything she'd left there, thank God! She sighed, almost shouted, with relief.

Then her heart was light. And she felt a warm, golden swell of excitement and joy. Yes—the feeling she had been waiting for all summer.

She rejoined Tina in the kitchen and fell into her proper place behind her, letting Tina take the lead through the house. Tina was stuffing a plastic bag of candy wrappers into an already bursting garbage can. She said they had been driving for two days, six hundred miles north from Iowa City. She picked up her cat and kissed it. Then she looked around the dim room with obvious pleasure.

"I can't believe it. This place is *big*! The only stand-alone place we ever lived in was a trailer," she said.

Annika blushed. Though even the comment, which might or might not have been intended as an insult, in this glowing moment could not really get her down.

In any case, she had her revenge. Tina lifted the window next to the oven, and Annika bit her tongue and smiled. When Tina took her hands away, the window slammed down and she screamed.

"We'll be out of our trailer soon," Annika said, thinking of the tight fit of the toilet in the single-wide's bathroom. Her own toes touched the wall opposite when she sat down; she couldn't imagine how her father managed it.

They were building something else, she told Tina. A gorgeous log A-frame.

"Oh . . . that's right . . . Sorry . . ."

Tina was still shaking from the window.

"Look how jumpy I am," she said. "You'll see why."

Annika followed her through the hall with its exposed wall joints and thick pink sheets of scratchy insulation. In the living room, where a couch had been dropped haphazardly, she bent down to pet the cat. The cat's long gray hair was snarled with burrs and Annika scratched them out gently and rubbed around her white ears with her other hand. She picked the cat up and bounced and patted her like a baby.

"Charlie's got a tick on her butt," she said.

"It's up here." Tina was waiting at the base of the stairs now, looking impatient.

Annika kneeled slowly to deposit the cat, hiding her face. She realized that the drawings she'd left here could simply have been moved to another place in the house, instead of being thrown away.

But on her way up the stairs behind Tina, looking at her tall, curvy figure in her skimpy clothes, Annika was also feeling grow within her the strange sensation that she hadn't spoken for years, that her vocal cords desperately needed exercise, and that the sound of her voice was as clear and true and sweet as a bird's.

She started chattering, informing Tina that the northern Minnesota forest was most likely a whole different sort of animal than what she would have known in Iowa.

"Oh—how's that?" Tina said.

"Well. We've got all the big carnivores. Bears, wolves. Big cats, too. And I'm not talking about bobcats. We've had those. But the lions are new. The DNR says people are seeing things, but everybody's seen them."

"Have you?"

"I think one night I saw a big black one going across the road!" Annika skipped up the last two steps. She kept talking until Tina interrupted her.

"This is it," she said.

They were at the door that led to the attic. A narrow door with a metal knob—Annika had never opened it. She had always stayed almost exclusively downstairs. The empty second floor was cold in the winter, unbearably stuffy when it was hot.

Now, a barrel blocked the entrance to the attic: a rusted oil drum, nearly four feet tall.

The pucker appeared again on Annika's forehead. She kicked the barrel with her toe, and it rang out like a real drum.

Tina was walking around it, her bronze-painted fingernails pressed to her mouth. "I got the top off. There's a whole stack of cinder blocks in there."

Annika inspected the barrel. What a chore it must have been to get it in the house and up the stairs, then all the cement bricks on top of that. Why in the world? She told Tina the Block family couldn't have left it here. She shook her head. No. It must have been Sherry.

Sherry—that sneak, that house thief!

On an afternoon this past February, Annika had arrived at the Blocks' house, a sheaf of new drawing paper under her arm, to find the handle of the screen door tied to the main door's knob with a piece of yellow baling twine. The door wasn't locked anymore, of course; Annika had seen to that herself, months before. And she could have slashed this rope with her jackknife.

But it was a hobo sign. Annika had turned and hightailed it away from the house. It was someone else's now.

A few times in the following months, Annika had seen Sherry going in and out of the house, poking around the property. The same way Sherry had probably seen *her*.

Once when passing the place in the dark, Annika had heard voices, a woman's and a man's.

In late May, Sherry had shown up to cut asparagus out of the same ditch Annika was in—also to ask with a leer about the nasty drawings she'd found tacked up all over the living-room walls of the Blocks' house.

Outside the attic with Tina, Annika focused on acting nonchalant. She told Tina the Blocks had left for North Dakota six years ago, but that this winter, Sherry, a skinny, drifter, crazy-talking woman, probably a drug addict, had moved in, spouting the lie that the Blocks had rented her the place.

In fact, she told Tina, you couldn't trust a thing this woman said . . .

A week or two ago—Annika did *not* tell Tina—she had realized she hadn't seen Sherry for a while or noticed activity on the place. But she hadn't yet gotten up the nerve to come by and see how things stood.

Sherry was the sort of person who could turn a space uncomfortable just by walking into it. When Annika was a little girl, an intrusive neighbor had used to do that at the place on which she lived alone with her father: while his skinny, sloppy sons played roughly with her toys and stomped the wild strawberries, fat, loud Alsvik from a few miles down the road made the horses scream just by approaching the corral. He would pull into the driveway right at suppertime in hopes Annika's father would fry him a steak.

If Alsvik didn't catch them outside, Annika and her father would duck beneath a window to avoid him. Of course, they almost always did the same thing with nicer people, too.

Yes, Tina said, she knew about Sherry. The Blocks had just found out about her being in the house. A former neighbor had mentioned her when they ran into one another in the Grand Forks shopping mall.

Unlike Annika, Sherry hadn't tried to hide. She'd shoveled the driveway, filled the late winter sky, blue and pink, with white chimney smoke.

"I don't know anything about that." Annika had told Sherry in the feral asparagus patch, Sherry cackling at her, following it with the kind of sharp, deathly rasp of a cough of someone getting over the flu.

"They told us that when we got here, we might have to chase her out," Tina said. But though Sherry had left a few things—filthy clothing and rags, already thrown in the trash—Tina said she'd been nowhere to be found when they'd arrived last night. Tina ran her finger over the scabrous rim of the barrel. It had been shoved up tightly against the door.

Up here on the airless second story of the house, Annika felt or smelled something odd. Sherry must have left an impression, a shade of herself. The same way Alsvik's pall would linger at the trailer long after they'd gotten rid of him, seeming to hang on the leaves of the lilac bush and the dogs' fur like a layer of grease.

Tina stepped away from the barrel and wrapped her hands around the back of her neck. "What do you think? You think maybe she had a big cat up there?"

"A big cat!" Annika snorted, though she was getting agitated; she wiped spit from the corner of her mouth. "How would a big cat get up here?"

Tina frowned. She bent her knees and pressed her broad shoulder against the drum. "Well. I don't know. Maybe a skunk? I might as well," she said and shrugged. "I'll have to see it sometime." She let out a big grunt and pushed harder. Finally, the barrel moved with a screech across the wood. It went another inch. Then it shuddered out of the way of the door.

The door let out a groan before suddenly swinging open as if it had been sprung. Annika jumped back. But Tina, accustomed, undoubtedly, to Iowa, which Annika imagined as a soft, undulating expanse of cornfields and fruit trees, never anything more ominous lurking in its lacy shadows than a rabbit or a butterfly, began to walk up an empty set of wooden steps.

Annika shook her head. A burble of nerves rose in her gut. "Wait," she said.

Tina faltered and looked back. Annika stood still, her heart beating quickly. A bit of daylight filtered down, the sound of a few flies buzzing. Dust hanging lazy and undisturbed in the air.

Finally, she nodded and followed Tina up.

The attic was a small, almost empty platform. The roof slanted so sharply Tina nearly had to crawl. Her jean cutoffs crept up the backs of her thighs, the paler flesh there bulging through shapes made by knots in the strings. Nails bristled from the dark water-stained wood of the attic walls. On the floor amidst mouse droppings and dead flies were curls of Christmas ribbon, a couple of empty pop bottles. No embarrassing drawings.

Though, it was funny—after all this buildup, Annika had almost been looking forward to seeing her scenes filled with flesh and figures again . . .

There *was* something unusual in the room. Laid out in a corner by the window, their colors long faded from dust and sunlight, a bed-shaped pile of quilts with the crumple of a form imprinted on it. The only window had been painted shut long ago, but the glass had been smashed out from the inside and the damp breeze was coming in.

Tina was studying the shattered glass and the hard bed. Even with the window broken, a sour smell clung to the room. Even stronger than the stale odor out in the hall.

Annika went to get a closer look. The soft wood of the floor gave a little beneath her feet. She stepped gingerly, stopping before getting all the way there. She didn't like to touch the scummy-looking blankets even with her shoe.

"What do you think?" she said, and in the same breath, "Maybe we should show my father . . ."

After only a second, she turned to go. Tina was quick to follow. Halfway down the narrow staircase, a creak made both girls jump and Annika felt Tina's warm hand press into the small of her back. She felt a dizzying urge to grab Tina, dig her fingers into her fleshy arm, and scream. As she ran faster down the stairs, she began to hear music outside. Also, the sound of a horse on the road.

CHAPTER 2

About twenty yards past the driveway, heading west on County 66, Mr. Haas was riding a swaybacked Appaloosa. The horse was visible at intervals through the pine windbreak, its head listing to one side. Mr. Haas held his burly body straight, his chin lifted.

Not Mr. Haas, Annika corrected herself: Gordon. Before her graduation, she had owed him that respect. Now, they were the same.

As Haas crossed County 4, another figure, tall and gangly, emerged from the southern ditch. So her father had come home. Annika couldn't say how much time had passed since she'd left the trailer in the late morning to escape the quiet.

She was struck by the way her father looked. Like a crane picking through the bog, its skinny head up in the air. Occasionally she saw him from such a distance, but never with someone beside her, watching him too.

A tremor ran through her. She felt giddy, though cold, even in the sun.

Her father had driven to Badger early in the morning. Usually, they went everywhere together. He'd asked her to come today, but she hadn't wanted to, she couldn't have said quite why.

Haas did not stop his horse, and Annika's father loped alongside the decrepit, halting animal. After a few feet, he stopped and cut sharply back into the ditch. He shoved through grass and weeds, lifted one long leg after the other over the wire fence, and returned alone to his cow pasture.

After a moment, Annika turned away—so violently she collided with Tina on the steps of the Blocks' house. All of the sudden, it made her almost sick to look at her father.

Hoofprints marked the Blocks' driveway. In the yard, a young man was walking the front length of the house, humming and playing a fiddle. Every few steps he stooped to peer at a gash in the paint or to sniff at the sprawling tangle of the wild rose bush.

While Tina continued into the yard, Annika stopped on the front steps. She stared at the young man. Of course, she knew what a fiddle was; she had seen them on *Hee Haw*. But face to face with one, she thought that before, she hadn't known what one was. Larger than she would have expected, at the same time more subtle and fine. A collection of curves and shapes pooling together just so.

Its sound was solemn. Not funny or cute, like the fiddles clucking at the rubes of Kornfield County. Full of sound, of a range of sounds, light and dark. Like two or three people murmuring at once. Perhaps the people were huddled nearby; Annika could almost, not quite, catch what was being said. The young man held the body and bow loosely, as if the two pieces formed a single creature that had climbed onto his shoulders of its own accord.

Tina seemed ready to burst with their discovery in the attic, while Annika hung back by the screen door.

Tina was just starting to speak to her husband when they heard voices. Two more young men were rounding the corner of the house. Their arrival was so unexpected, and her nerves were running so high, that Annika jumped.

The young men walked slowly, their hands in their pockets. Tina glared at the sight of them. Though they were probably out of high school, the boys lacked the beefy necks and wide, red faces most young men here developed immediately upon graduation. Even in hillbilly clothes, these boys, like Tina, had a sleek city look.

The taller of the two young men stopped in the driveway and planted his legs wide apart. He crossed his arms and barked out to the fiddle player, "Nope. What do you know? None of them are gonna work."

Then he shot a mean grin at Tina. When he noticed Annika, he smiled kindly at her, as if she were a little girl.

Tina looked another way, her swagger deflated. There was a brittle, anxious look about her now. She watched the fiddle player ask if there were any outdoor outlets at all. The tall man said there weren't. The third young man said he thought the well house was a possibility—it had a stove in it.

"A stove!" The tall man rolled his eyes and his voice rose as if he were continuing an argument he thought he had already shut down.

The third young man shrugged. Ambling over to the woodhouse, he reached out to gently rap his knuckles on the slab wall. "Even just in the summer, for playing around . . ."

"You can't record with a stove," the tall man said.

"And the house. You've got the whole house," Tina said to the fiddle player.

"But if he needs a place to go," the tall man said sharply, before turning and stalking up the driveway. He wore jean overalls, no shirt, and his feet were as bare and pale as his chest. Halfway to the road, he stopped to draw or write something in the sand with his toe.

The third young man bowed and patted his heart before sitting down in the grass. He told Annika his name was Thomas. He had long sideburns and a manner of diplomatic acquiescence. He told her the tall man was Polly—probably "Paulie," though Annika never could think of it that way—and gestured for Tina to introduce Annika to her husband.

That was the fiddle player, Jesse, who didn't seem to mind, hardly even to notice, that Annika had turned up out of nowhere with his wife. He was a good-looking young man, with a curly cloud of brown hippie hair squashed by a battered cap, workman jeans rolled loosely a few inches below the knee, and a crooked half smile.

An unexpected rush of embarrassment and resentment made it impossible for Annika to return the smile. Here he was, the husband—and her with nothing but a father at home!

Thomas asked Jesse who was on the horse, but that was made to wait. Tina would not be put off any longer. She spoke slowly and dramatically to her husband.

"You know what?" she said. "I found something. I think something bad went on in your new house."

The words did not have the effect Tina had likely been looking for. Jesse smiled as if he were thinking of something else and started another tune, Tina talking over him. When Jesse settled on the thick warm grass with his fiddle, she sat close beside him, and he absently patted her knee. Annika stayed by the door, moving aside for Thomas when he went to see the attic for himself, smelling of a faintly sweet woodspice soap or cologne. In the driveway, Polly was still messing around in the dirt.

"Some kind of game the kids were playing," Jesse said.

"No." Tina frowned. "Annika thinks it was the crazy squatter woman, too."

"Why?" Jesse looked at Annika, who froze and looked down at her child-sized tennis shoes. Well, she said, it was just a good guess—the Blocks weren't crazy people . . .

Tina said, "How else can you explain it? She was keeping someone up there."

"What for?"

"Someone broke the window."

"A serious game," said Jesse, winking at Annika and taking out a cigarette. He put it down when he seemed to get another musical idea and played a few more notes.

Beside him, Tina's face was going through a series of changes. First, she slapped Jesse playfully on the back of his curly head. He ignored her, so she subdued the bright popping of her eyes, clucked her tongue, stretched her jaw, and leaned back on her elbows. She closed her eyes like a cat in the sun and shook out her red hair.

Jesse lit his cigarette, and out in the driveway, Polly sniffed the air. He appraised his drawing before scratching it out with his foot, then padded into the yard, reaching out his hand for a smoke.

Watching the three of them from her perch on the splintery steps, Annika began thinking of the last few months the Blocks had lived here, before they moved to North Dakota. How often she had indulged in this particular memory, even though it was now six years old . . . Dale, the Block boy who, out of five, was the closest to her age, had spent that summer playing with a rangy, wicked-looking cousin from Grand Forks. Annika had spent a great deal of time spying on the boys, and one of their games had evolved to include her. As soon as she reached the corner of 4 and 66, pretending her intention was to continue walking slowly north over the gravel past the house and toward the lake, each boy would hide behind his own fir or jack pine in the single line of them that made up the windbreak between the road and the yard. When finally they jumped out to show themselves, drawing back the fine blades of their arms, threatening to shoot, one with only his imagination but the other with a real bow and arrow, Annika ran away.

Today, Annika imagined Dale taking his turn as Prisoner up in the attic, wearing the satiny soccer shorts he always had on in the summer. His colorless hair longish on one side. Locked up and alone, leaning back gingerly against the small section of wall not covered by a forest of nails.

In her fantasy, Annika climbed the stairs. She heard him get up. His sneakers turning up dust that would hang in the rosy gold evening light.

Maybe when she got up there, she compelled him back down to the floor . . .

Good lord, was that what had happened? Who might crazy Sherry have duped and led up drunk into the Blocks' attic?

Something like that certainly wouldn't have been out of character for her. It was known in the area that for a time Sherry had lived and worked at Norris Camp in the state forest but had been fired for drinking too much and for repeatedly climbing Faunce Tower in the middle of the night to harass whatever man was up there scanning the woods for fires.

Finally, shyly, hearing Thomas coming downstairs and down the hall, Annika moved from her spot on the steps and joined the others in the yard. Polly lay stretched on his back, smoking and pulling up grass with his filthy toes. The roots were clumped with black clay dirt.

Thomas came back outside shaking his head and saying it sure looked like some kind of torture chamber up there to him.

Jesse gave him a warning look. He glanced at Tina. "Well. It doesn't make any difference now, does it?"

Tina said she wondered if they shouldn't call the police.

"Are you kidding me? What a pain in the ass. If he's going to work in that dump, let him work," Polly said, still lying on his back, his eyes closed.

Now all of them except Polly turned their eyes to the house. Its peeling white paint trimmed with faded black. Behind it, flashes of the reddish barn and other outbuildings showed behind tall stands of timothy and draping silver grass. Beyond that, a wire fence guarded an empty pasture.

A wooden swing hung from a big ash in the side yard. Its trunk had been twisted in a storm. One rare afternoon when she was nine or ten, when her father had been over helping the Blocks vaccinate calves in exchange for the same favor, Annika had taken turns swinging from the deformed tree with Dale Block and his younger brothers.

She hadn't come over to play again. Why not? Well. Her father had dissuaded her.

For Annika, the afternoon drew on in a sort of dream. Surrounded by these strange new people, she grew pleasantly disoriented. Occasionally, she did shudder when she imagined Sherry emerging from the weeds, brandishing an incriminating stack of paper.

Any other plans she might have had for the day evaporated. Including her trip to the top of the Blocks' place, to a rocky strip of field where she'd been hoping to find something in green or blue. This north-central section of Minnesota, a few miles south of Canadian waters, had been leveled by glaciers ages ago. Where they were sitting used to be the northern edge of the inhabited world. The glaciers had melted into a lake, hence all the pebbles.

With the pretty rocks she might have dug up this afternoon, Annika could have finished the butter press she was making for the Lake of the Woods County Fair. The artful little press, made of carved maple and a handle of stones, she felt would stand a decent chance at winning a ribbon worth two, two-fifty, or four dollars.

Last year, a ribbon would have been almost a certainty, but this would be the first summer she would age out of the youth category.

For a moment, Annika sat up and fiddled with the strap of her leather bag. She flicked her eyes from the house to the woods some five hundred yards distant behind it, a line of straight-trunked trees looking as if they had been drawn there with a square.

Yes, she could finish the press as planned . . . On the other hand, she could also smash the whole thing with a log, she could do whatever she wanted, she could climb a white pine and stay up there howling all night . . .

How strangely her mind was working today! Annika felt she was in pieces—no longer one solid being, but made of thousands, millions of floating particles, sailing out of her in all directions like pollen, each one praying the warm, silky wind might catch it and deliver it somewhere it might stick.

She should have had more to do this summer. So much she wouldn't have had any time to brood. This was supposed to be the year the farm was expanded—but her father's plans for it hadn't come through.

She lay back on the grass again. There was the fence, of course. It had to be put up around the garden before they lost the whole thing. She'd used working on that fence as an excuse this morning to her father not to go along to Badger.

But no. She didn't want to go home. Not to cut boards for a fence, not even to play around with one thing or another in her pleasant workshop space in the garage.

For whatever reason, she wanted to stay here, doing nothing . . .

Annika got bitten by something in the grass and went to sit on the front steps. She was glad to be joined by tall, lovely Tina, who leaned back against the screen door, her eyes shut, her long tan legs stretched out. Her face golden brown, shaped like a diamond, her soft-looking yellow shirt cropped to show a few rolls of olive flesh.

Dark auburn freckles speckled her cheeks and what showed of her chest. Once when Tina shifted on the boards, making a faint noise in her throat, Thomas glanced her way, and perhaps she felt the look like a passing ray of heat; she smiled with her eyes still closed.

By now, Tina had let her husband and the boys know that Annika, despite her appearance—only four-foot-nine, with miniature breasts and hips that made her look like a figure in a dollhouse, an effect accentuated by her neatly fitting pioneer and cowgirl clothes, boots and a high-necked, buttoned blouse—was not a child, but a young woman herself. The information, however, hadn't made a difference in how any of the men looked at her.

On the steps, Annika stretched out her short white legs and slid them against Tina's. Tina's skin was as warm as it looked, and here was an astonishing thing: a brownish-blond down of unshaven hair, silky as the baby-green spring growth on a pine.

Close to Tina, Annika felt silly and girlish. Even light-headed—though it was the intoxicating kind of dizziness she felt when a ride turned her upside down at the fair.

Probably she could have a little more. She made to whisper something into Tina's warm neck. All she could think to say was that Polly's hair was longer than her own, but Tina laughed as if she'd said something hilarious. Annika giggled, too. She stopped before confiding that even with that and his silly overalls, Polly, with his calloused, filthy feet and snarly attitude would be her top pick of the three of them had she the choice.

Though she did wish Jesse would play his fiddle again. She breathed rapidly into Tina's ear. Now she was trying not to dissolve into laughter, but also to catch her breath. With one hand she kept Tina's lavender-scented hair out of the way, while the other gripped the rough edge of the step.

She had to lift her face to reach Tina's. Annika kept her lips near Tina's skin for so long that finally Tina pushed her gently away.

"It's hot," she said.

Thomas asked again about the man who had come by on a horse, and Jesse told him that Gordon Haas was the principal at the county school. His house was a mile east down the gravel 66. He'd asked if Jesse and Tina had looked their new place over yet; he was interested to see how they liked it.

Across two fields, the faint outlines of Haas's place were visible: Kapinsky's old farm. Annika and her father had used to care for Kapinsky's animals and gather his eggs whenever he was away, until the last few months he was here, when her father lost a bid on a piece of Kapinsky's land—Haas's land now. On the property was a chicken coop, a machine shed, a milk house, a well house, a yellow farmhouse, a barn, most of it wasted. As far as Annika could tell, Gordon Haas didn't use any of it except for the house and the well. The barn could hardly be counted when his two poor old horses were practically dead and gone.

Jesse said Haas had been out riding and was drawn to stop by the sound of the fiddle. He'd invited Jesse to come on a ride with him sometime.

Tina shook her head. Jesse shook his back at her. He told her that Haas played music, too. "So he's your principal, Annika?" he said, and they all looked at her.

"He *was*," Annika said.

"Is he any good?"

Annika wasn't entirely sure which question she was being asked, and it did make a difference. She decided to speak about the way the band director said Haas played the cello—apparently very well. She had never seen him play, herself. He didn't share his talents with everybody.

Which was too bad because she wasn't ignorant. She had played the euphonium for eight years in the school band.

For a moment, Jesse looked happy. Then he swept an uneasy look around at the landscape, flat as paper and damp in all directions.

"He laughed when I asked him if there were any good venues around here." Jesse's sigh had a grievance in it that he directed at his wife.

Polly snorted and rolled over in the grass.

"Well. That's not what you came here for," Tina said.

CHAPTER 3

The phone rang in the middle of the night. Annika thought she'd been wakened by mosquitoes until the ringer clanged again. She woke with her cheek stuck flat to someone's skin. Her eyes snapped open; she spread her hand.

No—it was the cool edge of the mattress. In her dream, she had needed to get somewhere, and in the process, she'd had to crawl over a mess of other sleepers on the floor.

From the other bedroom of the trailer, she heard the slow sag of the box spring. She began to see her bookcase in the dark. The damp night air brought in the high, dissonant chorus of crickets and frogs.

Dimly, from the living room, she heard her father's voice. She yawned and swung the bare leg not already dangling there over the edge of the bed.

The living room was dimly lit by orange light coming from the kitchen. Her father was on the phone. Tall, lanky Weston Rogers, thirty-eight years old, a faintly apelike curve to his back, long arms that agitated at his sides when they had nothing to do. Annika had his dark brown eyes, but she had inherited her short stature, small features, and the sunset color of her hair from her mother, who was dead.

Her mother had died before she could remember. But someone else could be dead, to merit a call in the middle of the night.

Annika leaned against the wall, watching her father talk. His eyes were so narrowed as to nearly have closed, and he was running his hand back hard through his light hair. She stood up straight when he hung up. He glanced at her, his tongue rolling in his mouth, before dropping into a chair.

"Who was it?" she said.

Her father replied bitterly, "Your new neighbors," and Annika lowered her head.

"I guess you gave them our phone number," her father said.

"Are they all right?"

"You get started with something like this, Nick, and then there's no end to it."

"What did she say?" Annika glanced shiftily at her father from the shadows of the hall.

"What difference does it make? What's gotten into you?"

"I don't know," Annika murmured, "something . . ."

"Jesus, Nick, I could hardly sleep as it was. You come home yesterday acting like . . . You just stayed there all day. Doing what? Who are these people?"

"They're just—people."

"Why are you looking at me like that?"

"Just tell me what she said," Annika said.

Her father was still staring at her in disbelief. "I guess she thought she heard something at the door."

Annika hesitated. Maybe she didn't want to be around for that—in case it was Sherry, coming back to the house? Her father was watching her closely. He gave her a feeble smile.

"They'll call the police," he said and sighed with relief. "That's all right."

But Annika's hackles rose. "You told her we'd come."

Her father shook his head, his brown eyes wide behind his glasses, his mouth hanging open. "I had to say it; that's the problem. You get put in that position, and then you have to. When you get in with people like this, then you're stuck in it . . ."

Annika stood looking at her father for a moment. "I'll go alone."

"No. You're not walking if there's something out there."

"Can I take the truck, then?" Annika almost laughed out loud. She could count on one hand the times her father had let her take his truck. And almost always only to go on some errand for him.

"You want to leave me here without my truck? No."

They stood staring at one another. Finally, Annika moved toward the hall closet.

"We're staying here," her father said. "It's the middle of the night."

When Annika grabbed her jacket, her father began to go toward her. She turned and looked at him.

"Nick. You're not even dressed," her father said and moaned.

Finally, he dragged himself into his bedroom, which held the same double mattress and iron frame her parents had bought over twenty years ago. Slowly, he pulled a pair of jeans on over his shorts while Annika watched from the doorway.

The night was pitch black with clouds, cool enough that she wished she'd grabbed some socks. The short walk across the lawn left her tennis shoes soaked, her feet slimy and gritty. She was wide awake now. The two dogs—mixes from the same litter, border collie, Australian shepherd, most likely a few other things, Mash grayish brown, Tippy black and white—came trotting out of the barn. Tippy, that crazy mutt, with her sweet and dopey glassy light blue eyes. In the last year or two, after getting kicked by one of the horses, she had gone a little funny in the head. She'd gotten so aggressive with the cows, biting their fetlocks hard enough to draw blood, nearly laming one of the calves, that her father had had to stop working her. Unfortunately, the lack of anything to do had only made the dog nuttier. Recently, she had started digging up the garden.

Annika bent and kissed her. "Hey, honey lovey," she said.

She patted Mash, a calm and steady dog, before jumping into the truck. Excitement was rising warmly in her blood. When she saw her father's shotgun lying in the back, she thumped her leg with her fist and cried, "Oh, can I get mine?"

Her father hunched his long torso over the steering wheel.

"No," he said.

Annika waited a mutinous second before shutting the door. The headlights cast a few yards ahead of the truck on the flat narrow road, gray-brown sand and gravel. A foot or so of weedy shoulder on either side divided the road from the sharp slope of the ditches. Annika slapped a mosquito on her neck and the truck's lights lit up a pair of red eyes in the long grass.

In her dream, a long, ropey, naked man, a mane of tangled hair falling around his face, had leered up at her as she passed above him. He reached up and poked her bare stomach, grinding in with a sharpish fingernail. His face was good-looking, his neck dusky with a film of dirt.

Annika had sneered back down at him. She hadn't been able to decide whether to stay or go. In the truck, she turned down her lips and clutched her body against the door. It made her almost nauseous to think of that dream with her father right beside her.

Her father drove the half mile, crunching slowly over the gravel. By the time they got to Jesse and Tina's, he was hardly pressing the gas at all. He stopped at the head of the driveway. He and Annika stared at moths flittering in the headlights as thickly as blizzard snow until Annika began to squirm.

Finally, she half stood up in her seat. "Don't you think we're probably scaring her!"

With a groan, her father turned in, the wheels shuddering over ruts, rocking through puddles.

The place was quiet, every light on in the house. Tina's bright face pressed to the curtainless glass of the front kitchen window. The brown truck wasn't there, only Polly's van.

Annika's father must have decided to go ahead and get this over with; he tapped the horn, then jumped out of the truck with his gun and told Annika to stay inside and lock the doors. When he disappeared around the corner that went around to the big ash, Annika revolved in her seat, peering outside. She focused on the eastern edge of the building, where her father would most likely come out.

When he did come, he called for her to get out of the truck. Tina opened the front door of the house. She was still dressed, in jeans and high-heeled sandals, plum-colored lipstick on. Her dark red hair backlit from the yellow glow of the kitchen. Annika's father hardly glanced at her as she ushered them inside.

Tina told them that she, Jesse, and the boys had gone out that night. When she'd gotten tired on the ride back from town, they'd dropped her off on their way up 4 to the lake bars.

She was getting ready for bed when she heard a scuffling at the door. At first, she thought it was only moths. But she was sure the knob rattled quietly.

"So you're thinking this was a person?" Weston had a hand to his forehead and was looking more miserable than ever.

"Yes. I don't know. Maybe," Tina said.

She said she had thought it could have been the boys, or one of them. The truck wasn't there. But maybe they'd gone into the ditch or been stopped by a moose coming off the bog to cross 4. When she called out, no one replied. The rattling stopped. Until maybe ten minutes later.

"They didn't knock?" Annika asked.

"No."

"And no one drove in?"

"I haven't seen a car all night." In her heels, Tina was only three or four inches shorter than Annika's tall father. She sighed, sat down at the table, and rubbed her face. Through her fingers, she smiled at him. "I'm sorry. Weston, right? It's nice to meet you. Thank you for coming. I'm sure glad Annika was over here yesterday. If she hadn't been, I don't know what I would have done. We haven't met anyone else yet. I guess I would have had to call the cops. But I thought it might just be Jesse or Thomas and they'd passed out on the lawn. Polly isn't even of age . . . Well, and neither am I . . . And I'm only nineteen, that's probably even worse than twenty . . . I didn't want to have to answer anything about drinking and where we'd been. A fake ID can get you in big trouble." Weston's expression grew stony and Tina hurried on. "I was too nervous to go outside and look. We don't have a gun or anything here. I'm sorry," she said again.

Annika felt another surge of excitement. They had IDs for Tina and Polly; maybe they'd get one for her, too.

Tina was smiling strangely, as if her lips were about to crack. Her red-brown eyes gleamed with relief, maybe tears, as she looked up at Weston.

"Maybe I just imagined it," she said. "That's what Jesse'll say."

"I'm glad you didn't go out there," Annika said and glanced at her father. "You didn't have to when we're right here."

Her father muttered something. Then he left the room. Tina watched him go before whispering to Annika, "Your dad's shy."

Annika looked at her in surprise. But this was better than admitting the truth.

"Yes, he's always like that," she said.

Tina leaned back in her chair and shut her eyes. Annika's heart, full of sympathy and emotion, was ready to beat fast again if it needed to. She noticed that with her father in the house, her disquieting feeling that had been born in the attic with Tina was gone. She felt capable and strong. She sat at the table and patted Tina's hand.

Tina shook herself awake. She got up to make a pot of tea and started to talk while Annika watched water spurt from the ancient faucet as if it were a spring in a desert. She'd always gotten water for her paintbrushes from standing pools in the backyard or by melting snow in a cup with a match. Only once or twice when she got thirsty had she gone to the trouble of heaving the cover off the well tank.

Tina spoke a little about herself, mostly about Jesse. They'd gotten married three months ago. Jesse, twenty-two years old, had lots of talent and an enormous brain. At that young of an age, it was really something that already his band, the Sycamores, which included Thomas and Polly, had gotten notice from some important people in Iowa City. These people had spread the word in even more important Milwaukee.

More specifically, Jesse had gotten notice. He had been featured in a national beer commercial playing old-time fiddle music at a barn dance. And now he'd come up here, to Lake of the Woods County, to work and write, with only Tina to help him.

Pride and pleasure broke through Tina's fatigue. Not that she was the only one who thought the move was a good idea, she said. Jesse had acquired an agent through this whole process, and it was that man who'd made the suggestion. Jesse was a genius—he could lack focus, however. In a more populated place, or back in Iowa with his bandmates, he might have been tempted to go out too much, screw around with silly group projects, and waste precious time. It was important they capitalize on the moment, before the commercial went off the air. Annika had never seen it as it was on a cable channel, but Tina said it was very good.

A friend of Tina's had used to come to the vast Lake of the Woods for ice-fishing, and that's how they had found out about this area, dirt cheap and remote, safely separated from the rest of Minnesota civilization by over a million acres of state forest. On their drive up on the flat bog road, upon seeing the sticks of dead-looking pine trees grasping their way out of peat and sphagnum and, when the sun went down, the lack of any light out in the darkness, Tina had felt certain they'd made the right decision. This eerie place would be a good creative fit for her moody husband.

Jesse's charge was to write new, original music that would get him to a certain professional level. If he had a shot for something else, why spend the rest of his life in VFWs playing "The Devil Went Down to Georgia"?

For the world, Annika wouldn't have let on how much she liked that song! She began to understand that Jesse didn't need to get a job, nor to farm, hire out, anything. He hardly had to leave his place at all. Tina said that for as long as they lasted, they were living off the residuals from the commercial. Annika nodded as if she knew all about it.

All the talk began to make her drowsy. She went to the kitchen window, cupped her face, and tried to see into the yard. Her father's steps crossed the wooden floor above her head. She looked at the ceiling, lined with heavy beams certainly slabbed from tall stands of the county's original timber. The outside was in, in a place like this. The ghosts of an old wild life clearly heard and felt.

The kitchen floor was only particleboard with a few scraps of old linoleum peeling out here and there, mottled with teeth marks. Dogs—or even goats, from the smell.

Annika took her own reconnaissance stroll through the first story. After that, she sat down again with Tina, who looked so tired now she might be about to cry. Tina took her bracelets off and laid them on the table as if she could no longer stand their weight. Still, she went on talking in a soft, blurry voice marked by the kind of high inflections that usually accompanied rocking a baby or stroking a dog. She told Annika about the job she'd left in Iowa at an old-fashioned candy store, where she had not only sold candy but learned to make it, pull taffy and divinity, flat peppermint sticks, cream caramels and thick crumbly toffee topped with cocoa dust and almonds.

Annika woke up then. Being out and about in the middle of the night had made her hungry. Her wet feet were growing chilly and she shivered.

"From scratch?" she said.

"Sure." Tina yawned. "Of course." She looked up when Annika's father came into the room. For a second, he looked back at her.

"So that's the barrel you got up there," he said, before looking away.

"Yes—what do you think?"

He shrugged. "Some kind of crazy thing."

"So this woman's really crazy?"

"She's something. She must've thought she had something up there. I don't know why she broke the goddamn window." Weston was quiet for a moment before staring into space and saying it was too bad: Sherry had left an ugly gouge when dragging that stupid barrel. Even given that, with some sanding and a couple coats of finish, the floor could still be pretty nice. It was good wood. It was a solid house and could be fixed up all right if anyone ever bothered to finish the walls and ceilings.

Only when someone else was present could Annika hear her father's flattened Montana vowels, and it happened so seldom it surprised her every time. She stared at him, shocked at this outpouring. For some reason, it also made her uneasy.

But Tina said that sounded nice. Her eyes, deep-set, elongated, a rusty color a shade or two darker than her hair, crinkled and almost disappeared when she smiled.

She said she wanted to work on her kitchen, the floor particularly, and the Blocks had told them to go ahead and do essentially whatever they wanted short of knocking down any walls.

Though, Tina added with a sigh, she and Jesse were going to have to watch their money. No matter how cheaply they could live up here, their income from the beer commercial would go quickly, what with a move, Jesse's new recording equipment, and renting a whole house besides.

Tina yawned. During her speech, the look on Wes's face had grown distant again. He had lowered his eyes and made his way for the door. He was fiddling with the loose tab lock with his long fingers.

Annika winced. The lock had been wobbly ever since she'd made a rough job of picking it with a pin.

Her father asked Tina if she'd seen anything else funny around the place. But no, she said, nothing until tonight.

"Shouldn't we stay around until Jesse comes home?" Annika said.

Her father stiffened. Tina had been starting on the buckle of her sandal, but now she dropped the strap, put her hands on her shapely hips, and looked hopefully back and forth between them.

"*I'll* stay," Annika said.

"No," her father said quickly, though softly, too. He had glanced at Tina before he spoke and she was crestfallen. Weston was looking agitated now, his arms twitching as he hovered around the door. "All right," he said finally and sighed, "I guess I could leave her the gun."

Anyway, Annika thought it had probably only been moths. The cumulative beating of a hundred tough little wings could resound eerily through a quiet house when you were alone. She had had the same scare once when she was eleven or twelve, one of the first times her father had left her home alone for a few hours.

Tina smiled shyly at Annika and said, if she wouldn't mind—and though Annika was too small to even handle it effectively, her father left his 12-gauge in the living room and escaped alone into the damp night.

It was now past three and still Jesse and the boys weren't home. When Annika's father left, Tina told Annika this wasn't unusual. If there was any kind of party going on in someone's garage or grounded fish house, they would have found it, and might not be back until morning.

The couch smelled of cigarette smoke. When Annika made to flop down on it as it was, Tina brought a pillow and quilts, sheets embroidered with flowers, and a towel to wipe her damp, grassy feet on. Tina tucked a blanket around her and Annika smiled and squeezed Tina's soft fingers between her shoulder and chin for a moment before letting her go.

Then she couldn't sleep for the life of her. Too many images beating around in her head . . . Tina's long, powerful legs in skimpy sleep shorts, her perky red ponytail, and those crazy boys tooling around on the brushy shore. The mammoth lake began its cold and murky swath far into Canada just a few miles north of here.

Annika was thinking of Tina so much, she thought she must want to *be* her. She had never spent the night at another girl's house. The room was pleasantly chilly. While she was cozy under the blanket, she imagined it would also be nice to cuddle up to Tina in her bed.

And she had never spent the night in this house. Once upon a time, her own private place. Annika grinned into the darkness. In a way, it was hers now more than ever.

She was thinking of the boys as well; soon, they would be here in the house.

Cool, honey-sweet air drifted in an open window near her head. In a tree close to the house, a whippoorwill was shrilly calling. Annika covered her mouth to smother a giggle when she was visited by a brilliant thought. Tomorrow, she would suggest to her father that the intruder at the door had been the female moose with the brainworm that had lately taken to rubbing up on a bachelor's house in Williams in the middle of the night.

She hadn't been asleep long when Jesse, Thomas, and Polly came home. She didn't hear them come in at the door, only when one of them spoke softly to the meowing cat. It was growing light outside. One of them turned on the bathroom light, shut the door, and groaned. Annika kept her eyes closed. Another one of them came into the living room and discovered her there with a soft "Oh" in the back of his throat.

As she fell asleep, she was thinking of all of them. Courtly Thomas, who dressed in the same bumpkin style as the other two, but in clothes that were pressed and clean; insolent, quarrelsome Polly, with his shrewd, dark eyes, moving nimbly on his bare feet like an ermine or an otter; and Jesse, a little shorter than his wife, which was interesting and unusual. His angled, unpredictable face.

As was the case with Tina, they were like a present Annika had unwrapped, and she couldn't tell at first what it was or what it was for. Only that she liked the look of its parts: uncommon, intricate, and sharp.

CHAPTER 4

A few hours later, Annika opened her eyes. Without bothering to
fully wake up, she quietly hefted the gun and tiptoed through
the house and out the front door. Thomas was on the living-room
floor in a sleeping bag. Outside, Polly was stretched out in the van,
his hand over his eyes. The back doors were open, one long, pale foot
sticking out. Annika resisted an urge to grab it.

At home, she inspected the garden. No fresh damage. Only the watermelon hill Tippy had dug up two days before. Did she think she
was digging for gophers? She was a Western dog. The lines of corn
she had destroyed Annika had replanted, but the seedlings looked
thin and pale. No, they wouldn't mature in time; the work had been a
waste. Annika had gotten the fence posts up, and the rails, plus three
boards on the southern end. That was all.

She was exhausted. She went back to bed and didn't get up until
noon. Her father wasn't in the house and she didn't see him anywhere
on the property. At two, she was outside eating a sandwich when two
tall figures came up the road.

Her father with Tina. Annika stood up. All of the sudden, she felt
dizzy. As if the ground had shifted beneath her feet or the world had
turned another color. Only when a neighbor, at her father's rare re-
quest, came to help with something the two of them couldn't handle
alone did she ever see him with anyone at the house.

Annika walked to the end of the driveway. "What are you doing?" she said to him.

Her father's jaw generally hung slightly agape, as he chewed peppermint gum with his mouth open almost every second of the day; it fell open further now. He was carrying a drill and a chisel.

He said gruffly, "I fixed the lock and put in a dead bolt."

Clearly he was trying to project the impression that, thanks to her, he had been forced into it. An unquiet look in his brown eyes made this hard to believe.

Annika studied him suspiciously. Had he ever guessed about all the time she had spent in the Blocks' house, sometimes as often as two or three afternoons a week?

No—she thought in a way her father was an innocent, at least when it came to her. Who could say what *she* was? If he knew about the things she thought about some of the time!

Always she had arranged it so it looked as if she'd only been in the woods. It was easy to come back with a sack of pinecones, scratches on her arms. Her father had never minded her wandering into the trees as far as her feet could take her.

His expression faltered and he turned from her. He took off his glasses, fiddled with the nosepiece. Tina was strolling beside him, her fingers laced behind her back, her eyes cast down. She told Annika good morning in her cigarette-rich voice. She said that since the boys were still lazing and useless, and Jesse in an uproar about being woken by the drill, she'd thought she'd escape for a while.

"It's not my fault he stayed out all night when we've got things to do," she said.

The dogs Mash and Tippy ran out to growl at Tina; Weston told them gently to be quiet. He kneeled to ruffle Tippy's thick fur, both hands working into it intensely. The dog shivered as he scratched.

The gray cat Charlie padded up behind Tina, then stopped to bat at a dead mole stiff and dusty in the gravel. A couple of their own cats crept out of the woodshed and were almost upon her when Tippy and Mash chased all the cats around the back of the house. A pack of them ranged between their farm and neighboring ones, depending on who had the most rats or supper scraps.

Tina was interested in looking at the garden, but the bald spots Tippy had dug out looked so bad that Annika steered Tina to the fat brown and yellow hens squabbling near their acrid-smelling coop, Mash trotting among them, wagging his tail and licking up a scrap of bread.

In general, over the summer Annika focused on the chickens and the vegetables, while her father tended to their herd of beef cattle and managed two fields of potatoes. When it was time, they both cut the third field for hay.

In the trailer, her father was the one to apologize. The two of them were decent housekeepers, but ever since Annika could remember, her father had stressed the temporary nature of their house. She had always accepted this without question, even though she had never lived anywhere else.

With a stranger's eyes on the place, she began to feel, too, that the kitchen window was too small, and that the dim orange light coming from a tinted fixture hung low over the table was not only inadequate but unpleasant. The carpet was old, dull green with a long nap. Her father had decorated a little with antique cracker and baking-powder tins, and Annika always kept a basket of dried berries on the table. She couldn't remember the last time anyone but her or her father had been in the house.

In the living room was a framed drawing of her mother's fantasy house. Her mother's full-color sketch: a chestnut-colored A-frame log cabin with a stone chimney and a curl of lavender smoke. Annika's parents had dreamed of building the place together; then the dream had been transferred to her.

Near the picture was one of Annika's artworks, a sandhill crane charcoaled and tinted with watercolors on the same distinctive butcher paper that until recently had hung in such volume on Tina's own living-room wall.

Weston seemed to want to get Tina out of the house almost as soon as he'd brought her in. He followed closely behind when Annika led Tina down the hall to the bedrooms. When the two girls stood for a minute talking, he tapped the toe of his boot and loudly blew his nose.

He looked upset when Tina saw a photo of Annika's mother. She made a startled noise.

"You're almost the same," she said to Annika.

Annika smiled. Yes. Her own and her mother's thin, precise features, looking as if they'd been sketched in faint pencil, were very similar, their yellow-red hair identical. They had the same small feet, for which it was impossible to find shoes outside of the children's section; short, spindly fingers; and white, angular, foxlike faces which drew to a point at a sharp chin.

When Tina left, Annika started on the garden, going back and forth between the fence and the weeds. The temperature went up past eighty. Tippy and Mash lay down panting in the shadow of the house.

The work wasn't giving her the usual level of satisfaction. A bad feeling began to creep over her, the anxious hopelessness she had noticed at times since her graduation, but until now, only when her father left the place and she was completely alone. Today, he was in the barn, only twenty yards away.

When Annika dropped her work and went to be near him, she caught him talking to himself. This happened sometimes; only he was not talking to himself, exactly, but to her mother.

He was in a stall brushing down Sparky, Annika's mother's gelding, ancient now. Working over Sparky's withers, her father asked her mother, Diane, for her opinion on the gelding's hooves. He waited, then said in the low, pleasant voice he used around a horse, "So it's still all right for a couple of weeks, you think?"

A few days ago, the gelding had cut his leg on the wire fence. A bad cut and bad timing—it had been three weeks since her father had last trimmed him. His wife knew better than he did on this and other issues, having grown up on this porous ground, the expert on what it would or wouldn't do to a horse.

Annika's father said now, in his own voice, though the words weren't his, "If you could think of a way to hold onto him so you weren't putting any pressure there—but it doesn't matter. If it's still hurting him, he won't want you to get anywhere near it."

He noticed Annika. He said, without missing a beat, "Nick, cut down on his grain for a while. We'll wait a couple of weeks and just keep an eye on it." As was often the case, Annika didn't know if it was her father or her mother saying it. This had never bothered her before.

Today, however, there was something new as well. An hour or so later, Annika saw her father, standing in the doorway of the house, make a gesture as if he were patting someone's shoulder, an invisible someone her own height. Then he pushed up his glasses and went outside, his long arms swinging, headed for the fields.

CHAPTER 5

Related to her father's logic that it was worth little at this point to spend money or time on rugs and fixtures was his determination that he and Annika would build a real house together, as he had planned to do with her mother. Two years after Annika was born, her mother got sick with a lung condition that made going out in the cold difficult and dangerous. She spent a whole long winter stuck in the little trailer and by the middle of May, she was gone.

In the months after he buried his wife, Weston had formed the concrete plan of buying the field directly across County 4. Since then, he had been putting money away toward that end. He wanted to expand the value of the farm with wheat. Enough money for cropland at a decent price was not enough to build a log house with a stone fireplace, honey-colored walls dripping pine sap, and one whole wall made of glass. But it could be, if the right thing was planted. Wheat yields had been high the last few years, no matter who you talked to.

Early on in her life, Annika had caught her father's fever for making and squirreling away money. She'd been doing small odd jobs for people in the area almost as long as she could remember. When she was twelve, her father had begun accepting the amounts she pressed on him to go into the savings account he kept for the land and the new house.

Annika's father had moved to Minnesota from Montana with his family when he was in high school. Of his brothers and sisters, only he had stayed, for her mother. Twice he had taken Annika to visit her relatives in Montana, once when she was four and again at nine. She remembered the first trip, when she was still being treated like a baby, most fondly. When she returned as a little person whose personality was already formed, her father's sister and brothers and their children, all teasingly affectionate with one another but reserved with strangers, had shyly given her the latter type of treatment; they didn't know her at all.

By five on the day Tina came to the house, Annika had finished weeding the garden and put up the southern wall of the fence. Nailing in the last board, she noticed movement in the shadow in front of the trailer, Tippy rising all at once from a nap, as if in response to a silent summons—louder, whatever it was, than Annika could yell—then running like the dickens toward the garden, a streak of black and white. First, the dog tried squirming under the rail of the unfinished western wall. Failing that, she dove through the open middle space, nearly knocking herself in the head. Once in the dirt, she dug into the green beans like a badger, her black butt up in the air.

Annika shouted. Tippy was unmoved. Annika came up and lightly smacked the dog's behind. She backed away, surprised, when Tippy turned and snapped at her. The dog had never done that before.

Tippy went back to digging, like a bulldog with a stick. Annika threw a stone, but it was only when a cat crossed the lawn that Tippy took off again toward the house in a shower of dirt, abandoning her work, whatever it was.

Annika patted soil around the plant that had been attacked. It had not been completely torn apart and might come through all right.

Later, in the kitchen, she stood gnawing on a radish and wondering what her father was going to do with the pack of hamburger defrosting on the counter. She looked around the trailer with her father's dissatisfaction. How might she get Tina to come back—and to bring the boys, too? What could she offer them?

In a bigger, prettier place, Annika could entertain. Her father, like an unpredictable or crotch-sniffing dog, during those times would most likely have to be sent away.

Yes, they needed that money . . . Annika sat down at the table and began a list of figures. With Tippy's ravages, they would be out on corn and onions, it was time to admit it. She went to the phone and began to call all the neighbors who had ever hired her to see if they had anything else they needed her to do. She announced herself in her father's way—"This is Annika Rogers, Graceton"—a qualification more necessary for her father than it was for herself, on account of the other Wes Rogers who farmed in Carp Township, but she did so like the sound of it.

She left a message for Chrissy Rebarchek, who lived near the lake. A minute later, the phone rang. Annika heard Tina's voice, low, rich, and panicky.

"Hi, Annika. Is your dad there?"

"No." Annika frowned. "What's up?"

"I'm locked in the house!" Everyone had left Tina alone again. She'd turned the dead bolt, but it was so new and stiff, she couldn't turn it back again.

·Annika felt a swell of pleasure. Also an echo of the dark, sweet, trembly feeling she'd shared with Tina going up into the attic.

"He screwed it in too tight," she said, delighted. "I'm coming over."

She changed out of her jeans into a long stiff khaki-colored skirt. In getting off the place, she sneaked like a thief, looking left and right before darting to the road. She spoke sharply to the dogs to keep them from following her.

She picked wildflowers, the small blossoms scattered like knots of embroidery amongst the thickly growing grasses of the ditch. Black-eyed Susans, yellow and pink lady's slippers. Annika's favorite, the sturdy little Indian paintbrushes with their hair all on fire.

It was illegal to pick a lady's slipper. Annika tucked the velvety yellow orchid under her buttoned blouse.

"Look at you, Laura Ingalls," Tina said through the screen of the kitchen window when Annika arrived. Annika knew at once Tina didn't like the fussy blouse and skirt. At the same time, she'd gotten the impression across good-humoredly, without being cruel.

Tina got Annika inside through the window, and while Annika was adjusting the lock, Tina reported that earlier in the day, Haas from down the road had stopped over to take Jesse out on a horseback ride.

As for Polly and Thomas, they had gone back to Iowa. They'd just come to help with the move, Tina said.

Annika felt a rush of disappointment so deep and sore it surprised her. She stopped her work and hid her face. "Aren't they coming back?"

She glanced sideways to see Tina make a sour face, a dismissive gesture. "Oh, maybe sometime."

Annika dropped to the floor, pretending to look for a screw. She gripped her khaki hem. Around her, the house was quieter than before the boys had come.

Finally she couldn't pretend there was anything else to do on the lock. She took a breath and drew herself up. Well. There was still Jesse. And Tina—who looked smaller than she had the other day, staring wistfully out the window down the empty road and rubbing her knuckle on her teeth.

"Maybe Jesse and I can get settled in now," she said.

She told Annika that Jesse had planned to be out with Haas only an hour or two. It had been twice that long, maybe just to spite her. Jesse was still being a child about the noisy drill this morning.

Anyway, he was hungover and hadn't taken any water and Haas was planning to take him into the deep woods on the top of his place, so they'd better not have gotten themselves eaten or something.

At one point, Tina looked up the Haases in the book. No one answered. She'd been hoping to talk to his wife.

But Annika told her Laura Haas didn't live on the place anymore; she'd left not long before Tina and Jesse arrived. No, Annika didn't know why . . . Probably there was no one in the county, perhaps excluding her father, who would have been less likely than her to have heard any gossip about it.

As they had the night before, she and Tina sat waiting in the kitchen for Jesse to come home. The table was still covered in boxes. Around them were the hanging wires, the exposed rafters, the sagging, water-stained cupboards, piles of plastic bags stuffed with wire hangers and toilet paper. Through the back window, propped open with a stick, came the sound of barn swallows chittering, crowding the length of the power line.

Tina asked about Gordon Haas, and Annika told her how he had been brought into the school from out of state two years ago following an emergency: the former principal had swerved to avoid a deer out on Highway 72, spun into a ditch filled with cold runoff from the snow, and drowned.

What was Haas like? Well. He was an unusual man. Not quite like anyone Annika had ever met before.

His two master's degrees had impressed the school board, as did his talk about raising the bar for students' intellectual achievement. A cultured man with a forceful personality, he might have rubbed more of them the wrong way if he didn't also have a down-to-earth manner and a rough-and-tumble look. A beard and cowboy boots.

The most notable thing he'd done since he arrived was to attract a posse of some of the smartest kids in the school. Annika hadn't been uninterested in signing up for that group herself.

Her father, though he didn't care much for Haas, hadn't vetoed her plan. It might be worth it for Annika to get in with him now that it was Haas who owned that field across 4.

Unfortunately, Haas's student group had remained unofficial, no application process ever advertised. A few times Annika had wandered near the new principal's office, but she never could find a time when the room wasn't either dark and locked or filled already with kids looking both animated and enchantingly at ease. Not as if they were in a room with a teacher at all. Rocking in their chairs, talking over one another, some even sprawled on the carpet.

In a corner, Haas would be leaning back himself, the cuffs of his shirt rolled up. His short, muscular legs stretched out, propped on another chair, his hand on top of his head. Often he was grinning or laughing, his big pink mouth wide open. Annika never could get herself to knock.

Once, soon after he'd first arrived, Haas had talked to her directly. At that point, he was coming up to all kinds of kids in the halls, she supposed to see who he liked.

He asked Annika about her talents, the things she enjoyed, how she wanted to shape her future. He was vaguely interested in her plan to get into the state forest more often to gather tamarack cones to sell to the DNR.

The fact that Annika liked to paint drew Haas in a little more. Suddenly and dizzyingly, he was leading their conversation to a bloody medieval battle and bringing her to the library to show her a painting of a demon getting whopped by the Virgin Mary. Staring aloofly ahead out of layers of windblown headdresses, Mary had trapped the creature's serpent body under her little foot.

Annika stared at the picture. She flicked her eyes to one on the facing page, a crude woodcut of a pack of dogs, sheep, and nearly naked people gorging on fruit out of a barrel.

She looked from the book into Haas's blue-gray grasshopper eyes, popping and rolling in his head. She began to tell about a garter snake that had once run over her foot in the grass. What had surprised her the most about the whole thing was her reaction: a deep, bullish bellow. She'd always assumed that given a reason, she would scream like a normal girl.

Also, she'd felt herself freeze. For several long moments, she was completely paralyzed. How disappointed in herself she had been—some woodsman she was!

Haas had stepped back and regarded her. He crossed his big arms and said, "Well. What do you wish you would have done?" He had a gruff, affable voice, like a friendly huntsman or pirate.

Annika looked back at him and said she didn't know.

"It couldn't have hurt you, but it did scare you. Didn't you want to catch it?"

"A garter snake? And do what with it?"

The excitement in Haas's eyes troubled her. Where was this going? Perhaps, in some indistinct, underbellied part of herself, she knew.

"My father says I did the right thing," she said finally.

The intensity in Haas's eyes flickered and dimmed. After a second, he sighed and told her to go get some lunch. Annika told him she wasn't hungry. She kept staring at him. He said he had work to do and sent her on her way.

Later, she wondered if he found out who her father was; she had avoided this point. Haas didn't single her out again.

In the house with Tina, Annika soon wearied of talking about all of that.

"Ancient history," she said.

Tina was on the same page; all her high-school teachers had been prejudiced against her. Not knowing a single thing about her didn't keep them from calling her a hippie pothead, sometimes right to her face . . .

The two girls smiled at one another over the glass jar of Annika's wildflowers, placed amidst the junk on the table.

Annika asked if they shouldn't do some unpacking, and they started moving furniture into place and unloading cardboard boxes, which

Annika broke down and tied into bales with twine from the dusty
yellow pile in the barn. At eight, when they got hungry, Tina asked if
Annika shouldn't call her father.

Annika shook her head. Here *she* was—and he was there. She
thought of the block of meat softening on a white plate in the trailer's
kitchen.

"I left a note," she lied. A moment later, the phone rang. "Don't,"
she begged Tina.

Tina gave her a funny look before answering and handing over the
receiver.

"That fence isn't going to finish itself, you know," her father said.
"What are you doing over there?"

"Helping Tina. Just like you were." Annika watched Tina move dis-
creetly into the living room.

Her father paused. He said sheepishly, "It's your night to make dinner, isn't it?"

Annika grew hot with anger. When he'd set out the beef himself!
"I'll be back soon—just a little while."

"Well, should I wait on you or not? I'm about starving here."

Annika couldn't remember a time in recent history when she and
her father had not eaten supper together. She thought of him alone
with his hamburger, sitting in one of the metal folding chairs.

"No. Don't wait on me," she said, low.

Her father spoke softly, too. "Nick. I don't like you being over there
by yourself. They're too—grown up for you."

Annika's face flushed again. She muttered that they would talk
about it later and hung up. Tina came back, and the two of them
made sandwiches and cut up nectarines. Tina put on some music. She
and Jesse had a big collection, mostly old cowboy records and cas-
settes, only a few CDs. Jesse didn't like what he called the mathemati-
cal sound of them and was waiting for the industry to either work the
kinks out or come up with something better. Annika didn't recognize

the bands from what she heard on the Roseau station, though most of the album covers looked like country music of one kind or another.

Tina put on a crackly recording, one man singing with a guitar. She gave Annika a wolfish grin.

"I bet you've never heard anything like that before," she said.

The song was filled with sounds that seemed to be mistakes, but the music made Annika's heart beat faster; it was quiet and yet it didn't feel quiet, and she was never quite sure where it would go.

The man sang that he would beat his woman until he was satisfied. Annika raised her eyebrows at Tina and asked shyly, "Do you know 'The Hoodooin' of Miss Fannie Deberry'? That's about the devil, too . . ."

It was fun to unpack to the music, yet part of her was relieved when Tina turned it off again, leaving only the sounds of horseflies and swallows, Charlie's mews and cries as the cat walked with her silky paws on the tops of their bare feet.

When they were done, Tina slumped to the floor and ran her hands over her dusty hair. Yes, here it was, finally—a house! In Iowa, she said, she and Jesse had been living in odds and ends and trashy little apartments. Tina was used to those kinds of places, as her mother had worked a low place on production at Hormel until she died when Tina was sixteen. Neither of them knew where her father had gone, and Tina had spent her late teens crashing with older friends and sketchy relatives while she finished high school, sleeping in closets and kitchens.

The whole time she'd been with Jesse, Tina had been anxious about their living conditions. Even though he didn't say so, she was sure that eventually Jesse was going to need more . . . He'd grown up in a family of Lutheran pastors who not only preached religion but wrote books about it. Jesse had even gone to college for a couple of years. His mother taught at the university in Iowa City, and his childhood home had a gorgeous cedar deck wrapped around the entire back length of the house.

To celebrate unloading the last box, Tina and Annika took a walk in the yard. They were in the back, Tina talking over plans for where she would put a big garden in the spring, maybe an experimental plot this summer, Annika explaining the constitution of the soil and making suggestions, when at the same time they looked into the shadow of the barn and where there had been no one, there was suddenly someone there.

Tina jumped. Annika only stared. The woman had been standing still, but now she started to walk forward.

"Where did she come from?" Tina cried.

Thin and flat-looking like a paper doll, Sherry pushed her way through the tall grasses, some of it higher than her head.

Something had happened to her. She held her torso at a crooked angle and was dragging one of her legs, with each step swinging it around like a rope. She stopped a short distance away. Against the level landscape, her figure was like one sewn onto a quilt or painted on the wall of a cave.

"Hello," Tina called. "We see you there."

Annika chewed on her finger. Sherry shaded her face with her hand and spoke sharply to her: "Who's she? Did you think I was gone?" Annika felt Tina look at her. She brought her hand down to her side and opened her mouth pretending she was going to speak.

Tina swore under her breath. "Yes, we thought . . ." she said after a while.

"Well. Here I am."

Sherry's voice was low and raspy. She wore a shirt that, like Tina's, was cropped at the midriff. Even from this distance, the lines of her ribs showed through her sunburnt skin.

Tina said in a firmer tone that she and Jesse were renting the place and the Blocks had said Sherry had better clear out.

Sherry said, "No. They never told me that. I was just gone for a little while."

"You haven't been staying in the barn, have you?"

"They never told me I couldn't," Sherry said plaintively.

"They never told you that you could."

Sherry's eyes were dark in the shadow cast by her hand. "Have you been trying to get in the house?" Tina asked her.

"You don't have to knock if it's your own door. Anything going on in there?"

"What do you mean?"

"Anybody else come to see you?"

Annika's anxiousness rose. She tried to think of a way to end this without opening her mouth.

"You guys aren't doing nothing tonight?" Sherry said. "Just walking around?" When they stayed quiet, she wrapped her hands around her skinny waist and blew air out of her lips. Her body sagged. She looked off to the west, showing a dark mark on the side of her face, dirt or a bruise.

"Well. Clear out a place for me," she said.

Annika stood looking at her. Sherry stared back. Then she put up her middle finger and took a step forward. Annika stiffened until Sherry turned abruptly and walked off in her listing gait.

Tina watched after her. "Well. That answers that."

Annika felt almost like crying. She watched Sherry to see where she would go.

"What should I do?" Tina said. "She's going into our woods."

"She's probably camping." Soon Sherry was only a small shape on the far flat horizon. She disappeared into the trees.

"I wish Jesse was here. I'm glad you are, Annika. Clear out a place for her!" Back in the house, Tina locked and bolted the door. She didn't like it when Annika went out to the side yard to toss the onion tops.

Then Tina couldn't stop chattering. About how, really, she could hardly talk, herself . . . It wasn't as if she'd never broken into some-one's place and partied there. In high school, she and her friends had used to do that in strangers' summer cabins all the time. Tina and an old boyfriend had even squatted in one for a month one winter when they'd run out of money.

Now that she was on the other side of it, however, dealing with someone who might very well have drug or mental problems, she could see how it could cause real trouble.

She debated about calling the police or the Blocks. She decided to wait to talk things over with Jesse. At eight, she called Haas's number again. No answer.

At Tina's pleading, Annika reluctantly called her father. "Well, hel-lo there," he said coldly.

Annika explained to him the need to make a plan, if Jesse didn't come back before dark, for the two of them to go into Haas's woods on the horses—"Sure, whatever, Nick," her father broke in, in a low voice.

"Tina's nervous," Annika said. In the silence that followed, she told him she would be in touch with developments. In a catch in his breath, she heard the possibility of him asking if he should come now, and as an afterthought, she told him how she'd had to come fix his work on the lock. That ought to shut him up.

She said goodbye and hung up quickly. She didn't feel good about it, and as evening came her gloomy feeling increased with each drop of light that left the sky. Her father was so cheap that he never liked to turn on the lights until he absolutely had to. She wouldn't put it past him to sit until bedtime brooding alone in the dark.

She had promised Tina she'd stay. And even when, at nearly twi-light, which came at after ten this late in June, Jesse finally came limping up the road, Annika didn't think of leaving.

Jesse seemed different than he had been yesterday. He looked irritated, ready to collapse. Yet also his eyes were gleaming with a panicky fire.

He greeted Annika indifferently, Tina not at all. Several times, Annika watched Tina try to maneuver her way into his view, but he would beam his agitation or despair over her shoulder or duck his face to the ground. He hardly paid attention when Tina mentioned Sherry had the raspy voice of a crackhead, not even when she noted that crackheads could mess you up even if they didn't look like much.

"You forget, this is a woman who had someone trapped up in the attic," Tina said.

"We don't know that."

"I've known crackheads. And here, out in the middle of nowhere . . ."

"You're a big girl," Jesse said.

The weather was calm, the late light sparkling on the windbreak pines. The three of them sat outside, Tina and Annika on the steps, Jesse leaning against the house, rubbing his legs and pulling twigs and burrs out of his curls. Each one he pinched between his fingers and studied darkly.

He and Tina drank beer out of bottles wrapped with an intricate, artistic label. Annika studied the illustration on one of the empties. She waited for Tina or Jesse to offer her one and wondered how she would answer, but neither of them did. Sulking a little, she ate a scoop of chocolate ice cream melting in a glass of root beer.

Jesse, wearing a thin white T-shirt torn at the collar, showing a ridge of skin and bone, held the neck of his bottle with his first two fingers and thumb and took his shoes off with only his toes and feet. Annika lit crumpled newspaper and kindling in coffee cans to keep the mosquitoes away.

Watching her work, Tina seemed restless. She would direct her eyes pointedly away from Jesse, at the flames, at the fields or the road, every once in a while letting out a sigh to indicate her complete intoxication with the beauty of the evening; or she would turn and stare baldly at him.

When a car drove by east on 66, Annika informed them it was Karlyn Johnson. The car's red taillights stood out in the greens and browns beginning to go black. In that direction, there was only the straight dirt road lined by the small wooden crosses of ancient telephone poles, many of them leaning at odd angles, and the metal pricking of pasture fences.

The low sky held onto its last glimmers of yellow and blue. The Rogers' cattle, making a warm, rustling sound, roamed through grasses and wildflowers in the pasture on the other sides of 4 and 66. Draping silvery green foxtails dotted the yard. A light wind brought the heavy funereal smell of dying lilacs from the side yard, as well as fresh purple clover from the ditch.

Tina was catlike, like little Charlie at any moment as likely to spring onto a cricket as to arch her back into a stretch. She told Jesse that Thomas and Polly had called to say they had made it the three hundred miles south to Minneapolis, where they would spend the night. They would see a show and sleep at the house of an old girlfriend—Polly's? Thomas's? Impossible to know from the way Polly told it. Maybe both of them had gone out with her, or had wanted to. Tonight, they would find out which one of them she liked better.

Annika was almost trembling with jealousy while Tina crossed her hands over her chest in a matronly gesture.

"They'll grow up sometime!" she said.

Jesse groaned, his head hanging down between his legs. He said he missed them already. It was too quiet here without them.

"Now you can get to work," Tina said. "Aren't you happy about that? Tell us about your day."

"It was great." Jesse gestured helplessly.

"Was it?" Tina watched him rub his legs and scolded him. He

shouldn't have ridden for the whole day like that, after not going out for months.

"We didn't ride the whole time," Jesse said.

"Why? What else did you do?"

"He showed me his place. We even played a little music. He's very good."

"What's he like? What did you talk about?"

"I told you." Jesse's eyes rolled and his voice rose. "We didn't—talk the whole time. We played music, we stopped a few times in the woods to eat—"

"What did you eat?"

"I don't know! A picnic."

"I could have packed you something. If I'd known you were going to be out so long!"

Jesse's lips curled. "We didn't need it. Stilton! Where in the world did he find Stilton? Good wine, too. He must have ordered that."

"Maybe not . . ."

"It would have been rude not to go."

"I guess so."

"Anyway, he wouldn't have taken no for an answer. I tried to leave a few times."

"You couldn't have told him you needed to help your wife?"

"You'll understand when you get to know him." Jesse's mouth twisted painfully. He looked away from Tina, adding in a sullen voice that anyway he could have done the furniture tomorrow. Wasn't that what she was peeved about? Furniture! They could do that anytime. There were things they would need more than that. People, if they weren't going to go nuts. Gordon Haas was an interesting, cultured person, stuck up here without anyone to talk to. Imagine meeting someone like that way up here. He even had contacts in the music world, and not just bar band stuff. He had used to play in a professional avant-garde group before he started teaching, and it sounded as if it had done pretty well.

"You wouldn't know it, but he's forty-six," Jesse said.

"That's about what I would have guessed," Tina said tartly.

"I would have said midthirties."

"I was worried. You didn't call."

Jesse swore in a way that sounded like "Aha!" before laughing unhappily. "Tina. Goddamnit. We're in the country now."

"What does that mean? Jesse. What happened today? What were you doing over there for so long?"

"If we have to be out here, at least I shouldn't have to worry about a schedule. I won't. And you shouldn't, either. Doing whatever it is you're going to do . . ."

Tina sat stiffly while Jesse turned away and spat. Annika held onto her ice-cream spoon to keep it from rattling in the glass.

"I wish you would have been here today," Tina said quietly. "We were scared."

"I bet Annika wasn't scared."

Tina got up and wandered the yard. She came back with a handful of tough-looking dandelion greens. "We can eat these, you know . . ."

"Not this late in the year . . . You know, Gordon's not sure it was such a good idea I came up here by myself."

Tina scowled. "You didn't . . . Anyway, he doesn't know you."

"He's not the first one to say it."

"Polly? You can't be serious!" Tina piled the leaves beside her on the steps. No, she said after a moment, speaking more tenderly, they had made the right decision. Certainly, she said, Jesse loved Thomas and Polly. Of course he did. They were his best friends. But they might have messed him up if they'd come along. They were fuckups, pure and simple. No ambition. Jesse must not forget that.

Jesse was attacking his beer label with his thumbnail. "Gordon thinks I could have made up for that. Every group needs a leader."

After a second, he set the bottle aside and relaxed back against the house again. Well, anyway, he said, at least he had Gordon now. It would have been fun writing with the Sycamores, though. Noodling around on tunes, tramping the good-smelling pine woods coming up with lyrics.

Of course, he and the boys would also have stayed up late, played out wherever and whenever they could, slept all morning. Consequently getting only an hour of work done in a day sometimes, or none, Polly always gone to go pick up beer or pot or some skank, Thomas puking in the yard, too messed up to play, and pulling Jesse into all of that crap. Yes. Tina was right about that . . .

But he sounded wistful. On the road, Karlyn Johnson passed by going the other direction and they all watched until her taillights winked out in the dark.

"Why didn't he ask both of us to go, I wonder," Tina said after a while, "if he's so starving for cultured company or whatever?"

Jesse smiled harshly. He threw a charred curl of newspaper back into one of the coffee-can fires, crossed his ankles, and flexed his big toe until it cracked.

"I would have thought you'd be glad about Gordon," he said. "He might be able to help me get somewhere in the business. Isn't that what you want?"

"Yes," Tina said slowly.

"Why do *you* think he didn't ask you?"

She began to look nervous. "I guess he only has the two horses."

"Or he could tell just by looking that you're nothing but a hick!" His deep-set eyes wide, Jesse cut a quick look at Tina, who, for a second, froze in place. Then she bounded off the step, laughing hoarsely. She came forward on her hands and knees, her curved rump in the air, sat back on her haunches, and slapped her husband in the face.

Jesse slapped her back. He laughed when Tina grabbed him and rose to her full height. She yanked him to his feet. She pulled him down again and pinned him with her long, brawny legs in the grass.

Then they were really wrestling, and Annika couldn't take her eyes off them. She drank big, fast, caramelly gulps from her sweating bottle. Tina grunted and laughed, Jesse howled about his sore legs and groaned, and once, when Tina rolled Jesse over only inches from Annika's toes, she saw, in the flames licking out of the silver cans, the flash of Jesse's wide, lusty grin out in the dark.

When it was finished, the two of them sprawled out panting. Jesse got up and stood over Tina, a bare foot on either side of her head. She looked up at him, her big chest rising and falling, barely contained in her cropped shirt. Jesse shrugged his arms out of the long-sleeved flannel he wore over his T-shirt. He tied it around his waist and bent over to help her up. Instead of taking his hand, Tina reached up one more time and smacked him.

When she saw Annika watching, Tina fell back onto the damp grass and closed her eyes. She smiled and ran her fingers over the exposed skin of her belly.

After that, the two of them were quiet. They listened with Annika to the big spider-legged mosquitoes, the mockingbirds in the black arrowtops of the windbreak, the brush wolves yapping near the woods. Out on the bog, a heron squawked. Sparky and the other horse, Fern, nickered, and the cat Charlie, stalking something in the cheatgrass on the eastern side of the house, made a quiet scratching there.

Jesse went inside for his fiddle and a red sweater. He wrapped it around Tina's bare shoulders. Then he sat close to her on the grass and didn't protest when her long fingers reached into his pocket for a smoke. They were murmuring to one another now.

"Yes. I love it," Jesse said, a catch in his voice, and nuzzled his wild hair into Tina's neck.

Tina sang with him on a song about a French girl falling into a well. Three boys came along demanding a favor before they'd pull her out.

Tina's voice was tuneful but shy, Jesse's high and clear, buttery and golden, though not sweet. Occasionally, he sang in his throat, slipping it in at the end of a phrase.

The fiddle carried far into the night. Both Jesse and Tina looked so attractive, with their somber concentration. Annika was so full of a tense, hot longing she thought she'd die. She shivered and pulled her stiff skirt more tightly over her knees. The fiddle had been built from a tree like anything else, but not to put something on or to hold anything up. Simply to cry out . . . Jesse performed the tune he had played the other day, but differently. The other day, it had rocked back and forth steadily like a boat. Now, it went forward for a bit; then it waited. It slipped behind a rock before it came back out.

Jesse and Tina tried to imitate some of the natural sounds. The frogs, the wolves, the tireless whippoorwill. Annika stared hard across the road, listening for the hiss of her father's phantom field of wheat.

After a while, Jesse stopped playing. Then Tina's touch seemed to provoke him. He looked jumpy and moved away from her again.

"Still, I might've made a mistake," he said.

"No. No, we didn't," said Tina.

CHAPTER 6

A week later, on the Fourth of July, Annika woke to find the north-ern quarter of the garden a massacre of roots and shattered vines. Tippy's destruction of the pumpkin patch touched not only the gardener in Annika, but the child. She fell to her knees and cried like a little girl.

When Tippy came to kiss her, she pushed the dog away, following it with a halfhearted clod of dirt. At the sight of her father coming across the lawn, an unfathomable click in her brain sent Annika into full hysterics. She had never felt anything like it. Her father tried to touch her and she screamed.

He backed away. "Jesus, Nick, calm down. The dog's not right in the head."

"Neither am I!" As the words escaped Annika's throat, a cold terror gripped her. She was suddenly quiet. She felt her father kneel in the soil a few feet away, but she didn't look at him. She held her breath, then kept holding it. If she kept it up, she might pass out. What might the world look like when she came to again?

With a blast, she let it out. Then, a pull of tender, leafy air. Her lungs were all right. Her limbs, on the other hand, didn't move. Quite pos-sibly she was paralyzed.

"It's the fence is what it is," her father said gently. "It's hanging over your head."

Annika turned to look at him. She watched him slowly blink his brown eyes.

"Maybe," she said.

When she got to work, she did feel a little better. At one, she came into the house and ate egg sandwiches with her father.

"Do you want to go in tonight, do you think?" she asked him.

Most years, the two of them didn't go into town for the Fourth at all, only took half the day off with a box of ice cream and a kite. They'd done that two summers before, when Annika was fifteen, though she had felt itchy about it. She hadn't wanted to see anyone she knew, but she'd thought about the black Rainy River lit up and refracting colored lights. Perhaps what she'd wanted was to drift all night on a raft with her father, past a series of celebrations blossoming out of the dark.

"I didn't know if you'd want to," her father said, looking at his plate. Because last year they *had* gone in, and it had turned into a rotten night.

Annika had not had an easy time of it in school. While her mother had been involved in things outside of the farm—a coffee column for the paper, a volunteer position at the library—and might not have allowed Annika to get away with how she'd handled school, which was to do her work and keep to herself, her father didn't have a problem with it.

Her father did believe in education, as unschooled idiots lacked the tools to do anything worth doing in life and were constantly being swindled. But school was something to get over with as quickly as possible. Then for the rest of your life, you could avoid most anyone you wanted.

Most of the kids at school had bad taste. Except for hunting and fishing, even the boys looked down on country things. To them, music, clothes, and slang words ideally came from the city. These kids might barrel through the woods in a truck and blast at something, but they'd turn up their noses at eating it. Like most of their parents' generation, they believed that things were better if they came from the store, and if they couldn't afford them there, they went without.

In the halls at school, Annika would sidle haughtily past the other kids, eating from a greasy sack of her handpicked hazelnuts, daydreaming about taking a hike at four to see if the white cow hadn't gone off on her own to birth that calf.

Some of the kids played nasty jokes on one another and they took endless cracks at Annika, even armed as she was with her shield of cold disregard. Her high-waisted prairie skirts and Wrangler bootcuts, the tall leather moccasins she'd sewn from a Ben Franklin kit, her Western dressage with fringe and mirrors stood out in a school full of girls in short suede skirts and silk blouses.

And her diminutive figure stirred up in a few of the boys what seemed like a deep revulsion. Two in particular liked to press into her small breasts a dirty shoelace and order her to tie it onto her back belt loop so it would hang like a tail. They called her a white rat and would twist her arm around her back when she wouldn't do it.

The boys were three years behind her in school, expounding the humiliation, and the torment continued into her senior year. Annika had spent the last twelve years longing for this summer, when plans for the wheat field and the log house were underway, when finally her real life would begin and she could be alone.

She did like the school building in town. Most of the businesses were housed in low, nearly windowless structures made of corrugated aluminum. The few originals left included the Rex Hotel and the school, dimly lit, three stories, with thin wood floors that creaked dangerously and undulated under her feet, its walls filled with mice and asbestos, built in 1915 of stately red brick.

At last year's Fourth of July, one of the boys who liked to torture her had found her on the street while she was dancing with her father and said something nasty about it. For years, he and his comrade-in-arms had left her alone when her father was around. Last summer, it seemed something had changed.

"How about this," her father said to her now, "you finish that fence today, and tomorrow night we'll go into Warroad for supper."

Annika sighed. "All right."

As she nailed boards into place that afternoon, she was thinking that even if she didn't feel good, exactly—pleased, lighthearted, looking forward to anything—at least it must be better that she was calm. The work was repetitive and steady. She had finished one more wall of the fence, and half of another, when a movement on the property to the northwest caught her eye: her father, striding through the cow pasture headed north, his black cowboy hat on.

Annika propped the board she'd been lifting from her pile and stared. At the property fence, her father climbed over. He wore his dress hat only when he was going into town, and not for any old visit to the grocery or feed store, either.

Annika checked her watch. Seven o'clock. She tried to see if her father was on the road now, but the brush was too thick.

In the house, there was no note where they usually left them for one another, by the telephone. But on her pillow was a scrawled message—did he hope she wouldn't be able to read it?—saying he'd gone to the street dance with Jesse and Tina.

Annika dropped the note. She fell onto her bed, the paper crackling beneath her, and squeezed the sides of her skull with her palms. She began to breathe noisily and rocked like a disturbed child she'd once seen in the middle of the road in Roosevelt when his parents tried to bring him to the flea market.

The gesture didn't bring any relief. It only filled her body with too much oxygen, which might have been helium; she felt she might float to the ceiling and hang there, her legs thrashing helplessly, hopelessly, trying to stave off, distract her from some unknowable pain.

She threw on clothes for town and ran to Jesse and Tina's. By the time she got there, their truck was gone.

On the way home, she walked slowly. No, work was not the cure for what ailed her. It must be this!

But she'd missed her chance. Why in the world hadn't she thought to call Jesse and Tina herself?

Go alone? How could she do it? The thought of the great tide of people that filled the streets for the Fourth made her eyes swim.

In the kitchen, she took her father's keys from the hook.

By shoving into the cold wash of people as if it were the lake—that was how. Once she dove under, the cold would feel all right, and when she came up, Tina would be there.

Annika felt better once she was driving, propped on her pile of cushions, the windows open in the warm dusk. Ripening alfalfa gave off a sunshiny smell. In the meadow by the boarded-up general store at Pitt, fat deer grazed under the violet sky. The faded sign read "Knives and Wild Rice."

In town, her good feeling went away. There was traffic. In the middle of town, the streets were jammed with cars and people; the tourist fishermen were driving in from the lake. Looking for a place to park, Annika went into a panic. Finally, she circled all the way down to the hospital, where the small wood-frame houses were dark on the quiet and wide paved street. She stood a long time alone in the late evening light jingling the keys in her hand before forging forward.

As she got to the center of town, Annika peered anxiously into clusters of people. In front of the stage on Main, blocked off for the street dance, a hundred or more people were drinking cups of yellow beer. She realized that not only might she have called Tina and Jesse herself, but she could have suggested they go into Warroad instead of Baudette, only twenty more miles for a dance filled with strangers.

When, after ten minutes of misery, Annika finally found them, Tina took her in her arms.

"I was hoping you'd change your mind. It's no fun being the only girl!" she cried.

Annika sighed. It was strange to be suddenly enveloped in Tina's expanse of flesh, her cool arms, her big, soft breasts. Annika's skinny body felt like a tense, wiry animal. Her shoulders relaxed. She let out a barking laugh like a cough that made Tina draw back in surprise.

Her father gave her a startled smile. He looked at his boots like a child. He nodded a few times and said nothing. When he finally looked up, Annika held him in a stare and he took it helplessly.

"You're just in time. We're getting tacos," Tina said.

She wore white shorts on the cool night, her big brown legs striking even covered in gooseflesh. In the midst of the celebration, even broody Jesse looked happier. He stood languidly in the middle of the street, wearing motorcycle sunglasses and a raffia pinchfront, his hand on Tina's waist.

For once, her father wasn't the only man in town in a cowboy hat. He was dressed to the nines in good dark jeans, a tucked snap shirt, a silver belt buckle, and Laredo boots.

"Where'd you end up parking?" he finally said to her. "You locked it, didn't you?"

Annika looked away, jingling the keys in her pocket. Let him worry about his precious truck. Maybe he should buy her her own car; then he wouldn't have to worry about it.

In the Uff-Da Taco line, they ran into Gordon Haas. Her father took a step away and lowered his head like a bull.

The whites of Haas's eyes stood out prominently. Even when he was quiet, they seemed to flash with forceful ideas, persuasive judgments. Tonight he stood alone, chewing with his mouth open. His squarish hands were greasy from the fry bread. There was sour cream in his mustache.

"Jesse!" he cried, throwing open his short but powerful arms.

His morose expression lit up, and Jesse looked starved to see him as well. He took off his sunglasses and the two men embraced like a father and son reunited after they'd been separated all night in the woods.

Haas turned to Tina, pulling her down to his level to kiss her. He was short but built solidly like a wrestler. The way he looked at Tina was hungry, too. No surprise there . . . How many times had Haas barged into industrial arts, shouting over the screeching band saws, to flirt with Annika's teacher in front of the class, irritating the young woman to no end?

Tina seemed irritated as well. Haas's look for her had also a kind of calculation in it, or resolve.

Finally, Haas acknowledged Annika's father, who came forward to shake his hand, greeting Haas with an angry hangdog look and avoiding direct contact with his bulging eyes. Haas gave Annika a similarly dutiful hello.

"Gordon," Annika responded coolly, happy when his eyebrows betrayed a trace of annoyance and surprise.

She noticed that when Haas talked to either Jesse or Tina, he seemed to like to get each of them alone and to speak softly. A few times, Annika barged in. Tina and Jesse didn't need any more trouble, did they? Haas looked cross every time Annika got close to Tina or Jesse. So she would go in a little closer.

But at the same time, with the school principal in their group, she could relax. The two nasty kids from school—she hadn't seen them yet—wouldn't act up around him.

At one point, the group shifted, and she and her father ended up near each other and alone.

"You could have asked me if I wanted to go," Annika said.

"I did ask you." Her father's face grew red. "Nick, would you say Haas is at their house quite a bit?"

She backed away from him. "What?" It *was* true that Annika would be the one to know. She had felt emboldened enough to drop in on

Tina and Jesse twice last week. She'd dropped off two pails of green beans and said she was checking in on the Sherry situation. The first time, when Tina was alone, she tried to get Annika to stay until Jesse came back into the house; but the second time, when she and Jesse were hanging pictures together, Tina had smiled at her reluctantly and asked about the work she had to do at home.

Annika liked Tina's pictures. Clipped from an artsy calendar, they were classical mythological scenes and fleshy figures in sensuous poses.

The first time Annika was there, Gordon Haas was as well, though he and Jesse had kept to themselves outside somewhere.

Annika shrugged and told her father it seemed that way. She looked back at Jesse, Haas, and Tina.

"That might work out all right," her father said. "You see, Nick, it don't hurt sometimes to know someone who knows someone."

When Annika turned from him, moving close again to the others, he stood as he usually did in a crowd, as if he hoped he was hidden in a fog.

Annika found the look on his face pathetic whenever someone broke through to talk to him. She, on the other hand, felt herself warming to the growing crush of people, the noise rising.

At one point, her father stepped out of his cloud to sidle up to Haas. He towered over the man, his long back bowed over. Haas glanced up with a bored look as Weston began to speak.

The wheat, what else . . . In the year before he moved, the previous owner—Kapinsky—of the field Weston wanted had said he might be willing to sell it. But when the time came, Gordon Haas and his wife, moving here from high-priced Denver, offered more than Annika's father could have paid per acre to keep the place together. Kapinsky took it. Now he must be living high on the hog somewhere.

On the street, Annika heard Haas say back to her father, "No. I'd just as soon see it go wild, Wes."

Her father shook his head.

"I'm going to plant trees," said Haas. "See what they can do when there's nothing in their way."

"I see you haven't done it yet."

"I'm going to plant them in the spring."

"There wouldn't be much point in that. As soon as anybody else got their hands on that land, they'd just come down."

"You mean when you got your hands on it?"

"We got plenty of trees, don't we?"

"Are you telling me that in this whole county, there isn't any other land for sale?"

"I can't be driving all over hell and back. I've got too much else to do."

"I don't see how you'd even do it. Are you going to hire somebody?"

"Now that Annika's done with school—"

"One little girl, that's how you think you're going to do it?"

"That's not your problem, is it?"

Haas shook his head and escaped, leaving Weston hanging back in the street alone in his hat and black boots.

Annika was snickering with Tina about a greasy-looking couple dancing obscenely near them on the sidewalk. She'd been doing her best to avoid hearing the conversation between Haas and her father. Here in town, it suddenly seemed like a joke, that house. A quiet house in the country—why in the world?

A glowing feeling was growing in her. The town had a shine to it. She couldn't remember ever enjoying the holiday this much, even as a child.

It was after ten and she wanted to get to the hill for the fireworks. As soon as it had swelled to bursting, Main began to empty. Jesse and Haas were not in a hurry; they had struck up a conversation with the woman plugging in her electric keyboard. The banner on the front of the stage named her as Judy—"Judy & the Outlaw."

Annika's father turned to Tina in the street. He said mournfully, "I sure am sorry about that dead bolt." Here he had come to help Tina feel comfortable and secure in her house, and look what he'd done instead.

Tina smiled kindly at him. Annika thought she could probably drag her father to the hill if she wanted to, but she didn't want to go without the others. A solitary red star streaked into the sky beyond the grocery and hardware stores and she found the tension nearly unbearable. How many times had she sat alone with her father and watched the sky break open into its first crackling color of the night? A signal somehow more poignant to her than any natural one that another year had passed.

Tonight, she could hardly keep herself from hopping in the street. Her father put a hand on her shoulder as if she *had* been hopping. He said they would be able to see almost all the fireworks from here.

But here was not sitting cozily on a blanket next to her new friends where everyone else was—where everyone could see!

Finally, Tina touched her, too. "Let's head over. Jesse'll find us when he comes."

This would be nearly impossible, but Annika didn't say anything, and neither did her father.

Her tingly, peaceful feeling formed a protective barrier around her. If the school bullies showed up, she would only laugh.

Tina had been treating Jesse with a queenly aloofness tonight; it might have been part of her strategy to walk calmly away without a word to him. Two blocks away, the bank sloped darkly to the black, shimmering water of the Rainy River. People and blankets covered the slope. They were lined up on the bridge to Spooner, the frontier name for the eastern side of town, as well. More than a thousand people. The population of the town was only a thousand, but the celebration was for the whole county, four thousand people in thirteen hundred square miles. Tourists and Canadians too. The scene was lit by a dim light near the two-ton statue of Willie the Walleye and the white Christmas bulbs strung on the eaves of the VFW. Across the water to the north were the lights of the International Bridge.

After weaving and fussing like a duck scoping her nest, Tina found the spot she wanted. She asked two groups of people to move to the left and right, Annika and her father hanging back until she had accomplished it.

Her father made to sit beside Tina, but Annika wedged between them and plopped down. Sighing, her father stretched out his long legs and crossed his ankles, the toes of his boots black points against the sky, brilliantly lit every thirty seconds by a firework or a cluster of two or three. Still faintly burning on a raft in the middle of the water was the flickering outline of a fish, the evening's opening spectacle.

Sparklers and glowing jewelry dotted the hill. The cool air smelled of bug repellant. Tina looked over her shoulder for Jesse. Annika wrapped a blanket around herself and Tina and they ate together, dropping bits of food, fishing them out of the yarn to wrap in crumples of napkin and wax paper.

Each boom resonated pleasantly in her body. The fireworks had never looked so spectacular. At the same time, Annika knew she had never paid them less attention. Watching with a friend was the real miracle, though she felt she was handling it like a natural.

This week, following tradition, half of the front page of each of the county newspapers, the *Baudette Region* and the *Northern Light*, would be taken up with a black-and-white photo of a glittering burst of stars.

Walking back to the dance, Annika noticed some of her former classmates looking at her curiously. They seemed even more distant from her life than before, not just because of graduation.

At the same time, all at once they seemed real to her. What would they do with themselves now? Who were they looking for in the crowd?

She and her father and Tina ran into Karlyn and Doug Johnson, who lived a few miles north of their trailer on 4. Doug in his Maple Leafs cap and black mustache was as amiably impassive as ever, but Karlyn could not hide a measure of surprise at seeing them there. When she was introduced to Tina, Annika's father getting the jump on that one, even putting a hand on Tina's bare shoulder, Karlyn looked at him as if an understanding had dawned on her.

This Annika could hardly bear. Karlyn erased the look from her face, but something about her reaction lingered even when things had been explained to her.

"Congratulations, Annika," she said, "do you feel old now?" After a glance at her father, whose head was down—he was trying to move them along—Karlyn added quickly, "We have a couple of baby goats now. Billies, too bad. But just a week old and still drinking milk. We got them separated from the nanny if you want to come see them sometime."

Annika studied the sharp comb lines in Karlyn's wheat-colored hair. It was pulled back neatly with a jeweled clip. She touched her bumpy ponytail with regret. The music was reverberating down the street.

"Oh, you mean you want me to do something with them?" she asked after a moment.

Her father had gone ahead with Tina. Annika told Karlyn to call her about the job, then ran to catch up. Back in the street, Jesse and Haas had started in on the beer garden. The road and sidewalks got packed quickly. Kids from school, cashiers from the pharmacy and grocery store, toddlers holding the hands of bigger children and wobbling to the music. Annika's teachers casually smoking cigarettes, and some faintly familiar-looking young Canadians, too. If you didn't cross the border regularly for town-hall parties or after-school poutine and éclairs, you would have seen them only at last year's Fourth of July. The sunburned strangers from the city who had spent the day on the lake wore visors and sweatpants, but everyone else had dressed carefully.

Judy & the Outlaw played "Fishin' in the Dark," "Friends in Low Places," "Black Velvet." By eleven thirty, the level of excitement was high. Young and middle-aged women on the asphalt dance floor had replaced the children, now asleep in their parents' arms. No one had to move carefully to avoid them. The women shouted the songs at one another, greeting each new number like a barely believable surprise as a song would seem to spur a secret memory of some great or tragic moment they'd all lived through together.

This was one of only two or three community-centered events in a short summer, a rare opportunity to talk to someone in a party kind of atmosphere. Annika's bus driver Harland, who had the gigantism disease, took a tall, thin woman in black leather by the hand and led her into the street. His grasshopper legs and sharp elbows took up a wide area. When he started to twirl her, everyone got out of the way.

Harland could yodel like a professional. If begged by Annika's senior classmate Pam Fadness, he would occasionally agree to perform in the dark mornings on the bus, for Annika always a happy and chilling moment.

The sour smell of the Fourth of July—cheap light beer, sweat, and smoke—had bothered her when she was young. Tonight, she enjoyed it. She would have tried a beer if she could have gotten her hands on one. But even Tina, drinking something brown she had mixed at home and poured into iced tea bottles, didn't offer to share. Because of her father? Annika wished he would move farther away down the street.

Sometimes the gaze of the crowd would shift from the band and the dancers to a particular part of the street. The mood would grow darker. A bottle might smash on the pavement. Often, it meant a Canada Day fight had been rekindled. But Americans didn't relish in a fight like the Canadians did; it was usually shut down quickly, this side of the river.

Annika felt the musicians were excellent and said so to Jesse. "Ha!" he jeered. But he couldn't pretend he wasn't having as good a time as anybody. He had even begun to respond to Tina's air of pleasant indifference . . . how she lightly batted him away when he tapped her bottom or slipped his hand up the back of her shirt. He began telling the story of the first time he'd ever seen Tina, at a music festival out in the country. She'd stepped out of a creek with a group of other pretty girls, wearing almost nothing. Later, she showed up in front of the stage he was performing on, crowned in purple alfalfa and performing tricks with a Hula Hoop.

At seventeen years old, she'd had a wild reputation. No one ever knew where Tina had come from, what rock she'd been sleeping under.

Tina protested that she hadn't been a complete savage during that time. She'd run a stand for the candy store at many of those festivals and sold her own herbs and seedlings.

Tonight, her hair was tied into two pigtails. Tucked into one a sleek braid, two strands of thread woven in, aqua and rose. Under the gaze of her husband, she laughed and toyed with the silky end of the braid, her red-brown eyes glittering under the streetlights with flecks of yellow.

Gordon Haas was getting drunk, and soon he was making his own cloddish advances. Haas wasn't unattractive, for an older man, but it was unpleasant watching him try to keep up with Jesse. Jesse, with his easy lean grace, the faint stain of stubble on his smooth skin, his body yet unmarred by the gray smoke issuing poetically from his lips, was a magnet for attention even when he wasn't doing or saying a thing.

Where was Haas's wife Laura, anyway, a distinguished-looking woman with a neat cap of graying brown hair and a handsome face? With Laura beside him, Haas's potbelly and florid skin had a dignity he could not seem to muster on his own, no matter where he had traveled in his life or how many books he had read.

Tina responded to Haas's innuendos in an imperial way. When he took her by the arm, she blew a stream of smoke straight down into his face. "Get off me, old man!" she cried.

Haas didn't seem insulted. He grinned and took an even firmer grip on her. Jesse's cheeks turned pink.

Annika's father had been standing a few steps apart from their group. Now, he got a little closer. He was talking with another farmer. He gave the man a distant smile, as if he'd been told a dirty Ole and Lena joke, but every once in a while, he was glancing over at Tina.

Finally, Jesse pulled his wife away from Haas. He pinched the tan roll of flesh at her waist. Encircled in her husband's arms, Tina relaxed and sighed.

She gave Annika a benevolent smile. "Oh, Annika!" She said she couldn't wait to take Annika to see some real shows, in Iowa. The warm little bars the Sycamores played in the winter, their old-timey music bluesy and electrified, Jesse and the boys stretching their legs out after a set, the smell of fresh, sweet tobacco. The tent-filled fields in the summer, early-morning sun in the poplars after an epic, sleepless night. Grazing rabbits watching them in the dew.

Speaking of wild animals, that had been Jesse himself. Until he met Tina, she said, he had always had two or three girls at once.

"But we're old married people now," Tina said. "I'm almost twenty!"

Haas moved in again and stroked Tina's arm with the back of his hand. He said he might be old himself, but he knew all about that kind of thing. Throaty warm-up chords on a gleaming upright bass, ice tinkling, dim, flickering lights in red, yellow, and blue. Oaky-smelling hippies crowded around the tables. Despondent tunes, the crush of strange bodies in the dark. "Cocaine," "Rosalita," "No Meat on the Bone."

"'Rosalita!'" Tina sighed. "I wish Jesse would write something like that."

Jesse took a sip of beer and wiped his mouth. He asked Haas about one of the other songs he had mentioned and let his wife go. Blowsy and breathing heavily, Tina wrapped her plump arms around Jesse from behind. He shifted his weight and kept talking.

Tina stepped away. Slowly, she bent her knees and set her iced tea bottle down with a clink on the street. When she straightened, she looked dull and sleepy. But in the next moment, she was towering over Annika. She grabbed Annika's hand and yanked on it.

"Come on, Annika," she said, "we're going to dance, aren't we?"

Annika was seized with panic. She knew how to do only the two-step and waltz with her father. She didn't know how to jump around the way Tina would expect her to do. She pulled her hand back and shook her head. Everyone she knew was here.

Maybe in Iowa, she was thinking . . .

"Jesse wants to," she said.

Jesse gave Annika a wan smile and held his hands up. There was a beer in each of them. He was holding Haas's cup while he went to the bathroom.

Annika's father arrived from out of nowhere. Annika had never known him to dance with anyone but her, though she had heard stories of him and her mother. Tina shot her a quick, pained expression as Weston held out his long hand to her and Annika felt a rush of regret and took a step forward, but it was too late.

The Outlaw was singing "Elvira." Out in the middle of the street, Annika's father and Tina, both so tall, her father in his slim clothes, his sharp boots, Tina's long bare legs, her golden skin and big majestic body, her dark red hair against her white clothes, caught people's eyes like Harland and his girl had done earlier, but without the otherworldly effect.

Tina's pigtails swung. She did not seem familiar with the two-step. She stumbled and stepped on Weston's boot, laughing awkwardly. With a strained look, Annika's father turned her over the pavement and began to sweat. His glasses, wire with a bar across the top, slipped down his nose and his hair dampened around the temples. His gaping mouth, which at times made him seem stubborn or wary, gave him tonight an almost childish, wondering look.

Watching them, Annika felt the ground open up and drop her into a seamy place. Stained mattresses strewn on a concrete floor, sour-smelling men, rotten-looking dogs.

Tightening his grip, her father pulled Tina closer . . .

Annika looked away. Jesse had wandered off somewhere, but Haas stepped forward. Annika glanced over when she heard the commotion, Haas trying to cut in on Tina and her father, Tina trying to slip out of the iron grip of both of them.

Annika turned into the crowd, which suddenly seemed not cheerful, but hostile. Then she heard something awful and familiar.

"There's the white rat," the voice said.

She had not even seen the boy there. She was sure he had been watching, waiting until she was alone.

She turned to look at him. He was not much taller than her but was also hideously ugly. The likelihood that his smashed, toadlike features made him miserable didn't make her hate him any less. He stood alone, swaying drunkenly on the sidewalk, his eyes nearly closed. A dirty bandana tied around his big head.

No, she should not have done the ponytail . . . With her big ears that stuck out low on her small head, the name fit. Her blouse was even cream colored.

Jesse had reappeared and was watching her with a sympathetic look. Annika turned away from him, tightly crossing her arms. What else to do when you were being humiliated by a child?

"Look, the rat's jealous . . . That's her boyfriend . . ."

Annika pulled her fists into her stomach and waited for it to be over. She would never step foot in that school again. She wouldn't even come to town if she could help it.

After a minute, her father walked off the dance floor by himself, not toward her, but to the line of portable toilets by the bank.

Not long after that, the dance was over. The town stood for a while in the street, kicking plastic cups. It would be a whole year before there was another one.

CHAPTER 7

The next morning, Annika caught her father as he was leaving the house.

"Do you think you got anywhere with it last night?" she asked icily.

Her father stiffened and picked up his thermos. His voice was quite loud. "With what, Nick?"

"The field."

"I don't know. I guess we'll see," he said and walked out without looking at her.

Well. He wasn't the only one who was upset. To think that even before Annika's humiliation last night, he had eclipsed the good feelings she'd been having by trying to take something that was rightfully her own.

All day she watched him. She followed him outside and kept a sharp eye on the spot where he was working in the fields. She worked in the garden picking peas, but when she saw her father's gangly figure getting close to the woods on the far edge of the potato patch, she called the dogs, quickly crossed the backyard, and climbed the wire fence into the spongy pasture.

When she was halfway across the field, she saw him bent over a far row. Good.

Annika relaxed and slowed down. She clapped Tippy back from running the bleating cows, then squeezed through a gap between the wooden post and the wire at the gate of the second fence which separated the cows from the woods. Mash soaked the already mud-clotted hair of his underbelly sloshing through a drainage ditch. When she came with the dogs under the shade of the first stand of white pine and poplar, Mash took off into the deeper woods after a rabbit while Annika lingered at the edge, just hidden in the leaves and branches.

Part of the shoreline of ancient Lake Agassiz was said to have run straight across this cow pasture. Almost every summer, some young scientist or another sent a letter to the house asking if he might go get soil samples, and every time, her father decided he'd better not.

They had about twenty acres of trees. Swatting flies, Annika went around checking a few of her usual spots for signs, keeping one eye on her father. Piles of deer turds everywhere, looking like small, leathery black eggs laid amongst the patches of pink twinflower trailing its stems along the ground. She and her father sometimes hunted deer in the fall, though some years they wouldn't get around to it. They shared an unfavorable feeling about deer season, that it brought out all the yahoos, local and otherwise, who hadn't handled a gun or even been in the woods all year. Two years in a row, hunters had shot at their horses from the road. Now all of their land was posted.

Annika preferred trapping to hunting. A fisher snarling a few feet from her face could not be mistaken for anything else. She set and checked traps all year. While the seasons varied for raccoon, ermine, beaver, otter, rabbit, and the rest, she was unofficially allowed by her father to track, trap, and kill any fox, lynx, weasel, or brush wolf that killed a chicken, even a timber wolf if it took down a calf. And anything that threatened the house. Annika had never shot a timber wolf and didn't know if she wanted to, though she did dream of seeing one up close, as deeply as she feared and longed for the day when the big cougars and panthers that had now slinked their way from the West into this part of the world again came out of where they were hiding in the deepest parts of the woods, not to simply slip by like shadows as they'd done up until now, but to show everyone what they could do.

If she ever did kill a wolf, her father had instructed her to bury it deep in the ground to keep them both out of serious trouble.

The peatland on the northern side of 66 and the western side of 4 was state owned, strictly protected, prohibited to walk on except when it froze. In the summertime, to step in was to destroy it. Annika liked to look into the bog from the road. The spindly spruces, their roots sucking acid, their sporadic withered or barely gasping branches. The blood-red pitcher plants that digested bugs in the same water they drowned them in. The whole spread had a sparse, moon-like look.

Annika liked farming, gardening, and cattle just fine, but she preferred being in the woods. On her birthday and Christmas for as long as she could remember, her father had been giving her novels about girls and their hunting dogs, mythological forest stories, and collections of rhyming nature poetry. The sentimental poems about nature's beauty made her father cry, while Annika liked those best with a menacing undertone:

> *A treacherous smiler*
> *With teeth white as milk,*
> *A savage beguiler*
> *In sheathings of silk.*

One thing she and her father really liked to do was to bait bears together. They had never gotten one, though once they had come close. Another hunter used their bait and trap and took their bear. When they checked the trap, it had been sprung and reset differently. This happened occasionally with other traps too, mink particularly, for which the season could be as short as six days. The incidents prompted Annika's father, based on strong suspicions, to develop hostile relationships with certain people in the area.

They found out for certain who the bear thief was. Everybody did, as he took it without a license and was shamed on the front page of the paper. That was a rare cinnamon bear, too.

Almost every day during the school year, after the bus had dropped her off and Annika had tossed her bag onto the steps, she would run to the top of their place, where the tall, straight white pines and birches, breathing in the wind, laced their branches over her head. Her father had always let her go into the woods as much as she wanted. Sometimes even when she shirked her chores. Just not on solo trips to the state forest, too far away to go on a bike, where she would have liked to go more often for berries, mushrooms, tamarack cones. The one time he had let her take the truck there earlier this summer, she had stayed for twelve hours. When she came home, he was anxious. Not so much worried about her well-being, she suspected, but simply lonely. When finally she pulled in after dark, her father was coming south on 4, his long legs pumping her small bicycle, having struck out to the lake. It seemed that though he wanted to tend to her mother's ghost on this farm, keep it alive and well, at the same time he didn't love to be left alone with it.

Was her father afraid that if Annika went too deep into that wildest of places, she might not want to come out?

The dark thought appealed to her and for a while, out tramping in the late-morning sun the day after the Fourth, Annika felt peaceful again. She stopped at the pile of rocks where her parents' first two dogs were buried. Her mother had patted, fed, and trained these dogs with her small hands; they had barked to alert her when someone was coming.

Now, somewhere under the ground, they were two small-headed skeletons that, without their expressive eyes and wagging tails, could have belonged to any wild animal.

Annika wondered what her mother's voice had sounded like. She felt for a sharp moment on the edge of tears.

She'd asked her father this question once. He sat like a stone for a second, his brown eyes darting behind his glasses like two swallows before a rain. He stood up and turned away, talking about something else. While Annika had always been encouraged to worship in the cult of her mother and contribute money to her temple, her father liked to keep anything real of her to himself.

What was going to happen now? Annika thought of an incident a few days before when she and her father had been driving home from Williams in the rain. They had run into Tina walking on the road. She had gotten stuck out in the shower. Her father had made Annika get out of the truck and move into one of the small rear seats in the extended cab. Even though there was plenty of room for her next to the gear shift, between him and Tina.

"No, just look at how long her legs are, Nick." If that was any indication of how he wanted the order of things to go!

If it ever came to that, Annika thought, she wouldn't be able to stand it. She would—well, she would escape into the woods for once and for all is what she'd do.

Anyway, her father wouldn't get Tina. Not in *that* way. Over Jesse? Annika's churlish laughter fractured the quiet warmth of the summer woods.

Although it might not matter. Her father might not be the kind of man who needed a body to hold to replace one woman with another.

Annika ran her hand over the pile of burial stones. Thinking about her mother gave her a tender and sore, yet mystical, feeling. They were so similar it was easy to pretend a transfiguration had happened upon her mother's death: they had become the same person. Annika had started drawing partially as a fulfillment of this magic.

If she thought about her mother in this way, nothing had been lost. Still, the idea left her lonely. If her mother was going to live both out in Sparky's stall with her father when Annika wasn't there and in her own essence when she was, logically she couldn't also ever appear in a glittering mist to give Annika womanly advice. How to conjure the ghost of someone she couldn't remember, anyway, a woman she only pretended to know when she held a photograph? Babies let people go so easily. As long as another set of hands had been available to change her diaper and stuff her face, what had she cared?

For her father, summoning her mother seemed simple, like poking his head into his daughter's room to tell her that her egg was ready or calling the mare Fern in from the field.

Annika lay back against a flat stone and breathed in the clean, spicy smell of the trees. Tippy came panting to sit with her. Annika patted the dog, her eyes closed, and pictured her mother. In her mind, her mother's strawberry blond hair was going gray, like her father's. In reality, she had not been much older than Annika and Tina when she died.

Annika felt a drip on her face. She pushed the drooling dog away, sat up, and threw her a stick. She glanced at a western cloud. If she didn't get the peas in today before it rained tomorrow, she might not get back into the soaked garden for a week.

Tippy was nosing around in the rocks when Mash trotted up and mounted her from behind, his paws wrapped neatly around her small dark hindquarters. Poor Tippy, his own sister, who could only turn her head and snap at him—she didn't want to climb the rough pile of stones. He had her trapped. Annika stood up and called Mash off sharply. When he didn't move, she swatted him.

She remembered to look again into the potato field. Her father was gone. Annika began to jog. She sped up into a sprint. She came up to the house, panting, where she heard something that made her want to turn around and head back into the trees.

Her father talking again, this time in the garage, his voice nervous, unnaturally bright. "Diane," he said to her mother, hesitating before stuttering over something about voltage and electrical cords.

Annika was disgusted. Not least because her father was a miserable liar, even to the dead.

Shortly after lunch, she spied him walking to the end of the driveway. She didn't stay in the yard long enough to see which way he turned on the road. She took off running through the woods for Jesse and Tina's.

It was still only noon. She would have plenty of time to get the rest of the peas in if she stayed only an hour or two. It was still light late into the evening. A rainy day tomorrow would be a good time to freeze. Spending this warm and pretty afternoon in a steamy kitchen would be a waste.

When she got to Jesse and Tina's house, her father was not there. Jesse was on the steps drinking from a thermos of water, squinting painfully in the sunshine, Tina sitting beside him, looking at her hands. Haas was there as well. His dilapidated Appaloosa wandering the yard untethered and getting fat on the uncut grass. Annika picked up the dangling lead and led the horse away from the side yard. Tina had dug up a small plot there, and a spindly line of spinach shoots was coming through.

The three of them were discussing a call Tina had made the day before to the Blocks to ask what they wanted to do about Sherry. The Blocks were understanding, but they said they hoped Tina and Jesse would be able to deal with Sherry on their own. They couldn't get over from Grand Forks themselves right now. If Sherry hadn't done any damage or threatened anybody, she probably wouldn't. Jesse and Tina should lock the doors and keep an eye out. And get a dog. Of course, they should do what they had to, to protect themselves. Still, the Blocks would prefer it if the police didn't come. If there was any safety code one was supposed to follow to rent out a house, surely that old place wasn't up to it.

One hand palming the side of the house, Haas said, "No, they're right. Don't call the cops. That's not how people do things around here."

Tina looked up at Annika, her eyes dull, her hair, a crinkle in it from the miniature braid she'd taken out, falling in a pretty way around her face. "Is that true?"

Annika shrugged. What would she and her father have ever had to call the police for? She watched Haas, who seemed to be feeling even worse than Jesse. Each drink of water made him sweat. He wiped his big arm across his forehead; his skin twitched. Flies—or he could feel Annika's eyes on him.

"We don't have a choice anymore," Tina said. "She's stealing from us now!" This morning, some of her clothes had disappeared off the line. Now she felt jumpy every time she left the house.

Haas brought his hand to his mouth. Casually, he offered to go up into the woods himself to see if Sherry might be camping there. He could have a talk with her. He said they must do something to make Tina feel more comfortable.

Tina gave him a tepid smile. "Do you know her, Gordon?"

Haas said he had run into Sherry a few times on the road.

"Well, what do you think—is she completely crazy?"

Haas's head wobbled into a clumsy nod. "Ah. When she's drunk, she is." When Annika stared harder at him, he leaned into the house, his head bowed beneath his arm, hiding his face.

Jesse said he would be interested in going on that expedition himself. Inspiration, you know . . .

Slowly, Haas straightened and said he wasn't sure. They shouldn't make it look like an ambush. If it were just him, he was only a neighbor making a visit.

"How well do you know her?" Annika asked him.

Haas didn't look at her. After a second, she grinned and almost laughed out loud. She thought of the time she had heard a man's voice over here at the house. She wondered why she had never considered this possibility before.

"Maybe he's right." Tina turned to her husband and took his thermos for a drink. "Anyway, I'd rather have you stay here with me. And you haven't gotten any work done today."

That settled it; Jesse was going. He stood up and said he wasn't sending Haas into who-knows-what alone.

"Can I come?" Annika said.

"I think we *should* take her." Jesse smiled kindly at her; he might still have been thinking about the bad time she'd had last night.

Haas looked at her suspiciously. "Don't you and your father have a farm to run, Annika?"

"She knows the woods better than we do," Jesse said.

"Oh—there's not that much to know."

Annika said, "I think I know where she might be."

Tina looked pale. "I'm not going out there. You're all going to leave me here alone?"

Jesse said he thought he and Gordon could take on one skinny crackhead if they had to.

"I'll bring Tippy over," Annika said.

She ran home for the dog to stay with Tina, and she, Haas, and Jesse walked out into the Blocks' woods an hour later. The breeze felt good in her hair. The grasses, swaying in the sun, smelled wheaty, delicious, their slim heads bowed over with seeds. The land was so sunken and flat in this part of the country that when you looked at the line of woods ahead of you from a fair distance, it seemed nothing was higher than your head apart from the sky, and even that started at the same place as your feet.

Haas kept a faster pace than Annika and Jesse. He looked back every little while to ask if he was going the right way.

Annika felt Jesse watching her and was flattered. A few times, she crouched to run her hand over the damp ground or, when they got into the trees, to examine a broken twig. In fact, she was simply headed for an old hunting cabin in the woods, for most of the way following a faint deer trail.

When they arrived, Annika yanked the swollen door open. No one was there. No blankets or water in the gray shadows, a few insects humming. There was only one room, a bench wide enough to sleep on built onto one wall. A card table, a metal folding chair. Dead flies on the windowsill, a live hornet tapping the glass.

But some signs nonetheless: empty wine bottles on the board floor, a couple of dark pink, dried-up berries.

Annika stood breathing in the warm, dusty quiet. Cloudy light came in through two windows, filthy with dust and bird crap. She pressed on a loose board with her toe.

Outside the empty building, the clearing smelled faintly of skunk. A piece of yellow baling twine was knotted to a branch of a red pine and Jesse jumped to try and swat it. His fingers missed by a couple of feet.

"Hanging some kind of meat, maybe? How the hell did she get up there?"

Someone had dug a fire pit in the clearing outside the cabin and lined it with pieces of granite from the masonry pile in Jesse and Tina's backyard. Annika ran her hand over the neatly arranged stones. A wide circle around the pit had been cleared of undergrowth and needles down to the dirt.

Annika glanced at Haas. "I bet she's watching us . . ."

The three of them stood quietly for a while. They heard only a fluting thrush and squirrels.

Haas stood with his hands on his hips in the dappled sunlight, looking around at the camp for a long time. He went back into the cabin and came out with one of the berries in his palm, rubbing it delicately with his finger as if getting the dirt off a piece of gold.

"A juneberry," Annika said.

Haas didn't look at her. After a minute, he sniffed the berry, then dropped it in his shirt pocket. "That's something, isn't it?" he said. He began to complain about how in general, he felt that most people in this county had lost almost every trace of the place's old pioneer spirit. Acres of berries grew around here. Didn't anybody dry them to sell? Or make any jam? What an enterprise something like that could turn into. At the grocery store in town, searching the jelly and peanut-butter aisle, he'd once asked a woman who worked there and she told him she didn't know if anyone did all that anymore or not; it was an awful lot of work. Her mother had used to do it. They were poor and she had to. When Haas asked if she did it herself, the woman was insulted. She swept her arm up and down the grocery aisle.

"It's not the eighteen hundreds anymore," she said.

After a while, Jesse said he should get back to the house if he wanted to get any work done before supper.

On the walk home, Annika watched Haas huffing it just ahead of her in tall black rubber boots. Today, she could hardly believe that for a time last night, she had decided she no longer cared about the dream of the rustically elegant new house. Jesse and Tina would love the place. They would want to be there all the time.

Who knew when she and her father would get that field out of Haas? In the meantime, why limit herself to selling tamarack cones? She could be doing morels in the spring, blueberries in July. Of course, selling berries wouldn't be a matter of just stopping at the forestry office with a sack of cones. If she let a few neighbors know she had berries, word might travel. She did not relish the thought of going door-to-door.

Annika noted, in a strong voice meant to carry past Jesse, who was walking beside her, that that was a nice cabin back there. It had gotten her to thinking about the house she and her father wanted to build someday. As soon as possible. With that house, her father could fulfill the promise he had made to her mother, as well as get out of the dingy little place in which she'd had to die. Only recently, Annika said, had she begun to understand how much pressure the whole thing had put on her father.

"Sure. Of course," said Jesse.

Annika said that she and her father had gotten ideas for how the inside of their new place could look from the abandoned pioneer homes and outbuildings dotting the county, as well as the sooty remains of the Graceton one-room schoolhouse, which Annika would have attended with seven or eight other children if a county-wide fire, fifty years, road-building, and the advent of motor vehicles hadn't gotten in her way.

She'd liked to explore these buildings and ruins since she was a little girl. She said wasn't it funny that some people, when they saw those decaying walls, thought the buildings looked empty, sad, or spooky, back a ways from the road, buried in the tall, wet grass. It reminded them of a time that was unsophisticated, dirty, dead and gone. Some people might rip off an unrotted gray plank to build a bench or planter for their house; but perhaps they put that taste of the old life there just to show that their own life now was quite different.

Annika said many of the people around here were like that. They kept their houses modern and nice, only a few country touches here and there, some antique kitchen implements, a pristine milk jug or spice grinder, arranged on shelves for decoration. A plastic goose clock above a plastic countertop, cupboards filled with cheap crackers and boxed macaroni and cheese. Ceramic candle holders molded to look like a section of a birch tree and, from the flea market, black or colored etchings on mirrored glass: wolves, moose, and loons. Most likely made in China!

The butter press Annika was making for the fair would make a nice present for one of the neighbor women, someone like Karlyn Johnson. But even if Annika knew her or any of the others well enough—if her father ever accepted invitations for card games, cookie exchanges, or watermelon feeds—Annika wouldn't give the little press away. Even if Karlyn liked it, she wouldn't use it.

Annika's aesthetic was different. She didn't want a taste of the woods and country; she wanted it all. To her, those old buildings didn't look dead, but private and inviting. Very much alive. She wanted log walls, a gleaming slab floor, at the doorway a tough round rug of braided straw, a wooden table and a black cooking stove, a driftwood bench, a carved bootjack, a big woodbox, and a smaller kindling box. On the windowsills, dishes of colored stones and mussel shells. In the summer, jars of daisies and goatsbeard, in the winter a tamarack bough. A rock fireplace and chimney, a toasting fork, on the mantle matches and bullets. Pine chairs around the table, a rocker by the window, a throw of stitched furs, a mending basket, iron pots hung on the walls, a straw broom stood up in the corner, and her shotgun over the door.

In her father's room and in her own private loft upstairs would go the beds with thick posts and headboards knotted, split, and edged with bark, the mattresses secured in slings of knotted deer hide. Crazy quilts and feather pillows of goose and duck Annika would embroider by a lamp at night.

In the peak of the house, its sharp A-frame roof sloping nearly to the ground, would go the rosemary, yarrow, clover, strawberry leaves, and venison jerky hung up to dry. In the root cellar, pumpkins and squashes, drawers full of onions and potatoes, carrots stuck tops down in a box of sand, and jars of high-bush cranberry juice and wild-grape jelly, relish, maple syrup, mincemeat, birch water, wild rice, pickled beets, pickled asparagus, pickled green beans, pickled pickles, and jam.

And a milk cow tethered in the yard . . . Once they'd raised the money to build the house, they'd hardly need any more. With a place like that, one wouldn't have to travel for either goods or beauty. Not with Jesse and Tina inside, singing and playing the fiddle.

Privately, Annika imagined her father playing the host like a proper old man, serving popcorn and crêpes before getting out of the way of his daughter and her friends.

Walking through the tall grass with Jesse, Annika felt better now than she had since the good part of the dance the night before. "Sounds like you've thought it all out," Jesse said and yawned. Annika thought to look again for Haas. He'd gotten far ahead and she wasn't sure he'd been listening.

CHAPTER 8

She fouled things up with the peas. She didn't get home until evening, and it was her turn to make supper. While she was fixing
Scotch stew and the peas she'd picked in the morning, slow heavy
clouds moved in.

The rain started pouring and didn't stop for two days. By the end
of it, water was standing in the garden. Even when that subsided, one
step sucked her down into the dense clay soil nearly to the top of
her boot. There was no ideal spot in their low-lying yard for the plot.
Annika had waited to do this pick until there was enough to warrant
a full freezing day. Now, not only would they miss growing a whole
week of new peas, but the ones she did eventually get to would be
bitter, fat, and mealy.

The rain kept Tippy for the most part holed up in the barn. There
was some relief in that. But peas were her father's favorite vegetable;
he was so annoyed he told Annika she was getting lazy.

He was one to talk! Who had left the house at two to pick up a salt
lick, then come home after five having forgotten all about it? (He'd
stopped to ask Tina if she needed anything from town.) Who had
spent nearly all of one of these rainy days gazing out the northern
window, holding a needle and thread and a pair of jeans he failed to
patch?

"We'll have to buy peas now, Nick," he said, "and they won't taste
half as good."

"What do you care?" She meant, what was he saving money for? He didn't take the bait. Her father seemed reluctant these days to talk about her mother's house.

For a day or two, they were aloof with one another, though not cold. There was too much fire running through both of them for that. Annika wanted badly to talk about the restive ache that grew in her at the sound of the evening's first poignant frog. Every morning, she woke up already yearning for and dreading the sound. When she heard it, would she still be the same person, in the same place, as she'd been the night before? In her sleep, she scratched her nails over her belly so hard she drew blood.

The suspicion that her father was feeling the same way at times made her feel sick to her stomach. Or she wanted to punch him in the gut. No. She loved him. She loved him as he had been before, anyway. Even if she won this particular battle, would he be like every other man now? One night when she imagined her fist going into his belly, she gagged while she was brushing her teeth.

She was growing into something. At the same time, it seemed she'd never known she was young.

One night at supper, her father asked what she wanted to do for her eighteenth birthday, which was in the third week of July.

Every year on her birthday, her father took the day off and usually Annika picked the same thing for them to do: drive over to Warroad for lunch at the Dairy Queen. Afterward, they went to Zippel Bay, and back at home, they ate as much of her father's lasagna and yellow cake as they could until it was time to go to bed.

"Whatever you want to do," her father said, looking at his plate. His hair, the mix of birch colors that showed he had been a towhead as a boy, was thinning on top. "We could go to a movie if you want."

The nearest movie theater was in International Falls, eighty miles away, and her father couldn't stand the sulfur smell of the paper mill there. He had forgiven her for the peas. The moment felt important, the tension between them broken. Annika was not surprised when her father's brown eyes brimmed with tears. Remembering all the nasty things she'd been thinking about him, she felt overwhelmed herself.

She thought briefly about a day at the lake, though not at quiet Zippel Bay. This year she thought she would prefer one of the busier resort areas, where the boys were. They came to the county from dozens, even hundreds of miles away. Morris Point had a nice swimming beach, a bustling dock, and a couple of inlets her father could wander off to alone and cast from the shore. Any boy or man Annika hadn't known her whole life had the look of an exotic animal from the jungle or desert. More importantly, those young men didn't know anything about *her*.

That night in bed, Annika thought of her father and of everything the two of them had here. How content and happy she was; what a brat she had been! She drooled and cried into her pillow. She thought it over and decided that instead of going to the lake on her birthday, she would tell her father she wanted to go out for blueberries. Blueberries he liked even more than peas. And the patches that often developed by the old homestead sites near Norris Camp held a sentimental significance for their family. He and her mother had taken Annika there only days after she was born.

The next day, Annika mentioned it to her father. If she had been expecting a special moment, she didn't get it—her father agreed, but looked surprised.

After a minute, he seemed to be lost in thought. He was tidying up the living room, picking up stray shoes and papers with his long-fingered hands, and when he turned, she would sometimes catch the corners of his mouth moving. Various practiced expressions were crossing his face.

Perhaps he was imagining a conversation not with her mother, but with Annika—for a short while later, he asked if she wanted to have anybody over to the house in the evening.

"A few of the neighbors?" He avoided her eyes.

"I don't think so," Annika said coldly. "And after lunch, I don't want to do blueberries anymore. I want to go to the lake."

After the lake, she didn't say out loud, if she did anything, it would be to go to Jesse and Tina's. Alone.

When her birthday came, she and her father were both anxious and depressed, even while she was walking across the rippled sandy bottom at Zippel Bay and sidestroking through the cold water. She wore her mother's colorful suit, pinned to fit snugly in the bust. Her father paced the shore in his jeans, kicking at driftwood and swatting fish flies, which with their big, slippery wings had crowded the truck's windshield in a silvery drove the moment they pulled into the lot. Now they clung by the dozen to the back of her father's white shirt.

At home, her father gave her a woodburning pen and art supplies, as well as a new mink trap and the book *Young Audubon*. The next morning, Annika woke feeling she deserved more.

Her father might have been feeling the same, that he had messed things up somehow. At breakfast, he suggested that since it was sunny again, they should go to the blueberry patch in the afternoon.

It was extraordinary for him to suggest taking a second day off work when they had so much to do here in the height of the summer. The fence still stood unfinished. Since being cooped up by the rain, Tippy had become nervier than ever, though every time she went near it, she turned her nose up at the layer of moisture sheening the garden. Annika still had time. Did it even make a difference what the dog did now anyway, when nearly half of what she had planted was already gone? She shrugged at her father's suggestion. As soon as she finished feeding the horses and chickens, she hastily picked some onions to throw into a bucket and started to go over to Jesse and Tina's.

At the edge of the driveway, she heard steps coming up behind her. She started to walk faster. Then her father grabbed her arm.

Annika twisted out of his grip. "Get off me, what do you want?"

Her father put his hands on his hips. He took a step back from her. "Nick. Do you not get this? Tippy's going to get into that garden again."

She shielded her eyes from the sun. "Not today."

"Then today's a good day to finish that fence, don't you think? Nick, this is the food we live on all year."

"I thought you wanted to go for blueberries."

Her father stuttered. "That's food."

"We've got money," Annika said.

"Money," her father said and rolled his eyes. "Money? Let me tell you, money's got nothing to do with you being goddamn eighteen now. If you don't want to do your share of the work around here, I guess you wouldn't mind getting on at Marvin's instead. You think you'd like that better? Working in a factory all day?"

Annika looked at him for a long moment. Then she smiled.

"How would I get there?" she said.

Her father rolled his eyes again. He made a noise in his throat and dropped his gaze to the ground. When he didn't speak, Annika kept walking south on the road.

In her head, the conversation continued to roll until she was shaking with anger and talking to herself on the road.

"Money?" she parroted her father. "I made some of that money."

Coming up to Jesse and Tina's place, she made an effort to shift her thinking from her father and the farm. It was only making her look like a crazy person. She oriented her thoughts instead to the last time she had been to Jesse and Tina's house. Several things about the day had made a deep impression on her.

It was the day the rain had cleared. In the still-bright early evening, Gordon Haas and Jesse were in the living room, drinking pink cocktails and playing music. Jesse frowned at a piece of sheet music propped on a wire stand, stopping often to ask Haas about a note or a dynamic. Haas answered while continuing to play, slicing away with the big cello bow.

Then he would bark out, "Now find me and come back in!"

Which Jesse, his face bent close to the music, his lips turned up toward his nose like a duck's, would struggle to do; if, after he played a few notes, Haas shouted again, Jesse's green-brown eyes would shoot to another place on the page, and only when the song was done would he sit back and sigh, his face turned to the cracked ceiling, the red spot where the fiddle rested showing on his neck.

Annika stood back in the hallway, Tina, who had let her in, hovering somewhere behind. The living room didn't look as spacious as usual with Haas's big gleaming cello in it, its peg driving a dent into the unfinished wood floor. Still, the instrument, or Haas himself, magnified the house, electrified it. The two men struggled to get their footing while sunk into canvas deck chairs—"Goddamn chair," said Haas, scooting his behind forward on the back-slanting seat for the hundredth time. The tones vibrating deep from the bodies of the two instruments, then buzzing into one another in the air between them, so near to Annika they seemed sometimes to be coming out of her own body, caused a tremor in her chest. She laid her fingers there. The music was so daring and dark and complex that it made her feel untethered, almost mad.

And yet the mechanics were simple. The strings, the hollow wooden chambers, the men's arms and fingers working, the creaking of the chairs and the floor—

"Come on, Annika," Tina said. "Come sit in the kitchen with me."

Jesse gave Annika a perfunctory salute with his bow while Haas thumbed through a pile of music. He was cursing the chair under his breath, his stout thighs planted apart, his roper heels on. His glass sweated on the floor. He reached down to take a big swig.

Suddenly, though, he looked right at her. And spoke. "You like Hoffman, Annika?"

She stared at him. Tina said her name again, and finally, Annika followed her. But in the kitchen, as Annika pulled Charlie from another chair onto her lap and tried to listen to what Tina was saying, her heart was going faster than usual and her ears were in the other room.

Today, Annika again found Tina sitting alone at the kitchen table, listening this time to the sounds coming out of Jesse's studio. He'd set it up in one of the bedrooms upstairs, the second biggest in the house. The largest room they slept in, on the ground floor. It occupied the house's northwest corner.

Annika's father had warned Jesse about his mistake. The northwest room was not only scantily insulated, but it would get almost no sun and the brunt of the wind. They shouldn't be surprised if they woke one January morning with frost coating not only the outside but the inside of the window glass.

But those two rooms were the only ones the bedstead would fit in, and Jesse thought the cold and damp might affect his gear. Annika had been over when Jesse was arranging his studio. She helped him carry equipment up the stairs. Two fiddles, a drum kit, a long keyboard, microphones, a guitar, a battered trumpet, a recording console. When everything was in place, Jesse paced the room chewing on his finger, his other hand in the back pocket of his Tom Sawyer jeans, rolled up high and showing his hairy legs.

"So now what do I do?" he said and laughed shrilly.

Today, Annika listened with Tina as Jesse recorded the final tracks of a new song, different from his country and blues tunes. No lyrics, and Jesse had arranged the song for three fiddle parts. He was recording them all separately by himself.

When he played the demo for Annika, she didn't care for it. Each of the parts was in a high register and overall it had a screechy effect.

Three wicked, squalling children who were also Jesse, as each track carried his signature chords and licks. He wanted the song to sound sinister. When Annika heard it, she *was* afraid: of picking up an axe and throwing it around herself.

When he asked what she thought, she hesitated, and Jesse seemed angry. He said sulkily that he was just messing around. This process was all new to him. Before, he had always written in a group.

Either in desperation or retaliation, Jesse had made the piece louder and more aggressive than ever. In the kitchen, Tina draped herself over the wooden tabletop. She said Jesse had been working night and day on the song. He wanted to send a copy to his agent by the end of the week.

"He's too good for this!" she said.

But would he listen to her? Of course not, what did she know? He had written a beautiful song about her once. If only he would go back to the sort of thing that meant something . . .

The skin under Tina's eyes was dark. She crossed one of her hands over the other and nervously thumped the heels together to the syncopated rhythms of the fiddles upstairs.

She had done a little work on her kitchen. A few colorful plates and cups were lined up on the boards nailed to the wall. She had started an indoor herb garden and a line of drying yarrow and strawberry leaves.

But each task had been abandoned. A cardboard box of dishes sat on the kitchen counter, and a clay pot half-filled with dirt. Above a heap of wilted greens, pieces of looped twine hung empty from nails like small nooses.

Annika didn't sit down. If she had known Tina was going to be in this depressing mood, she might not have come.

Then again, where else could she have gone? Even if, say, she had thought to go to Morris Point by herself, it would be embarrassing, at her age, to show up at the resort sweaty after seven miles on a bike.

She sighed. She was over at Tina and Jesse's, but still Annika felt more chained to the farm than ever.

She suggested a walk, but Tina was tired. "Jesse's been keeping me up with that racket until late every night."

On top of all this, Sherry had made another appearance. Yesterday, Tina had caught her sneaking out of the well house, hugging a coffee can sloshing over with water.

"She stole a can of gas, too, and that's expensive. We needed it for the lawn mower. I'm afraid if I leave the house unlocked even to just go out and get the mail, I'll come back and all our food will be gone. Or she'll be standing in here! Then what do I do? Jesse refuses to do anything about it."

"Is it Haas telling him not to?"

"Well—Gordon thinks if we call the police about these little things, they'll only talk to her. It'll just make her mad and then she'll cause real trouble. Who knows, he could be right. Do you think she's dangerous, Annika?"

"I don't know . . ."

Really, Tina said, she was on her last nerve!

"If you're not too tired to drive," Annika began, "or I can, if you have a couple phone books I can sit on—"

"Are you taking me away from here?"

"You want me to?"

"Yes!"

Annika smiled as a wicked thought formed in her brain. "I'll show you a secret blueberry spot. Secret," she said.

"Who would I tell, Annika?"

"Jesse."

"Never," Tina said with a watery smile, and Annika emptied the onions she'd brought into the sink.

Coming up to the trailer, she felt excited and sick. When they were passing the house, her father came out of the barn. He stopped to

stare at the truck, his long arms hanging down. From the passenger
seat, Annika met his eyes for a second. She didn't think Tina had seen
him. But a hundred feet past the driveway, her head drooped. She
slowed down and glanced in the rearview mirror.

"Do you think your dad might want to come?"

Annika dug her fingernails into her thighs. She shook her head.

"No. He's got too much work to do."

Tina nodded and sped up. Her elbow out the window of the battered brown truck, her sunglasses on, one hand stroking brassy spots
on her hair where the sun pooled, humming to the Roseau station as
she complained about the commercial music they played, she started
to look a little better. The gearshift was as crotchety as a tractor's; she
had to put muscle into it to get it to click. At the railroad tracks, she
stopped to light a cigarette.

The sun and breeze were warm and peppery sweet. Even the
smoke smelled good, yet still the feeling in Annika's gut was bad. She
grabbed a bag of peanuts off the dash. They turned her stomach. She
cracked some for Tina, let the wind lick shells from her hand, sucked
salt off her fingers.

They took the two-lane blacktop Highway 11, County 3, County 2,
and a couple of Faunce roads into the state forest. As they bumped
through ruts, Annika thought that maybe she should have stopped
for her .22.

But that would have been impossible!

If they had stopped, she also could have grabbed more buckets for
enough berries to freeze or sell, if that's what she was going to do . . .

Passing through a cedar swamp, she asked Tina to pull over. She
got out and breathed in the air like an aromatic medicine. If she was
ever very sick, she had once told her father, take her there and lay
her out beneath the trees. With almost no undergrowth, the trees'
trunks, most of them straight, others mysteriously quite crooked, de-

fined the space from their dense canopy down to their roots showing darkly in the ground.

When she got back, if he were acting nicer, maybe she'd present the blueberries to her father as a surprise. That might be all right.

They passed the old Civilian Conservation camp, now headquarters for the wildlife management folks, Sherry's old stomping ground. They tooled around the homestead sites of the Norris settlement, no buildings left but one barn. It was easy to tell where the houses had been, though, still clear-cut after sixty years, here and there a gnarled white rose from the old country or a lilac bush.

They pulled over and got out to walk. Annika was interested in the barn. This past spring, there had been a fire just beyond it; that might be good for blueberries.

Heading toward the pine woods a short distance behind the building, Annika stopped to poke around. One of the hay doors on the second level hung by only one hinge, and the door swayed lightly in the wind. The ground-level door, warped by weather, stood slightly ajar, the bottom corner driven at an angle into the soil. In the weeds was a short length of rebar as well as a few squat beer bottles of brown glass, a rusted button, and other pieces of antique garbage.

Annika looked up at the second level. The structure seemed fairly sound. She wondered about the stairs that would lead to the loft. She turned to Tina, standing at a short distance looking into the glimmering aspens, and called to her. When she turned back to the door, she saw, as if for the first time, a matted path going into the opening of the barn. At the same time, the wind changed and she got a bad whiff of something.

It was pungent and acrid. Annika smelled it, and then she thought about it. An uncomfortable sensation ran down her body and she felt soft and exposed, like a beetle spinning on its back.

In the shadows of the barn, a slight movement and a soft growl. A hooded stare. Yellow eyes in the dark and a long body rising on four slender legs.

"What?" Tina called back.

Annika stood still in the tall warm field grasses waving slightly around her.

"Turn around and walk back to the road," she said.

Tina stood a second, then went quietly. Annika backed away from the door. She bent to the ground and picked up the rebar. She pulled out her jackknife, popped the blade, and dropped the rebar. She picked it up again, slipped it into her back pocket, turned, and followed Tina.

Several times as she crossed the distance of a hundred or so yards, Annika turned in a circle and peered into the bright quiet of the day. She glanced overhead. She thought to look for more lions in the leaves. The swaying branches were empty. In front of her, the curves of Tina's tall, tan body in jean shortalls over a lavender bandeau top moved in a not quite dreamlike way, a charged vision more real than real. At times, Annika felt she might stop, close her eyes, and simply wait for it . . . It seemed better than moving. It felt like torture to go. She pushed her legs forward through the tall weeds. Tough pieces snapped back at her like a whip.

Tina reached the truck first and got in quickly. Annika caught up and stood holding onto the open passenger door. She ran her eyes over the rippling brown grass in front of the barn, then over the birch, pine, and soft-looking foliage behind it, a mix of delicate colors ranging from bright green to gold. The building was quiet. Yes. But not empty.

There was one soft sound out of place in the fragrant air; Tina was hissing at her. Annika heard it only now. She turned to see Tina gripping the key in the ignition, then looked at the barn again. She took a few steps off the gravel and back into the grass.

Tina barked out her name. After another minute or two, Annika finally climbed into her seat and slammed the heavy and cantankerous door.

"What were you standing there for?" Tina said. "What was it? A bear?"

"For cripes' sake!" Annika grunted and squirmed in discomfort. She pulled the rusted rebar from her back pocket and dropped it clanging to the floor. She pressed her hands over her eyes. "A bear!"

"What, then?"

"Did you not smell that?"

"I didn't smell anything."

"Like a big old cat box. Like a big old sandpile filled with cat shit." Annika hardly ever swore. It felt good and she did it again. "Wildcat piss. Wildcat shit," she said. It had been dark, but so close. The big yellow-brown cat had looked right at her and she'd caught a glimpse of another one behind it.

She thought of the snake that had once run over her shoe in the grass. She shivered and smiled. She hadn't startled this time, had she? So this was growing up, was it?

"If I'd just brought my gun!" she said.

Tina looked at her. "What, you would have gone after it?"

"For cripes' sake!"

"With a .22."

Annika's grin faded. She glared ahead at the road.

"Even I know that," Tina said.

She started the truck, and with many small, precise motions that took several minutes to achieve turned around on the narrow forest road, trees scraping the vehicle on either side. She began to drive back in the direction from which they'd come. Slowly. It wouldn't do to hit something and break down here. "Do you think maybe they've packed up?" Annika speculated softly after a while. "Like wolves?"

Tina was still annoyed. "How would I know?"

"There were two grown ones in there at least." Annika didn't know much about cougars. They hadn't been in this part of the country for maybe seventy years. "They didn't come after us. In the winter, it might have been a different story," she said.

Still, she had gotten them out of it.

"Jesus Christ." Tina glanced into the rearview mirror and let out a long breath. "You had me so scared!"

"You should have been scared."

Tina let out a shrill laugh. Then she screamed, and Annika jumped and swore again. After a second, they screamed together. They fell into hysterics, and when that was over, the drive was full of a pleasant, breathless silence in which they listened to the wind in the clattering poplars.

When they hit the blacktop, Tina started to head back to 4, but Annika couldn't go home yet. Not even to Tina and Jesse's. No. She was too wound up. She told Tina she still wanted to go picking.

At first, Tina said not on your life. But she looked lively now. Even happy. Far better than she had looked sitting at the table in her kitchen.

She drove where Annika told her to, a quarter of a mile behind a neighbor's place, Frank Gamache. He was too old to go out for berries anymore. It was common knowledge that anyone in Graceton was welcome in the clearing of his small pine grove, even old recluses like Annika and her father.

Most of the patch had been picked over. There were a few berries, not half as many as in the hot spots by the settlement, her father's blueberry heaven. That stinking cat box! The low bushes growing out of the duff there were so full and heavy, some of the berries big, too, almost as big as in the grocery store. Most years it looked as if not even the bears had discovered it. The way Annika remembered things now from last summer, an ice-cream pail could be filled without hardly moving ten feet.

The bears had discovered this patch. One came crashing through the brush on the far edge of it. Tina was crawling in her bare feet gathering pinecones, the lavender bandeau riding up over one of her big breasts, when she heard it.

"What's that, a deer?" She grabbed her sandals and rose. She adjusted her top.

"Maybe a really big one." Annika was laughing again. She felt as though a funny drug was coursing through her veins. The bear, still hidden in the trees, grunted and clacked its jaw.

Tina made to run away. Annika stayed still, peering into the foliage; she would have liked to get a look at it. Tina said her name sharply. Annika waited another second.

Tina whimpered and Annika put down her bucket and clapped her hands. "Ah, yah yah! Go on now, you. Go on!"

The bear huffed a few times. There was another smaller crash. The crunching in the brush got fainter until it was gone.

Tina moaned. "Annika, do you know what you're doing?"

"You can trust me." Annika giggled when Tina glanced at the truck parked several yards away on the trail.

"I don't like it," she said.

"It's just a little bear." Poor Tina! But how incredible Annika felt today—as if she were not only out in the warmth and the sweet, loamy smell of the afternoon, but had swallowed it. The berries a bright periwinkle in the sunlight dappling the patch, the green leaves splashed with reddish purple. She thought again of the way the big exotic half-crouching cat had held her eyes as its head came down low to its paws.

Tina had not sat down again. "I'm getting bitten alive, anyway."

"Just calm down."

"I guess I could just leave you."

"I guess I could walk from here."

Tina stayed on her feet for a long time. The woods were quiet except for a raven making a call like hammering on wood; another responded with a sound like dripping water. Finally, Tina shrugged and dropped to the ground. This time, she left her sandals on.

"Fuck you, Annika," she said.

Annika felt a shiver of shock and pleasure. Tina lay back with her plump arms stretched out, her knees up, and little by little Annika covered the bottom of her pail. She glanced from time to time at Tina lying on the reddish needles, close to the color of her hair and eyes. Tina groaned and rolled over, bits of bark and leaves clinging to the backs of her freckled legs and falling up the cuffs of her shorts. Sun glinted on the blond streaks in her hair.

Watching her, Annika thought again of the evening Jesse and Haas had played music in the living room, keeping at it as shadows began to fall. Soon after Tina turned on the lamps, the two men came into the kitchen. Annika heard them pass by. She was in the bathroom. Calling out to Haas that he was going to get something, Jesse ran back upstairs.

When Annika came into the kitchen, Haas was leaning over Tina, a damp dish towel crumpled in his hand. Tina looking at him with an acerbic smile as she had on the Fourth of July.

Her hand was up, blocking him. Haas was yanking on her arm, trying to get his mouth close to her ear.

When he saw Annika, he stepped away from the table, but lazily; he smiled, his lids drawn down heavily over his protruding eyes. He wore shorts that sagged under his belly. Finally, he turned to toss the dish towel into the sink.

After a minute, Jesse came in and handed Haas a harmonica. The two of them began a conversation about it that promised to go on for a while.

Haas's gray-golden beard, nearly meeting the sideburns that came down low on his cheek, had come so close to Tina's neck that maybe she'd felt a faint scratch there before Annika scared him away.

Haas blew a few splatty notes on the harmonica. "And as a blues instrument, what do you think of it, Jesse?"

"Well, the blues," said Jesse jauntily—how happy he was in the house when Haas was there!—"influenced every kind of folk music that came after it." He squinted and scruffed the back of his head, fluffing his curls. "I mean, in America. So you can't do any kind of— you know, even some kind of—with a washboard and a saw—without it. Well, you could, but not naturally . . . You could, but I don't know why . . . I don't have any interest in music that tries to be pure. You don't get anywhere with it. Backward, that's where you get. You might as well be dead. No. You take the music and you overpower it. With your own consciousness . . . Your own volition . . ."

"Your what? Where are you getting this crap?" Tina was talking to Jesse but glowering at Haas.

The two men looked at each other, hooting with laughter. Tina rolled her eyes and got up to fold some towels heaped on top of the washing machine.

Out in the blueberry patch, a couple of squirrels squawked over a branch. They shook the elastic pine bough against serrated patches of sun and sky and a few brown needles rained down. Down from Gamache's came the faint hum of a motor and the slam of a car door. One of his kids come out to make sure he hadn't died since the last time.

Annika was picking quietly when Tina cleared her throat. "Nicky. Do you think Jesse's changed?"

And Tina was using her nickname now, too! Annika smiled. She had hardly heard the question. "How do you mean?"

"What do you think of his new music?"

Annika hesitated and Tina cried out, "I knew it! Do you think it's Gordon's fault?"

"You want Haas to stop teaching him?" Annika thought this could be a mistake. Haas was pulling strings for Jesse; he'd already set him up with shows with people he knew in Chicago and South Dakota. Jesse could sight-read better now as well.

Haas had used to play professionally himself, at one point in a group with his wife Laura. But he said he'd gotten tired of doing that all the time. It wasn't for him to always have to stay in top performance shape, to perform every night. He would rather help along young people who were burning to do it.

"Jesse works too much," Tina said.

"I thought you wanted him to work."

Tina said coldly, "I just don't see what was wrong with what he was playing before. I don't want him to lose himself is all. He's wasting his time here. Annika, they're taking Jesse's commercial off the air. We're getting the last of the residuals checks next month. Our savings are running out and what are we going to have to show for it? That crap song? Does he think they'll be able to sell something like that? No words! Who wants to listen to that?"

"Could you get a job?"

"I already have one, don't I? If I hadn't been here, the money would be gone already. If there's one thing I know how to do, it's economize. That's what being poor for so long will get you. I could grow lettuce out of a sidewalk. Out here, you don't have to spend money. If I can do it right, I can keep him going long-term. But he can't make things so hard for me."

Tina said that back in the old days, Jesse had made life much easier. Perfect, even. When they first met, Jesse was so hot for her that he was out of his mind. Night and day, he would be driven to search for her in all of her little hole-in-the-wall spots, shouting from the street that he was looking for his alley cat. That put him in mind of a song, of course. Tina's song. The one all the girls loved, though they knew it was about her and to keep their distance.

Before Jesse, things had been rough and lonely for Tina. Maybe Jesse thought living recklessly was fun. Yes, and after today, Tina said, eyeing Annika, it looked as if he weren't the only one.

But Annika and Jesse were wrong. Had they ever been so hungry they couldn't think straight? Had they ever lived in a house without a proper door? Been woken up in the middle of the night after a party to the sound of someone's madman friend racking a shotgun? Had to appease him however she could when he told her he was bored and needed something to do?

Annika looked over at her, startled. Tina's eyes were closed.

She'd had a few ragtag friends in those wild days, Tina said, and usually there was some dirtbag boyfriend hanging around. That was all. Jesse had been a real chance for her. He'd married her to protect her and give her a home. That was what he said he wanted.

Annika stopped picking berries. She put down her pail, angled her foot over a pinecone, and slowly crushed it.

Yes, she thought, Jesse did seem something—harder—than he'd been when Annika first saw him sprawled on the lawn with Thomas and Polly. Not to say more muscular, but less easy and supple. Like a wheelbarrow being run over rough grass, a rigid, disjointed machine shoved forward faster than it wanted to go.

She said sulkily, "I'm sorry. But a little black bear isn't going to do anything . . . Have you told Jesse?"

"About what I think of the music? No. Not really . . . At least, I try not to . . . I have to be supportive, don't I?"

Annika put a berry into her mouth. It was too small, hard and tart. She chose a plump one out of the bucket and crushed it over her tongue to sweeten the first one away.

CHAPTER 9

When she came home, Annika no longer felt sick, but her eupho-
ria was gone as well. She felt annoyed with the entire world.
She had toyed with the idea of hiding her pail until her father had
gone out to work, then putting together a blueberry crumble. When
she came home, her father was reading in his chair. He started to look
up and she brushed past him, leaving the berries on the kitchen table
and heading into her room.

That evening, she washed them, picked out bugs and twigs, left the
bucket in the refrigerator. At breakfast, she put a bowlful on the table
and heaped them on her cereal. Her father grabbed a handful of Chee-
rios dry and went outside, leaving his black tea still hot and steaming.

Just her luck, today Annika had woken up feeling that she wanted
to work. Too bad that now she couldn't on principle. If her father
wanted a fence, he would have to build it himself.

She spent the cloudy morning on a bike ride, a stretch of road lined
on both sides by a tall, pure stand of black spruce. The forty- and fifty-
foot trees rose straight to their pointed tops, blocking most of what
there was of the light. Pedaling slowly through the weave of misty
green gave her a cool, underwater feeling.

She passed a field of green rye grass, a stack of bee boxes. She mean-
dered, ending up back on County 4 heading to rocky Graceton Beach
on the Lake of the Woods.

At Karlyn and Doug Johnson's driveway, she thought of the little billy goats. Karlyn had never called after the Fourth of July to say if she wanted Annika to sell them for her or clamp them or what. Annika paused there a minute, her toe on the gravel.

She went on to the lake, where she parked her bike in the sand beneath the trees and climbed the biggest rock. The waves sprayed her ankles, the mossy-smelling, green-brown water lapping as far as the eye could see. Seventeen hundred square miles of it. Small seagulls swooped and dipped by her seat. A pelican scanned the water, its heavy head looking as if it would bring the bird careening down like a dead airplane. With her binoculars, Annika picked out the fuzzy tree line of a distant island where she and her father went sometimes in the early fall to pick wild grapes. Despite the size of the lake, it was generally gentle in all but the worst weather and shallow in many places; though the maze of islands was intricate, treacherous to the lost and the drunk, and there were a fair number of them.

From her perch on the rock, Annika worked at contemplating a fat leech near the water. It was the length of her hand. Back a ways from the water, a lilac-colored flower grew amongst the rocks and black mussel shells. As she brooded, she swatted at not only the mosquitoes and fat horseflies they contended with on the farm, but clouds of gnats, blackflies, and sand flies, which swarmed her bare ankles and stung her scalp until blood dripped down her face.

Very quickly, she got bored. She was too antsy to brood. Her mind was blank on ideas. She wished she had brought a fishing pole, or at least her swimming suit. Around eleven, she felt a drop from the sky and leaped off the rock as if she were being released from jail.

A mile from home, she was caught in a torrent of rain. Even in the midst of the deluge, as soon as she swung into the driveway, she could sense something funny on the place.

Another small piece of the garden had been dug up. The divots where several of her new corn plants had been rooted were filling with water. Piercing through the clatter of rain, Annika heard a gulping, mournful sound; slunk down halfway into the doorway of the barn was Tippy. The dog was howling. Her long fur getting soaked, her paws plastered with heavy garden mud. She didn't want to go all the way in, not even when Annika petted and coaxed her. Back in the barn a ways, Mash was standing by, staying dry but watching the other dog. When he saw Annika, he wagged his tail.

Tippy was staring at the front of the house. The dog stood up when Annika's father came out onto the steps, a towel wrapped tightly around his hand.

Then she began to snarl. Annika spoke to her, but Tippy's muscles stiffened under her hand. Annika left her and began to walk to her father, shouting through the rain.

"What's wrong with the dog?" she said.

She stopped walking when she saw the light green towel was soaked clear through with blood. Her father's pale face was slick with rain, his face and clothes smeared with soil. He looked past her at the barn with red eyes.

"You should have been the one who had to do that," he said.

Annika stared at him. When he turned around again for the house, she followed him, walking slowly. Near the door, shivering now in the cold rain, she sped up. "Did you drag her? Did you have to? You didn't have to."

Her father didn't turn to look at her. "After all the work you put in? Tina called," he added in a harder voice. Annika looked up from taking her tennis shoes off and stuffing them with newspaper from the kindling box. Her father was headed for the bathroom.

"For me?" she said.

"Why else would I be telling you?"

"How's your hand?"

Her father closed the bathroom door behind him. Leaving her shoes on the mat, Annika took the cordless into her room and shut the door. She unbuttoned her sopping blouse, pulled off her jeans, and dropped them both on the carpet. Her teeth were chattering when she called Tina.

"Nicky, are you all right?" Tina said. "Do you think you can come over tonight?"

Annika sat for a second. "All right."

"Things aren't good today." Tina's voice shook. She didn't explain, only begged Annika to come for dinner and a listening party: Haas was coming to hear Jesse's new song and offer suggestions. Tina said she was getting sick of having that old beast around, but what else could she do? On the off chance he'd be able to save the wretched thing . . . but she wouldn't be able to bear it without a friend!

Tina said she had to run into town; if Annika got there and no one was around, could she let herself in and start slicing zucchini? The extra keys were hanging in the woodshed.

After hanging up, Annika lay back on the bed in her underwear and stared at the ceiling. When she came out of her room in fresh clothes, her father was working in the kitchen. It was even dimmer than usual in there. The rain had made it cool and he had on a blue zip sweatshirt with the hood up. He was making a cake; he licked batter off his thumb. With the fingers of his uninjured left hand wrapped in a paper towel, he began awkwardly rubbing shortening in a pan. The hand that had been bit he'd wrapped carefully in the dun-colored gauze they used on the cows and horses. A small spot of blood had stained through.

"How deep did she get you?" Annika asked. "Let me know when you change the wrap. I want to take a look at it."

Her father shrugged. "It'll be all right."

"Well."

"I took care of it myself. What else was I going to do?"

Annika frowned. "You didn't have to do it," she said again. She looked at the red mix box on the counter, made of Formica or some other cheap, sturdy plastic. The bowl was plastic, too, the double mixer sunk into the freakishly yellow batter like a leaky boat.

"What did Tina have to say?" her father asked.

"Nothing. Just saying hi."

"No trouble with Sherry? Everything's all right?"

Annika waited before saying in a low voice, "If she had wanted you to know, she would have called you."

Her father stopped with the shortening and stared into the pan. Annika's heart began to beat fast. She braced herself and walked into the living room. She grabbed a hunting magazine and dropped onto the couch. She couldn't pay attention to what she was reading and only pretended to. After a minute, there was the whir of the mixer, its loud scraping against the plastic bowl.

A little while later, she came into the kitchen for a snack and told her father she was going to Tina and Jesse's for dinner. He had been standing with his hands on the counter, looking down at the ugly laminate. He tapped the pot holder he was setting out for the cake.

"No," he said.

Annika looked up. Her father wouldn't meet her eyes. She shut the refrigerator door.

"What?" she said.

"I'll need you to clear the trough ditch."

"Only if it stops raining."

"It's going to stop raining." He lifted his bandaged hand. "You want me to do it with this?"

"Tina needs me to help with supper."

"Well. You should have asked before you said yes."

"I don't have to ask to go over to Jesse and Tina's," Annika said.

Her father was now gripping the edge of the counter hard with his good hand. He finally looked at her, his brown eyes distant but hot. Shaded by the sweatshirt hood, his pale face was alarming. "You think so, do you?"

"I never have before," Annika said softly and stepped back.

"Well. Maybe things are going to have to change around here."

They stood looking at each other for a minute. A minute more. Nothing happened. It was unbearable. Finally, Annika took the piece of bologna she had pulled out of the pack and left the room without even getting any bread.

When he had set his cake out to cool, her father threw on his slicker and went out into the flood. At three o'clock, Annika heard him coming up to the house; she dashed into her room and shut the door. She sat on the edge of her bed, unable to read or sew or draw or punch the holes for a leather pencil case, gritting her teeth with fear and rage each time she heard her father's step across the floor. She stared at the walls but didn't see her carving tools, her new woodburning pen, her embroidery hoop, all hung on leather hooks, or the shelf with her shell and bone collection, or *Little House in the Big Woods, Bones on Black Spruce Mountain, Tatterhood, Pyrography Workbook*.

The rain stopped; then the sun came out. Annika lay back on her bed watching drops of light scatter into the room. Her father did not come in, and after a while, she dozed off.

When she woke up, it was time to go to Tina's. She went to leave, but her bedroom door wouldn't open. She rattled the knob and shouted, "Dad!"

"Nick." His voice was so near, he must have been waiting outside. Annika felt a swell of revulsion and stepped back. "You're eighteen now. You've got to start stepping it up around here."

She pressed her face to the cool door and knocked with her fist. "Let me out."

"Are you going to clean the trough ditch?"

She closed her eyes. "Those corn plants weren't going to come to anything anyway."

"Nick," her father said.

"You don't want me to see her."

"Well, they're too—"

"We're the same age!" Annika kicked the bottom of the door hard with her little foot. She had begun to cry. She kicked again and the flimsy paneling cracked. Her father shouted at her to stop. "What difference does it make," Annika said. "Aren't you going to build us a real house?" For a moment, her father was quiet. Annika listened to her own sobs. "No, that's right. I forgot. There's no way you were ever going to make that happen," she said.

After a silent moment, she heard the key turn in the lock. Then her father walked away. Annika waited another minute. She flung the door open, letting it bang against the wall. The hall was empty, and she went out the back door without a word. Her father was right about one thing: she was eighteen, wasn't she?

As she was heading to the road, Tippy ran up and followed her so closely that she tripped. Annika went down on the gravel on her knees. She tried to order Tippy back. But the dog wouldn't stay on the place without her, and Mash wanted to come too.

The world was sloppy and sparkling. Annika tried to see it, but she couldn't. She tried to let the sunlight warm and relax her. The ditches were a third full of water, high enough to rush into the culverts. Water lay in the low places of the fields and road, and everywhere in the dirt and mud were hundreds of tan, pink, and liver-colored worms.

Tippy ran ahead with Mash. They knew where Annika was going. Annika was sorry she had brought the dogs when she saw Jesse on the front porch dangling string for Charlie. Mash's charge at the front steps sent the cat flying behind the house.

"Hey, old dog," Jesse said to Tippy, rubbing her fly-bitten ear. "Hey, old Masher." Annika sat down with him. Tippy put her muddy white paw up on Annika's chest and tried to push her over. These had always been good, loyal dogs who had allowed her father peace and quiet when Annika was still too small to be left alone. When he was working in the house or garage, he was able to leave her playing in the yard since the dogs would herd her back if she tried to wander away. At some point, Tippy's left ear had been half chewed off by some animal or another, Annika and her father didn't know what. Ever since, even after the ear had healed long ago, the horseflies and blue bottleflies and the nasty little stable flies wouldn't let the scar alone, no matter what they or Tippy tried to do to drive them away, the poor darling.

Mash tried to lick Jesse, who made a face and pushed him away. Annika apologized, the dog had been rolling in something dead.

Jesse was acting so calm, it was a few minutes before Annika noticed that behind the screen door in the kitchen, Tina could be heard quietly crying. Jesse was gazing blankly at the lawn, his elbows on his knees. Finally, he rubbed his face and spoke to Annika.

"Why don't you go on in there and see how she is."

Tina was weeping into one hand, her fingers slick with tears. With the other, she held a lit match to a wood tick, tan and swollen, that was trying to crawl away on the cold iron top of the heatstove. Annika watched with her until the tick slowed, writhed, and burst open. Tina cleaned the mess up with a rag and closed the main door.

"Jesse and I had a fight. I asked him if he could stop working on the recording for just a minute—I had a headache. He said if I didn't like it, he'd go do it somewhere else."

"Where's he going to go?"

"Where do you think? He says after tonight, he's going to move his equipment and do all his work over there. When am I ever going to see him now? All he does is work."

Tina stopped herself up; a new clarity came over her face.

"Anyway, I've got to make dinner," she said.

First, she went into the bedroom and stayed there for ten minutes. When she came back, her hair had a faintly skunky smell and she seemed a little calmer. Dinner would be zucchini chips and fried saugeye sandwiches. On the wooden countertop, its edges dark and moldy, Tina laid out two towels. With a deliberate peacefulness, she lined up the pale green slices in even rows and salted them. Soon, they glistened with beads of moisture. A pot of oil heated up on a burner, the table was set with mismatched plates for four. Tina cooked a few chips to season the oil and Annika lifted them out with a slotted spoon.

Her father had caught the fish for Tina in Kakagesick Bay. Annika had been along, but her father had hooked nearly everything within reach of the boat, filling the fish trap within an hour and barely restraining himself from howling with despair when the trap, tied by a line to the throttle, slipped off when he gunned it and was lost in the water. It was already getting late, but they stayed until the floor of the boat was covered with a second crop of fish flopping in the sand and grime and the line between lake and sky faded, then disappeared. Then the only other remaining boat, trolling to the west of them, seemed to float on a dimensionless wash of blue-gray paper, the only orienting points the darkening tree-lined shore and the sun falling low and glimmering orange pink in a quivering line on the water.

In Tina's kitchen, Annika could not look at her father's blush-colored fillets. She had to turn in another direction. She got on her knees, patted the floor to call the cat, lay back on the pieces of stray linoleum, her hands on her stomach, and let Charlie walk over her chest. Watching the little gray cat, she thought of the big, soft-looking paws of the lions out by the blueberry patch.

Outside, the dogs started growling. Annika got up to go see. Jesse was leaning back on the step watching the road while the two dogs romped around the yard. They stopped roughhousing to bark when Haas arrived on the beat-up Appaloosa, whose hooves looked close to foundering. And Haas hadn't rubbed him down with anything—his dry hide twitched at the flies.

Still wearing his empty look, Jesse stood up and watched Haas come. He was still for a few moments, before walking up the driveway. Haas got down from the horse and the two men talked alone for some time, at one point Haas taking Jesse by the shoulders and hugging him.

The dogs wouldn't stop barking at the two men and the horse. Finally, they went so wild that again Annika was sorry; now she had to run them home. She took them only two hundred yards and ordered them back.

Mash obeyed, but not Tippy. Annika had to jog the whole way with her. Coming in the driveway, she felt a wave of nausea come over her at the familiar smell of the chickens and the sight of the muddy barnyard, the white tin outbuildings, the homely little trailer. Now what was she supposed to do?

They kept collars and leads in the barn for when they had to keep the dogs out of the way. Annika tied Tippy up and had to listen to her carry on almost the whole way back to Jesse and Tina's.

By the time she returned, the three of them had already sat down to eat. Tina was acting strangely. Every few moments, she laughed, whether or not anyone had made a joke. Sometimes she hummed, gently blinking her heavy-lidded eyes. She was chugging a beer. She had changed out of cutoffs into a pale blue sundress that showed her freckled shoulders.

Jesse was acting drugged too, his face more relaxed and peaceful. Both he and Tina ate the crisp zucchini chips with an oddly concentrated pleasure, and once or twice Jesse let his wife twine her fingers with his. When Annika got up for water, she noticed on the countertop a small plastic bag that held a grayish brown dried thing. A mushroom. At one point, Jesse got up to clear a plate, and when Annika looked again, the bag was gone.

Haas was festive, his eyes lit up, rolling and snapping as he pontificated on one subject after another. A few times, he clapped to get Jesse's attention. Tina he left alone, except to offer her a glass of wine from the big red bottle by his plate. His lips and teeth were stained reddish gray.

Annika started on her sandwich. The fish was very good; but she couldn't focus on it. Haas she was used to having ignore her, but tonight she could have been dead to them all.

After dinner, the two men went up to the studio. "What are you on?" Annika demanded of Tina, following her to the sink with an armful of dishes.

Tina dropped her gaze to the floor, looking uneasy. "Nothing. I'm trying to be more relaxed."

"You took something. What was in the bag?"

"Don't you think I've been too uptight lately—a witch?"

"No."

"Well, Jesse—"

"I liked you better the other way," Annika said, adding viciously, "And what do you think I'm going to do—tell my father?"

At the sink, Tina drooped a little. She rested both of her hands on the rim and watched the basin fill with water. Her hair was braided into a glistening auburn knot at the nape of her neck. She touched the growing mound of suds and said softly, "Well, Annika. I don't know. Maybe you shouldn't be here tonight."

Annika felt her stomach go hollow. "What? Why? You invited me."

"I know I did. I know."

"You want me to leave?"

Tina shook her head. She hiccupped, then began to giggle. In the moment before Annika got really angry, she wanted to die. So that was it, was it? They'd been laughing all this time, had they, at the little baby who lived with her daddy?

She took the cup she was holding and dashed it to the floor. It was only plastic, it hit with a cartoonish pop on the particleboard, before bouncing up and knocking lightly into Tina's bare shin. Even as she kept laughing, Tina gasped as if she'd been shot. She grimaced. The laughter wracked her tall body, dissolved over the flowery soap and steam. Annika turned with disgust and went to find the men upstairs.

They were listening to a tape a friend of Jesse's had sent him from upstate New York. A medicine show band. Annika wandered the studio while the men talked. On the top of an amplifier, she found a photograph featuring a teenage Jesse playing his fiddle, caught in a bow-legged position. He wore black jeans and a bolo tie. His curls were clipped short. With him was Thomas holding up the bass. Two other boys and a pale water stain partially obscured the lanky, sneering Polly on the drums.

Jesse was watching her. "That's the Sycamores," he said. Downstairs, they could hear Tina still giggling witlessly to herself in the kitchen and the clinking of dishes in the sink. Jesse turned the volume up. At one point, Annika asked him to turn it down again.

"Listen," she said.

Tina was calling, "Jesse. Jesse! Get down here." Annika looked out the window. Sherry was standing on the top step, her face pressed to the screen door. When she looked up, Annika dropped the curtain and backed away.

In the kitchen, Tina was holding a steak knife. Jesse took it from her and laid it on the table. The only other exterior door in the house was swelled shut, so they had to use the front steps, Jesse telling Tina and Annika to stay in the house, Haas telling Sherry to go on and get back.

"Well, hello, stranger," Sherry said when she saw him.

Tina and Annika followed the men out. Sherry had on the same clothes as before, shorts and a stained aqua shirt that showed her ribs, embossed in white with the words Palm Beach. She had a gaunt, volatile face, with sharp, birdlike features and yellow teeth. Though beneath her animal look, she wasn't old or even unattractive. With her big green eyes, her long lashes. She was no more than ten years older than Annika and Tina. Slender and dirty, her hair cut in a scraggly bob, dyed a lurid cherry red with light brown roots. The men who had worked with Sherry near Faunce Tower used to call her Wood Nymph and Swamp Minx.

She was giving Gordon Haas an insolent look. "I saw your horse," she said.

Sherry turned and walked off the steps when Haas and Jesse drove her that way. It had been so long since Annika had thought to worry about it that when she saw a folded piece of butcher paper in Sherry's back pocket, her mouth fell open.

Sherry hardly seemed to notice Annika. She lasered in on Haas. She stopped on the double line of planks that formed a walking path through the mud from the driveway to the house, her feet bare in ripped tennis shoes. "You got a cigarette?" she asked Haas in her rasping voice.

"Is that what you came here for?" Haas's voice was loud and unsteady. His face kept changing, as if he were trying to find and set the right tone. He came off the steps to herd Sherry farther back. Jesse came down, too.

"I asked you to get off our property," Tina said. Sherry looked up at her, then lowered her head.

"I ain't been here," she said.

"I saw you at the well house!"

"That ain't here."

"Where are you from?" Tina said. "Don't you have anywhere else to go?"

"I told 'em," Sherry muttered. "I told 'em, and they said they took care of it."

"Told who? Took care of what?"

Sherry scowled at the ground. Tina asked what she was living on up there in the woods.

"What there is."

"You know how to do all that?"

"I worked in the goddamn woods at the goddamn camp!"

"Do you have any money?"

"Tina," Jesse said. Sherry's eyes had brightened. She even tried to crack a smile. Tina stared at her. Gradually, Tina's look grew more intense, the same way she had looked at each of her zucchini chips before putting them in her mouth. After a minute, Sherry shrank away. Tina came down the steps to tower over her.

"Where did you live before here?" she asked Sherry.

"All right." Sherry frowned and waved her hand. "It's your house now."

Tina, her hands on her hips, agreed that it was. "And don't take any more of our gas. You think we're rich? We're not."

"You got this place. I told 'em, and they said—"

Tina interrupted to ask if Sherry had had raccoons or something in the attic. Jesse, on the lawn now, groaned and told Tina to forget it. He glanced at Haas.

Sherry's lips parted. She straightened up. "You got raccoons? Don't be leaving food around."

"You had that big barrel against the door," Tina said.

Sherry stared for another second. Then she laughed. It was such a deep, harsh sound that Annika jumped. Sherry looked at Haas with delight. He shook his head.

"Not in front of the girl," he said and gestured to Annika. He told Sherry sharply to come on. He wanted to talk to her in the driveway.

But Sherry was now screaming with laughter. She said she didn't see any little girl. She dodged around Tina to climb the steps and sidled in next to Annika. Wrapped her bony arm around Annika's shoulders. Her skin was sunburned and filmed with dirt; the rank, dark hollow of her armpit nestled near Annika's face. Her overwhelming musky smell held the whiff of sour wine. Annika tried to pull away, but Sherry held on.

"Who—this girl?" She was still chortling, almost gasping. "This is my girl. The *artiste*!"

"Sherry, come down," Haas said.

"She's my woodsy girl . . . She'll be a smokechaser like me when she grows up." Sherry's rancid grip on Annika tightened. But her other hand was reaching behind her. The brown paper was smudged, and so soft at the creases it had almost torn, but there they were . . . a whole parade of the wild naked creatures from Annika's dreams. Drawn more crudely than her painstaking horses and birds, in a hot, self-conscious rush, her pencil gone all the way through on the two figures in the corner. One a woman, the other with the face of a man, the body of a bear.

"They weren't all as good as this one." How fondly Sherry looked at it!

"Don't—please—"

In an instant—God!—the drawing was gone—back in her pocket. "If that's what you want," Sherry said and shrugged. Haas came forward and took her by the arm. She rolled her eyes at Annika but went with him down the steps, her walk less crooked now than it had been earlier in the summer.

Annika watched them, trying to breathe normally. In the driveway, they stood talking, Haas gripping Sherry by both arms now. "For God's sake, you stink," they heard him say before he lowered his voice.

Sherry wasn't whispering. Her words carried across the yard like the squawking of a crow. "You think I was gonna wait there forever? You think I was gonna shit on my own floor?"

Haas said something, and Sherry threw back her head with another guffaw. He'd gotten tied up with Laura, had he? For a whole day and night? She glanced over at the rest of them and spoke proudly. "You bet I showed up at the house and told her all about it and she saw the glass in my hair . . ."

Haas's face was crimson. Sherry pulled one of her arms free; then she gave him a rap on the head. "You gonna punish me? You gonna lock me up?" Haas gritted his teeth. He trapped her arms again, more tightly this time. Sherry grunted and started working to get out of his grip. Finally, she stomped his foot. He swore at her and after a second released her and backed away.

Sherry staggered on the driveway. Before suddenly turning to stare coldly at Tina. Tina was looking back at her in shock and amazement, as if Sherry had turned out to be a ghost.

Sherry turned back to Haas. "Is that why you ain't come to look for me?"

Haas stood still, his breathing a little labored.

Sherry spoke sharply: "Don't even think about it. She wouldn't like it." She got up close again and gripped his coat in her dirty fist. "Especially when you started to talk. Oh, lord," she moaned, "you should hear this dipshit! Selfishly existence exists . . . moochers and loonies . . . No one gives a fuck about that philosophy shit, you dip-shit. At least I know I'm fucked up. I don't try to make it sound like something better. Let go of me, you fuck." He wasn't holding her anymore. Sherry let go of his coat, then shoved him away.

Jesse motioned to Annika and Tina and told them to go back into the house. Neither of them moved. Jesse came onto the steps, reached around Annika to open the door, and nudged her from behind.

"Come on, Tina," he said.

"At least I know I'm fucked up," Sherry said.

In the kitchen, Jesse couldn't stop them from looking out the window. "He's giving her money," Annika said.

"Well, he has to now." Jesse looked at Tina.

After a while, they saw Sherry walk unsteadily and alone to the road. Watching her, Tina said in a low voice, "Now you've heard what she sounds like. Jesse."

"She's not a crackhead, though," Jesse said after a pause.

"You don't think so?"

"No. Just a drunk."

Tina shrugged. She looked very far away. Jesse began to leave for his studio. "That's how you're gonna sound someday if you keep smoking so much," he said.

Tina asked him, "How well do you know Gordon, do you think?"

Jesse stopped walking but he didn't turn around. "The woman's crazy, Tina," he said. Tina stared at his back. After a moment, he went on, and Tina dropped into a chair.

Tina and Annika stayed in the kitchen quietly for a minute. Finally, Annika said, "Tina." But it was like speaking to a stone. After a minute, Tina got up and went to finish the dishes. She ran more hot water into the sink.

When Haas came back in, he stopped near her, looking sheepish. "I don't think she'll bother you anymore."

Tina was quiet for a while.

"All right," she said.

It looked as if Haas would say more. He glanced at Annika and rubbed his eyes, then went back upstairs. Tina washed slowly as Annika wiped invisible residue from her arm with a towel. She felt that Sherry's smell was lingering.

"What are you thinking about?" she asked Tina.

Tina shrugged. It was as if she were alone in a deep chamber now. Annika made to follow the men upstairs to the studio. Instead, she met them coming clambering down.

"Come on, come up—Gordon's going to listen to it." Jesse grabbed her arm and pulled her.

Haas continued going down. Already his shamefacedness had disappeared; he beamed out his celebratory suppertime look. His short, muscular legs gave him a bandy-legged stride and his big arms were crooked out at the elbow like a wrestler's looking for a fight. His tight yellow-gray curls had frizzed in the humidity. He seemed even stouter than usual. Annika stepped aside, it was like getting out of the way of a horse or a bull charging into a herd of cows.

"I'll let Tina know," Haas said.

Annika looked after him; Jesse kept pulling her up.

Upstairs, however, he paused at the attic door, which was standing open. The barrel had been moved to the side, though it was still loaded with cinder blocks. Annika stood with him, looking up the staircase in the waning light. At the top of the narrow steps, the space was dark.

Blue-gold light still touched the second level of the house. Outside, the last of the sun glimmered on the wet leaves of the ash. Through the warped glass of the window, it shot rainbows into the hall. Jesse followed one with his deep-set eyes. He came out of his stupor to ask, "So do you want to be a smokechaser, Annika?"

"What?"

"Did you give Sherry something? A drawing?" He was studying her. "Annika, did anyone ever talk to you about going to college?"

Annika stared back at him.

"No," she said.

Tina and Haas arrived, Tina jogging a few steps ahead of him on the stairs. When he caught up at the top, he grabbed her from behind and held on, running his hands up her bare arms. Then he kissed her loudly on the back of the neck. Tina looked at Jesse. She pulled herself out of Haas's grip.

"Gordon, stop it!" she cried.

She hurried into the hall and bent her knees. Pressed her head into Jesse's chest. He held her lightly and chewed his lip with a nervous half smile.

Haas barked out a laugh. "I'll be right back, Jesse. I promise." He thundered back down the stairs. "Lavatory."

Tina stepped back from her husband, still gripping his shirt in her fist.

"Jeez," she said, a strange softness in her voice, "he's a real ass sometimes."

"He's just playing around." Jesse looked uneasy.

"Could you please tell him I don't like it?"

"Well. Anyway, let's just wait at least until he—"

"Helps you fix that shitty song?" Tina said.

Sharply, Jesse pushed her from him. Tina went down hard on her behind. She was close to the edge of the stairs. She scrambled to her feet and shoved him back. As he lost his footing and fell back, bracing himself with his hands, Jesse looked surprised. But once he was on the floor, he looked up at her, sneering.

"If it's shitty, it's your own fault. I knew I wouldn't be able to come up with anything on my own. I've never done it that way and I never wanted to. You wanted to be married to a genius, I guess."

Tina's angry look was already gone. "No." She took a step toward him.

"You wanted me all to yourself, anyway. What did you think that was going to do? Why did I listen to you, Tina? You can see where it's gotten me. You just set me up to fail."

"Set you up?" Tina repeated, and for some reason, hearing his own words in Tina's mouth made Jesse turn white. "Jesse?" Tina looked frightened, too. Her voice cracked. "You shouldn't put yourself down like that," she said, trembling.

"I'm not." Jesse covered his face with his hands. His voice was high and brittle. He was still sitting cross-legged on the floor, and Annika found herself staring down at him, too.

After a minute, he shuddered. He jumped up, dusted himself off, and strode into the studio. Tina put her head down. Then she rushed into the empty bedroom across from the attic and shut the door.

Alone in the hallway, Annika caught her breath. She sniffed her shoulder. Yes. Some of Sherry's colossal stink had definitely rubbed off on her. She was still the only one in the hall when Haas came back from the bathroom. She felt him recognize this on the center stair; he heaved a gusty sigh and slowed down.

When he was on the landing, Haas stopped in front of her, and they sized one another up like two boss cows meeting in a field.

After a long moment, he asked, "How did you like your senior year, Annika?"

Annika stared back at him. She grasped for something interesting to say. An impressive project, something in another language. Her French final had been a videotaped play she'd made with her old Barbie dolls, *Drame á la Plage*.

"It was good," she said finally.

"Good, good." Haas went on to the studio.

Annika stood a minute alone, trying to gather her thoughts. She felt insubstantial, flimsy, as if her head were about to float off. Finally, she went and knocked softly on the door of the second bedroom. When Tina didn't reply, Annika stepped slowly into the room, empty but for a few battered aluminum suitcases pushed against the wall.

"Tina," she said.

Tina didn't move or speak. She stood with her back hunched, looking out the bleary window. The room was coated in a layer of dust. Stray sheets of newspaper littered the floor and one wall was only drywall with splotches of white compound. Annika stared at her back, tan and bare in the blue halter.

From the studio, Jesse called Annika's name. "Jesse wants us," she said.

"He wants you. Go ahead."

"Tina . . ."

"He doesn't want me."

"That's not true. Everybody wants you."

Tina's posture softened and Annika moved forward. Her head came up to Tina's shoulder blade. Just to try it out, she pressed her face close, not all the way onto the polished skin and bone, just into the heat that was there.

"I'm scared," Tina said. "I know what it's like to be alone out there."

"Out where? You won't be. Let's kiss," Annika said breathlessly. She spread her hands on the soft, pilling cotton of Tina's dress. When Tina tried to move away, Annika held on fast, as Haas had done.

"Oh, Nicky, no." Tina gasped deep in her throat as if she were going to be sick. Annika gripped harder even as Tina squirmed.

Finally, slowly, she let go. She stood a moment staring at the floor and flexing her fingers. "Sorry," she said softly, drooling a little and sucking spit back into her mouth.

Her eyes burned and she ran out, not looking at Tina, not looking at anything. She hurried down the hall. In the studio, she crouched on a wooden crate in the corner and kept her head down. At first, she couldn't hear what Jesse and Haas were saying. There was a loud, echoing emptiness in her ears. She sat with her elbows on her knees, her fingers clenched in her hair, her feet jiggling. When she'd calmed down a little, she lifted her head. Jesse and Haas were rocking in wheeled office chairs in front of the recording console, discussing the music industry and artists who couldn't easily be defined, Jesse chattering nervously about the experimenting he had been doing. Haas shouldn't get the wrong idea, he said—he wasn't under the delusion he was anywhere near to being finished. Maybe he shouldn't even be sharing this piece of junk. But he didn't know where it was or where to go from here. He'd promised his agent he would send something out by the end of last week. So he hoped Haas would know what the hell to do.

"Play it, Jesse," Haas said.

The fiddles started shrieking. Jesse stared at his hands while Haas's eyes played over the console, watching the changing lights.

There was a flash of light blue in the hall—Tina lurking just behind the partially open door.

When the track was finished, Jesse sat up straight, the backs of his hands on his hips. Haas sat there screwing up his eyes.

Finally, Jesse prompted him. "What did you think about all the tracks being done on the same instrument?"

"Well. The blend is good."

Jesse blanched. "And you liked it?"

"Stop it. I'm thinking. How are you going to perform it?"

Jesse said sulkily, "I'm not worrying about that right now."

"What are you planning to do in Chicago and Aberdeen?"

"I get it . . . You hate it . . ."

"Jesse. Don't be a child. Just because it's not finished doesn't mean it's not good. You've got a monster here. A real monster. It's wicked. Sure! It's got teeth! But still. Let's put a cage around it. Let's bring in some other instruments."

Jesse's eyes watered. He sucked in a breath with a whistle. He said slowly, the angles on his face standing out, "All right."

Haas reached over and squeezed Jesse's hand. "You'll see. We'll do it right now." He sent Jesse to the drums and sat down at the keyboard. Jesse moved slowly. Stubbornly. Then he sat down behind the drum set with a sigh. Haas started the track and he and Jesse played along.

Immediately, even Annika could hear the difference. She thought Haas must be some kind of genius. Those nasty children were still hollering in the cold and dark. But they weren't so powerful now. They danced in front of the fire; Jesse and Haas made them do it. The little monsters could keep dancing or they could dive straight into the fire and burn. Haas dug a guttural line out of the electric piano and Jesse sped up on the trap. Jesse shouted out a few things over the music, sounding happier already.

When the track was done, Haas moved straight into something else: the voyageur tune about poor Margoton falling into a well. The piece now had a soft, creeping sound. Voodoo-style, he said. He sang, until Jesse replaced him with his finer voice,

> She fell into the empty well,
> *Ai, ai, ai! Margoton.*

Then three boys came riding on.
Ai, ai, ai! Margoton.

The boys demanded a kiss—Margoton promised—

But once she was out, she was gone.
Chased to the woods by Paul, Jacques, and Jean.
Ai, ai, ai! Margoton.

That's the way girls trap young garçons.
Ai, ai, ai! Finit la chanson.

Halfway through the song, Tina came swaying into the room. Now she was an even bigger mess. She stumbled over nothing on the floor, her supple arms flapping like a bat's wings. Her lips and teeth were stained red like Haas's, as if she had been eating a dead animal. Her face sagged. She peered dolefully at Jesse and Haas out of the tops of her eyes. A lit cigarette trembled in her hand.

Tina didn't look at Annika and Annika could hardly look at her. If this sloppy, drunk woman had been a stranger Annika was approaching on the road, she would have lowered her head and hurried past. If Tina had spoken to or touched her, Annika would have said as little as possible, avoided meeting her eyes, and jerked herself away.

Annika decided that she hadn't even wanted to kiss her. No. Not really! It would have been *someone's* hands on her. But it wouldn't have been her first preference, Tina being a girl!

"Jesus, Tina, don't smoke in here." Jesse got a good look at his wife's stained lips and stopped playing. "Oh, for Christ's sake—wine, too? That's too much."

Tina's speech was slurry. But a clear, bitter look passed over her face.

"You'll take care of me," she said.

Jesse screwed up his eyes and refocused on the music. Tina's head drooped. She went to stare at the keyboard. She reached for it with her cigarette, stabbed it out on a low note, and rolled her fist hard over the keys. Without looking at her, Haas reached out a hand and lightly pushed her away. Tina stumbled backward and clocked her head against the door.

"Jesus, Tina. Are you all right?" Jesse put his sticks down and rose. Haas wrapped his arm around Tina's waist and pulled her onto the piano bench.

"Come on, Tina . . . Grab something and play with us. We've got the trumpet here. The tambourine."

"Go to hell . . ."

Jesse watched them for a second, before sitting back down. Tina wiggled out of Haas's grasp. Careening into a corner, she crumpled into a pile of empty cardboard boxes, her long legs kicking up as a box broke, showing her white underwear.

In her own corner, smelling Tina's cigarette, pretending to examine pink patches of calamine dabbed on her mosquito bites, Annika slowly scratched her arms. She scratched a spot on her knee through a hole in her jeans. When she felt a nudge, she looked up into Jesse's green-brown eyes.

"Come on, Annika. Maybe it's time you got on home."

She wanted to go, but she didn't. This was Jesse's house. She couldn't stay here if she was no longer welcome, no matter how old she was.

But home. At home, it would be different than this. Would it be better or worse? Any way you looked at it, it was a rotten position she was in.

She had to stand up and follow Jesse, so she did.

It was after ten o'clock. Jesse didn't turn on any lights as he went wordlessly through the hall and kitchen and out the front door. When Annika came out of the bathroom, she was in the dark. Her head still felt disagreeably unscrewed. It kept replaying with deafening sound and fine visual detail her encounter with Tina in the empty room upstairs. Instead of following Jesse outside, she felt her way into the kitchen and took four bottles of beer out of the refrigerator. Hugging them to her chest, wrenching a cap off with her teeth, she crept into the living room, crawled into the closet under the stairs, and closed the door.

The taste was surprising. Something like black licorice, bitter but more natural and earthy-tasting than pop, not bad. She felt the effects almost immediately.

After a while, she didn't know how long, the exterior door in the kitchen opened and closed. At the same time, the wooden stairs creaked over Annika's head.

Then bits of a whispered conversation between Jesse and Haas at the base of the stairs reached her. Jesse wanted to go ahead and move his equipment to Haas's tonight. He couldn't stand working here anymore. He would keep sleeping here if Haas thought it was really necessary. But Tina was stifling him creatively. He couldn't even think with her skulking around the place. At least she could get a job, if for nothing else than to get her out once in a while. Though certainly the money would be nice as well. It was uninspiring and unhelpful, how she hardly ever went anywhere or did anything other than putter around the house like an old lady. At the moment, she was out cold on the floor of the spare bedroom. So really, the timing was ideal . . .

Haas sounded annoyed and impatient. What if moving the equipment woke her? How would it hurt to wait a few days?

They lowered their voices. Then one of them was following the other back upstairs. As the two men moved equipment, trying to keep their feet quiet, whispering harshly about the angle at which one or the other of them held this or that bulky object, Annika got drunk in the closet. Once or twice, she almost lost her head and leaped out to tell them how lovely it felt.

After a while, she dozed off. She woke once and heard Jesse say, "I'm not saying yes . . ."

When she woke again, the house was quiet. She crawled out of the closet and, giggling quietly, teetered to the threadbare couch. Out the window, she saw the spark of a cigarette. She thought it was probably Tina; the men must have taken their last load to Haas's. She watched the orange light for some time.

Then she heard a murmur from Tina upstairs. Annika thought to hide in the closet again. But by now, she was quite drunk. She couldn't remember exactly why she had thought she needed to hide in the first place.

The spark moved back and forth across the dark yard. Upstairs, she heard a man's voice. Then another sound.

She listened until there was no doubt about it. She had seen enough television, and while she might be drunk, she wasn't stupid.

Annika grimaced. She wanted to leap up and run outside—at the same time, she didn't want to. She listened, leaning back, her hands on her thighs. Fascinated, riveted, dissolved into the couch. She let one hand come up and over a little.

At one point, she shuddered and stopped. She shook her head like a dog getting out of the water; she had remembered that Haas didn't smoke.

She listened more carefully to the breathing and moaning. Then she was sure.

Would Tina want to get back at Jesse—like this?

Tina had told her to leave. If it were up to her, Annika wouldn't even still be in the house.

So Tina could fend for herself now, couldn't she?

Deciding what to do with her head swimming like this was like getting through a door she wasn't sure how to open or picking a shape out of the dark. Annika thought of running up the stairs, grabbing Haas's hairy feet, pulling him off Tina. What if both of them screamed at her?

Suddenly, the front door was opening. The kitchen light was switched on and someone called her name. But not Jesse—her father. God!

Annika jumped up. No matter what had happened already tonight, there could be nothing worse than her father coming into the dark living room in his Carhartt coat and Montana State Rodeo cap, Annika sitting there tipsy and alone, staring at nothing out the black window. With what was going on upstairs!

She flinched when the living-room light came on. The creaking of the wooden floor over their heads didn't stop.

"What are you doing in the dark?" her father said.

He heard it; his expression froze.

"I was"—Annika began to look around the living room as if to locate something—"just sitting here."

Her father seemed to be trying at all costs not to look up at the ceiling. He didn't want to look at Annika, either. His eyes settled on an empty beer bottle. He spoke brusquely. "Do you know how late it is? You've got to come let that dog loose. She won't let me anywhere near her."

Annika swore and her father looked at her. "You haven't been drinking, have you?"

"Yes. I'm sorry!"

"All right, well. Find your coat. You're coming back, aren't you?"

"I don't think I wore it."

Her father put his head down and started to leave. "Well, hurry up, for God's sake."

Finally, Annika started to move. Her feet were still more unsteady than she had anticipated. At that moment, the cigarette light bobbed past the window. Her father stopped and stared at it. Annika switched off the light and headed for the kitchen.

After a second, her father followed. They heard the front door opening. Upstairs, the creaking suddenly increased. There was a man's long and throaty cry.

Jesse started to come in. When he heard it, he stopped, one foot over the doorway. In the dark, Annika couldn't see the look on his face. None of them said a word and her father pushed her from behind to hurry her out of the house.

CHAPTER 10

Annika's dreams were loud, garish, and uncomfortable, and she got up several times in the night. When she woke the next morning, she was still exhausted and foggy, but she couldn't sleep. Her nose was clogged, her mouth was dry and tasted terrible. When she finally dragged herself out of her room, her father was not in the trailer. She dressed as quickly as she could and got outside.

There, was the dirt under her feet. With each step, she took a gulp of fresh, damp air. There, was her breathing it: Annika. Annika Rose Rogers. She pronounced her name under her breath.

She had a headache and she felt like crying. She went to clear leaves and sticks out of the ditch that ran down a slope from the rain-swollen horse trough. But when she got there, the job had already been done.

She went to work on the fence. At one point, the sweaty work made her so woozy, she threw up. She dropped to the grass. Two of the big tomcats came to lick up the puke. She petted the less skittish one before shooing them both away.

She saw her father walking from the cow pasture to the horses' field. There was no use waiting; she sat up, then trailed after him.

He called from a distance that he was going to see about trimming up Sparky. He got the gelding and tied him at the woodhouse. He usually secured him on the west wall of the barn; perhaps the switch would put the horse off guard.

Annika asked him, "Are you sure you don't want to wait? With your hand."

He spoke without looking at her. "It's gotta get done. It's not bleeding anymore."

Annika shut the dogs up in the house, even though they had been slopping in the ditch. She didn't have the heart to tie Tippy up in the barn again. The dog had still been howling when they came home last night.

The sore on Sparky's leg was healed, but her father spent a longer time than usual talking to him, running his hands firmly, soothingly, over the animal's body, focusing especially on the legs, reminding him the tender spot was gone and this would not bother him a bit. Before her father went to the barn for his tools, he asked Annika to stand at the horse's head and keep talking to him. When he came back and pulled out the long file with a dull point on the end, Sparky got jumpy.

Annika worried her father would get kicked in the jaw. It had happened once before. She stroked the horse's beautiful gray head, which felt like a miracle in her hands. The hint of a hopeful feeling warmed her chest. In fact, this whole scenario seemed miraculous. If she and her father had first run into one another this morning at the breakfast table, or when one of them was coming out of the bathroom, it might have seemed impossible not to talk about the night before, at least to make a plan for talking about it. Instead, they had simply jumped into working together on something important. All of yesterday was in the past. They didn't have to talk about anything. They had other things to do. Neither of them had changed or ruined everything. They were both still the same people they had always been.

With how raw and mixed-up Annika felt today, this seemed the best outcome she could have hoped for . . .

She loved the horse's hot breath, his oily armpit smell. Even his anxious snorts and tosses. She knew them well and just what to do. She pressed the top of her head into the muscular warmth of his neck.

Sparky huffed and ran his big rubbery lips over her shoulder. Annika stumbled and found herself looking in the direction of Jesse and Tina's house. What were things like over there, this morning? When her father said to, she stepped away from the horse. There was one second before her father began that he looked off in the same direction with a poignant and bitter expression. He took off his glasses, rubbed his eyes and wide forehead. Annika's stomach turned again.

After a moment, the look faded and her father got to work. He wedged the horse's right front leg between his knees, for a moment only holding it. Sparky stumbled and righted himself. With the dull end of the file, her father began to scrape clumps of clay and muck from the center of the hoof. Sparky kicked loose. Her father stood and patted him, talking quietly until the horse was still. He took the hoof up again and the gelding snorted but didn't fight.

Sparky protested when he got to the injured leg, but her father managed after several tries to get the hoof cut with the big nippers. When he had finished trimming and filing, he wiped the sweat from his face and checked the wounded spot on his hand. He stroked the gelding and told him he had been a nice fella, even though at one point the horse had stepped down hard on his boot. The pile of curved clippings her father pushed away with his other foot. He limped to the barn with his tools while Annika led the horse away.

When she went to let the dogs out, the old green carpet in the living room was covered in tracks and muck. Outside, the dogs tore the hoof clippings apart to get to the juicy insides, then chewed on them for hours in the shade.

Annika waited all day, but nothing happened, except her father seemed to vacillate between moods of ease and awkwardness. At times, during a conversation about how long they had before the fair or while discussing concerns about the way the rain was affecting the potatoes, they would smile tentatively at one another and after that act almost exhilarated.

At other times, her father's expression grew stormy and he avoided her. After supper, Annika went into her room and tried to focus on picking a pattern to tool onto her pencil case. She hammered lace into a needle but couldn't focus on the sewing, either. After a few minutes, she got up and paced the short length of the house.

In the living room, her father was dozing in the more comfortable armchair, printed with a line of ducks lifting themselves out of the water. Her father's mouth yawned open, one long, gangly leg stuck out on the dirty carpet. Annika began writing a grocery list at the kitchen table, planning her meals for the week on a separate piece of paper. Once when she got up to check the pantry, she let the door bang. On another trip, she did it again.

The second bang woke her father. He yawned and stretched. He took off his glasses and polished them. "You thinking of anything in particular for supper this week?" Annika asked him.

"How about a meatloaf?"

"Last night at Jesse and Tina's, we had fish and that was pretty good."

Her father reached over to the end table, where he had stuck his chewed piece of gum to the rim of his water glass, and put it in his mouth. He picked up *Jaws*, skimmed over a page. He asked if it had been the saugeye from Kakagesick and Annika said it was. He asked how it tasted and she said white and clean, delicious.

Finally, he asked, "Nick, did you drink a lot of beers last night?"

She almost laughed with relief. "No. Just one or two!"

"You're not going to do it again, are you?"

"No. I felt terrible today."

Her father gave her an anguished look, his jaw hanging open. He said, "If I ask you to clean the ditch or anything else, you do it," sounding less as if he were making an order than simply stating something he had always believed to be true.

"I know it," Annika said feelingly. "I'm sorry."

Her father said in a low voice that she couldn't just be staying out all hours of the night, either. "You think maybe it would be better if you didn't go over to Jesse and Tina's for a while?"

"I don't even want to," Annika said, and she was feeling so world-weary, it was true.

At least until a few days had passed—after she had finally finished that stupid fence, complete with a clunky, primitive gate on the northern side; she'd almost forgotten that part and nailed herself out of the garden—when she had the time to grasp what she'd lost.

As autumn loomed, it didn't, for the first time she could remember, seize all of August in its grip. The yellow squashes beginning to swell under the leaves, the cozy look of the dogs with their thickening coats did not fill her with dread touched with a tender longing. Neither did Annika feel the threat of school squeezing each drop of excruciating beauty out of the late-summer light on the wild plums.

If she *had* been going to school, she might have been clutching the smugly happy feeling that this year when she got on the bus, she would have with her the existence of Tina and Jesse. Something no one else in school had, or perhaps could even imagine. Maybe when Tina went into town for groceries, she would have swung by the school in her loud, conspicuous truck, her elbow out the window, Jesse's motorcycle sunglasses on, shouting with her pretty smile to ask Annika, waiting for the bus, if she wanted a ride. Jesse might have visited Haas in his office, and certainly he'd have come to her band concerts. She imagined him drawing everyone's attention by scattering guitar picks on the gym floor when he pulled something out of his pocket. If nothing else, Annika could have thought and even yapped about them all day long.

They had come a year too late. Sometimes in the evenings, when

Annika would have been going to Tina and Jesse's smelling of dirt and corn silk, she sat in a lawn chair in front of the trailer watching the sun go down, snapping a rubber band into her leg and wondering what in the world she had done with all this time before.

She would study her father sometimes. Had he felt this way for so long he was used to it by now?

A dark thought nudged her from time to time. She would think about hearing Tina and Haas in the empty room upstairs.

Everything had happened so fast, before she'd had time to make a real decision!

A few times, Jesse and Tina's old brown truck passed on the road. The first time, Annika didn't see it fast enough; she lowered her head and watched out of the tops of her eyes until it was gone.

She supposed Tina must be all right. There she was, sitting up straight, driving the truck as usual.

The second time she saw the truck approaching, Annika ran around back of the house.

With her father, it felt as if he and Annika had crossed some kind of threshold together. He looked at her as if she were a deer that was about to skitter away. And maybe he was right. Maybe more trips into the state forest, whenever she wanted, could become a reality. Maybe there were even other places where she wanted to go. The time was ripe. Annika proposed a deal. If she raised half of the money, could they take the other half out of the house fund to buy her a car?

Her father groaned. He sighed. But he gave in, almost in the same instant. As if he'd been expecting it. The old man must know it was time; he had to suck it up, accept an occasional lonely day if he was going to keep anything. Especially now that with Tina, it appeared he had come in third place.

Annika never heard him talking to her mother anymore. She wondered if all of that was over for good.

She also noticed that both she and her father tried to keep themselves even busier than usual. At the fair in the second week of August, her father rode Fern in the poles and barrels and took the blue and red. There were some decent riders in the county, but her father could outdo most of them, having come from ranches in the West. He showed both Sparky and Fern in the Quarter Horse Division. His peanut-butter blossoms didn't win a prize, and neither did Annika's venison jerky, but she did well on her butter press and several pieces of embroidery and leatherwork, winning ribbons totaling seventeen dollars. This year, the Fair Board had added a new category in the Open Division, photography. All of the categories that required portraiture, Annika made her father stand for. In one, she arranged him in his Cattleman hat, one foot up on the fence in a classic cowboy pose.

In her drawings and paintings, she was trying a new style. She figured one of the big red and white bulls floating on a background of gold and encircled in a wreath of stylized pink flowers. Before opening day, her father squinted at it critically and said she might do better in competition if he was standing on something. Also, she would certainly get docked points for leaving off the bull's ears, which she had decided he looked statelier without.

Her father turned out to be right. First place in Acrylics & Oils went to a buck lacking her bull's muscular depth and soulful expression, but grazing solidly on a hill.

For his thirty-ninth birthday in late August, Annika bought her father a copy of the thick glossy magazine *Log Home*. A painful nostalgic gleam lit up his brown eyes when he saw it.

On the afternoon they brought in the season's second crop of hay, Annika piloted the truck, the big Army surplus trailer veering behind it, over the lawn and into the alfalfa field, Mash and Tippy running alongside barking, the half-wild cats scattering out of the empty woodshed and from under the boat trailer as she passed. It felt good, being in control of that big outfit.

With the fence up, Tippy had found a new thing to be crazy about.

She'd started running circles around the woodshed when the cats were inside. In a week, the dog's track was two inches deep. After being wrestled down, smacked, and dragged by Weston the day of the listening party, she still barked and ran whenever she saw him.

Annika and her father had baled the hay the week before. Now, they would pile a big load into the trailer, which her father would drive north later in the day to trade for logs. Tomorrow, they would begin cutting them for firewood and, they hoped, get the load done before it was time to slash the potato tops. Her father was happy Annika didn't have to go back to school. He said he couldn't imagine how he'd ever gotten through harvest and butchering time without her.

It hadn't gotten over eighty-five the whole summer and now, soon, the first frost would come. Annika pried her fingers under the bands of twine and swung the rectangular bales up to her father, who stood in the trailer arranging them into rows and neat, prickly stacks. To get up there, he pulled himself into the trailer bed via one of the wheels, swinging his long leg easily over the side rail. Despite his ungainly walk, he was agile in that kind of way. And when the cows and the two bulls had trampled their wire fence and wandered bawling onto the road or into the yard—or, in past years, into the garden, where they sunk up to their spindly knees in the black, wet dirt, slobbering on Annika's corn until she whacked them with a rake—her father, with Mash's help, drove and roped them like a real cowboy.

II

CHAPTER 1

At the end of August, Chrissy Rebarchek hired Annika to harvest and put up her garden. Every day for a few weeks, Annika headed out at seven thirty on her bicycle north on County 4. The road cut through the pine bog to the west, denser woods to the east. Poplar and other junk trees near the road, spruce, tamarack, and birch farther back. Annika spent the day in the stunted vegetables, pulling vines out of the grainy, beachy soil, listening to Chrissy's small son holler in the house, freezing corn, and eating her sandwich with Chrissy at noon.

A year ago, Annika might have hunkered down in the garden to eat the lunch she'd brought, or even disappeared into the woods for a half hour just so Chrissy didn't see her and come out to invite her in.

This year, she realized Chrissy was not an uninteresting person. She had been a musical-theater star when she was in high school, about fifteen years ago. Now, she sang and acted in the community plays.

Every day, Annika knocked off work at two before coming home to tend to her own diminished plot and to help her father. On an afternoon early in September, Annika had to wait at the highway for a school bus to pass. She caught a glimpse of the football team inside, headed to a game.

The rest of the way home, she was trying to shake out of her head a humiliating ninth-grade memory. A bus trip to Grygla—the band was going to play at a football game. Annika spent the hour-and-a-half ride there sitting behind a tenth-grade couple. For part of the way, the boy had his arm around the girl. For the rest, she laid her cheek on his thin shoulder. Every time the bus jolted, her face slammed into the bone.

Getting on the bus earlier, Annika had paused at the seat of a boy whose parents worked a soybean farm north of Williams. The other farm kids were probably more like Annika than they let on but at school, no one put on bigger airs or scraped their shoes more carefully than they did. The boy stiffened and spread his body over the center of his seat. He scowled out the window looking angry and afraid, like every boy Annika had ever shown an interest in. The black-haired hockey player with a French name, the loudmouth in band who played the saxophone.

A boyfriend would wait for her outside of class, and she'd come out smirking to see him. When he put his arm around her waist, she'd push her skinny body right into him and he'd love it . . . She would run her hands up on his chest, push him into the wall. He'd laugh, but not be able to hold her back. He would know her full name, and love to say it, too. *Hey, there, Annika Rose. Do you know what you do to me, Annika Rose?*

In the dark on the way home from Grygla, the couples did more, hidden under blankets and coats. Even some of the girls curled up and fell asleep drooling on one another. Some of the cheerleaders rode the band bus, as the team and coach were cranky about losing and the girls found them unbearable. There was less room. Everyone had to double up; a boy had to sit with Annika. He was short and a little fat, in the seventh grade. She didn't know him. Maybe he didn't know anything about her either. Annika talked to him, and for a while, she thought it was going well. Then he fell silent. When he closed his eyes, Annika asked if he wanted to sleep. If he wanted to, he could use her shoulder to lean on. If he was really tired, he could even lie down in her lap . . . The boy didn't say yes or no. He sat with his face forward and didn't open his eyes. Annika laughed. Well. That didn't look very comfortable. She grabbed his chubby shoulders and began to pull him down. She was small, but strong enough. The boy's head was nearly to her thighs when his silent struggle finally got the best of her and he broke away.

But there was nowhere for him to go; he slid to the edge of the seat and teetered there. Annika sat with her throat aching, trying to smile and pretending to laugh it off.

On her bicycle the day she saw the bus on the highway, Annika pumped hard and fast to sweep the memory from her head. By the time she coasted breathless and dusty into the driveway, she felt a little better. The muscles in her legs had a pleasant ache, her fingers smelled of sun-warmed tomatoes, and she never had to get on a bus again.

The air took on the rich and sweet papery smell of dry leaves; the maple trees showed splashes of red and yellow. One evening when Annika was coming to the house with a load of wood, her father shut off the snarl and whine of the chainsaw and the chilly air that smelled of sawdust and bark seemed unusually still. She realized the last night of frogs had passed, she didn't know when.

When Chrissy Rebarchek paid her, for the first time in her life Annika put all the cash in an envelope and stowed it in her room. She stole away from the farm another few days to pick plums and highbush cranberries, then roasted up the kitchen making more jelly and sauce than she and her father could have eaten in three years. A purge of the kitchen cabinets made room for the rows of jars, which she had no idea how to price.

Annika rode up to Chrissy's place one afternoon to give her some jelly for the little boy, but she put off letting the other neighbors know. She liked coming into the kitchen to dust and gaze at all her beautiful purple jars.

On an afternoon at the end of September, her father came home from a trip to town having heard Haas was in some hot water at the school. In the first week of classes, he had taken some of his favorite kids to Minneapolis on a field trip that quickly became infamous. Rumors spread that he took them to a scandalous play and drank a lot of wine before barreling his car through a construction barricade just to make the girls scream. When the kids were questioned officially, they denied it.

Perhaps to distract everyone, Haas went on a cultural crusade. He tried to rouse the school against the two teachers who supervised Academic Triathalon for having nicknamed it "Nerdathon." An insulting name was no way to get kids excited about intellectual achievement, he said.

Someone gave Haas a list of more names. These were teachers who sometimes used the offending term in passing. A few teachers were taking the initiative to sarcastically defend themselves or tearfully apologize.

If it was firing Haas was after, things didn't go well. The whole thing only left a bad taste in people's mouths. Haas moved on to demanding the band play more serious concerts instead of acting like the athletic department's lapdog. This time, the kids complained. Pep-band music was the most fun to play.

Annika liked one of Haas's ideas: putting up surveillance cameras in the weight room. Some jerk was scratching off and defiling names on the "High Performance" plaques. Her name was listed for bench-pressing 90 percent of her body weight and she didn't like teasing and liked to see it punished.

As they talked about Haas that evening, Annika and her father avoided looking at each other. Annika imagined they were both thinking about that last night at Jesse and Tina's.

Not long after, her father started looking for opportunities to bring up Tina's name. He liked to drop it into carefully unemphasized place references: he had seen grouse tracks in last week's dusting of snow "in the ditch by Jesse and Tina's."

Sometimes, from a distance, Annika saw Jesse or Tina. Once, when passing the house on her bike, she stopped abruptly. She didn't see anyone, but she felt she was being watched. Another morning, she saw the brown truck idling at the end of the driveway. She peered through the pine windbreak and saw Tina sitting in the cab alone. Annika waited a while, hidden behind the trees that lined 4. After five or ten minutes, the truck slowly backed up to the house.

Where was Tina thinking of going? Was it possible she was leaving Jesse?

Annika waited a little longer. If she went to see her, would Tina recoil from her the way she'd done in the empty room upstairs? Nothing stirred in the driveway. Tina stayed in the truck. Jesse did not come out of the house. Finally, Annika moved on.

Near the end of October, she came in from nailing up a board on one of the pole sheds to find her father excited and trying to hide it. Tina had stopped by.

She had come to apologize. She said she hadn't been surprised when Annika and her father had stopped coming around after she and Jesse had fought in front of Annika. The next day, the two of them had felt ugly about it. Tina had started to call many times, but she knew they were upset and she was afraid. She was throwing a birthday party for herself in November and she hoped both of them would come.

"Huh," Annika said. She took her work gloves off and tossed them on top of the woodbox. She felt herself being followed by her father's hopeful eyes.

That last night at the house still lingered like an odious dream. Yet now it also seemed like a million years ago, as if she had been much younger then.

So. Tina did want to see her. Well.

Did Annika really want to get messed up with those two again, with all their problems? She was happy with her jam. She'd started a big new painting of pines by a dusky lake. She was trying to find more work and poring over advertisements for used cars in the paper.

Annika had even started to think seriously about what Sherry had said that last night at Jesse and Tina's. Maybe she did want to be a smokechaser. Or watch for fires from the state-forest towers. To be in the woods all day and get paid for it. She had picked up a pamphlet and an application at the DNR booth at the fair. Two young loggers were there, talking to the official in his olive uniform and flat-brimmed Smoky-the-Bear hat.

They were trading stories about a nasty biting beetle they called the jack-pine savage. When it took a chomp out of you, it felt like murder. Knock down a tree and it slipped from the heaving branches down the back of your shirt. Often, you had to strip down just to get it off.

Annika stayed there listening to the men for a quarter of an hour. Her father had to drag her away.

You didn't need a forestry degree for a smokechaser position, only your own vehicle and a fitness test. If she kept picking up work, she'd have her car, and the state trained you for free. She was sure she'd pass everything, no problem. She wondered why she had never thought of this before. It was exciting to think about . . .

Her father, however, with the potatoes in—having Annika at home all the time now didn't seem to be enough. Maybe it would have been, a year ago. But no longer. What did he have to look forward to?

That afternoon, Annika felt him continue to watch her as she washed dishes and put the coffee mugs away. Of course, they shouldn't go, her father said. They didn't need to go.

"No, we should," Annika decided finally. "It's her birthday."

That night while Annika was cutting leather in the kitchen, her father, setting the table around her, let the silverware drop with a cheery kind of ring.

The next morning, Annika woke up looking forward to the idea of the party a little more. Thomas and Polly might very well drive up. She hadn't considered that before. And who knew who else Tina might invite? It might be nice to see Tina again. They had gotten to be real friends, hadn't they?

When she was a smokechaser, Annika would meet the other people who worked in the woods. Until then, she didn't have anyone.

She wondered how Tina was faring with Jesse working at Haas's. Maybe it was better for her. Not so much noise. Yes. It would be good to find out if Tina was doing all right.

Annika became interested in the question of what she was going to wear, and in the following weeks, she spent time most days trying on her jeans, long boxy skirts, and prissy blouses in various combinations, then looking at herself in the mirror. Finally, she settled on what she had been leaning toward from the start, a dress she'd bought this summer at a rummage sale she'd gone to with Tina. The lady at the sale said it had been her aunt's in the 1950s and would make a fun Halloween costume.

Tina said that if it had been her size, she would have worn it anytime. Stiff brick-colored fabric, a short flared skirt, a tight revealing bodice. It fit Annika so well that the first time she looked in the mirror, she had to look away.

Then she didn't want to stop looking. She appraised her pointy face as well. Maybe her cheeks were starting to fill out a bit. She was no raven-haired, buxom beauty like the girls at school who were consistently crowned homecoming queen, but she had some curves in the right places. She began to warm to the idea. Yes. The boys at school were crazy, the way they hadn't been all over this.

Annika's shoulder-length hair, which her father cut at home, never looked nice hanging down. The day of the party, she asked him for help and he wrestled the uneven strands into a bumpy French braid. Annika yanked out a few pieces to try and cover her ears.

Later, she asked him, "Do you think I have to wear the pumps?"

He was rolling meatballs for the party. "Nick, I don't know . . ."

Annika came out of her room in brown cowgirl boots. "There you go," he said.

At seven, her father asked her to go over with the meatballs so they could be reheated before eight. He had run out of time and wasn't dressed.

Annika checked the mirror again before leaving. No. A French braid wasn't ideal. But what choice did she have? As she walked up the dark road, her legs cold in tights, her stomach began to flutter. If Tina brought up how Annika had acted in the upstairs bedroom that last night this summer, she must be prepared to laugh it off. She would say it was all a joke. She could even lie. She could say that, unbeknownst to Tina, Annika at that point had been drinking too. She hadn't been in her right mind. She couldn't be held responsible for what she'd done. She peeled off her glove, ate one of the cold meatballs, and licked peppery cream sauce off her fingers.

When she got to the house, Tina and Jesse's truck was not in the driveway. There were no cars at all, with Iowa plates or otherwise. A living-room lamp was on, and the hall light on the second floor. Annika knocked for a while, then got the spare keys from the woodshed and walked in. Most likely either Jesse or Tina was in here somewhere.

She couldn't find anyone. The living-room floor, stained black years ago from an oil stove in large, amoebic patches, had been swept clean. An unfamiliar record played on the turntable. A high wildcat voice asked, "Why lick up behind him and take his mess?" The bathroom was dark, the door ajar. Tina's hairbrush, cinnamon-colored strands wound into the bristles, had been dropped on the big bed. Her red cardigan hung over the back of a kitchen chair.

On the second floor, Annika saw that Jesse had moved his equipment back into the studio. The attic door was pulled to, but not closed all the way. She knocked on the door and called hello. She couldn't hear anything, but went on up.

At the top, she made out Tina asleep on the floor. Annika pulled the chain light. She felt queasy when she saw where Tina was lying: on the pile of faded blankets that had held, until Tina had rumpled them with her own body, the imprint of Sherry's.

Annika clutched her bare arms in the drafty room. Nail points poked from the wall near Tina's head. Tina stirred and pushed off a pile of quilts, rolling onto her side. Her hand was on her stomach. A knit shirt was pulled tight over her protruding, round belly. She opened her eyes and covered her belly with both hands.

"Hey, there, Nicky." She sat up, staring at her.

Annika gaped back at her. "Are you pregnant?"

"What?" Tina's eyes were working furiously. "That's mean. Why would you ask me that?"

"What are you doing up here?" The broken attic window had been stapled over with burlap. Annika walked over, pulled up a corner, and put her eye to the cold blackness. It helped dissipate the flush of heat prickling her skin. Tina wiped the sleep from her eyes with her sleeve. Nervously, she fondled the child's ring painted with a daisy that was hanging on a chain around her neck. Jesse had found it in the ditch this summer.

"Are you really pregnant?"

Annika wanted to ask, whose was it . . .

Tina's mouth was spread wide and hard in a kind of painted clown smile. What did it mean, that awful look?

Annika turned away. If Tina knew she had been there the whole time and had done nothing!

Even with the strange look on her face and her arms and face puffy, Tina was still beautiful, her burnished hair, her henna-colored, glittering eyes. The snappy voice and guitar were still going downstairs. Annika took a step away from the window.

"It's cold up here," she said.

"Is it? I probably didn't notice because I'm getting so fat." Tina's smoky voice was even thicker than usual. "But look at you," she added bitterly. "Look at you, you cutie. You look like June Carter Cash." Annika stared at her. Finally, Tina gave it up.

"Fine. It's true, Nicky." She sighed. "But please don't say anything. We weren't going to tell anyone for a while."

"Why not?"

"Well, it's still early, and the situation is kind of funny. How did you get up here? Jesse's not back, is he? Oh, of course. The keys. Well," she said, brightening, "I can't say it's not a relief to tell someone. But please—"

"I won't tell."

"Not even your dad."

Annika shook her head. She settled on the floor in her dress while Tina described how sometime in September, she had started to barf. She thought it was just nerves or an allergy, some dumb thing. She and Jesse always used protection. Though this just went to show you, condoms weren't always 100 percent.

Annika's face must have changed as she tried not to give herself away. "Don't worry, Nicky." Tina looked at her sadly. "I think it'll be all right. Let me tell you the whole story."

It was true that when she found out, she wasn't happy. She didn't know what she thought about ever having children. She knew she didn't want them now. She didn't have anything particularly against babies. But as a teenager staying with distant relatives and friends after her mother died, she'd often gotten stuck taking care of everyone else's. Everyone thought she owed them in this way.

She wanted a break. She wanted to be young and just take care of herself and Jesse for a while.

Jesse wasn't too thrilled about the baby, either. "So we were talking about getting rid of it. Then Gordon had the idea—"

Annika started. "Haas knows?"

"Jesse told him," Tina said slowly, "and he and his wife are going to take the baby."

"What?"

"I know . . ." Tina's voice shook. "It sounds funny, doesn't it . . . Giving your baby to the neighbors . . ."

But Haas's wife Laura, Tina said, had always wanted a baby. Years ago, when Haas and Laura were still playing music in a group together, they had decided to quit and build more stability into their life for supporting a family. Haas started teaching and Laura went to nursing school. But Laura had lost several pregnancies. Now she was in her forties and they'd all but given up. They'd tried pursuing overseas adoptions several times, but always they'd run short of money or things fell through. It wasn't as easy as you might think.

"You're giving your baby to Haas?" Annika said.

"Annika."

"You hate him."

"Well. Jesse doesn't. Jesse says—"

Tina didn't finish. Annika's hands shook a little. She sat on them and got a sliver. She pulled it out and sucked her finger.

"I didn't agree to this without thinking it over," Tina said.

Annika shook her head.

"No," Tina said, "I didn't. Once, I was ready to go to Fargo and just take care of it. I made the appointment. I was about to drive away." Tina told her she couldn't let on to Jesse or the Haases that Tina had slipped up and let Annika know the secret. Laura disliked Tina enough already as it was.

"Why?"

"Oh, I don't know. Nicky. Do you promise?"

Annika looked at her for a long time. "You'd think she'd love you. When did she come back? I thought she left him."

"Well. She came back for this," Tina said.

CHAPTER 2

Tina wasn't thrilled about gaining weight—"I was fat enough before"—and giving up drinking and smoking. But she said she could see that giving a baby to Gordon and Laura would put both of them in Jesse's debt forever. For the rest of their lives, they wouldn't be able to do enough for him.

For tonight, Tina said, she would just enjoy her party. She said Annika couldn't imagine how much she had been looking forward to it. She and Jesse had used to throw parties all the time, in whatever rickety old thing they were living in. How crazy that they hadn't done it yet here, in their first proper house! Jesse had been reluctant about the idea, but Tina stood her ground. For the first time in what seemed like forever, she was feeling well. And she'd hardly seen anyone except Jesse and the Haases for months.

"Nicky," she said critically, "can I try something with your hair?"

They went downstairs into the bedroom, where Tina pulled out the messy braid and ran a brush through Annika's hair. Annika closed her eyes. The stiff bristles and Tina's strong fingers on her scalp felt nice.

She tried to think . . . Tina didn't want her to know what had happened with her and Haas. That was clear. She certainly wasn't going to tell Annika whether she'd wanted it or not. Unless Annika came out and asked her.

When she opened her eyes, she smiled. A curling iron hid most of the unevenness in the cut of her hair. The curls, plus some brownish pink on her lips, drew attention away from her ears.

Tina changed into a green and white dress with a wide skirt like Annika's. The bodice came sneakily down just below her ribs. Her bronze skin was only a little paler than it had been in July.

Jesse came home with a bag of ice. He seemed a little distracted, but not unhappy. He had rolled his jeans up in his old summer way and when he poured himself a glass of wine, he let Tina have a sip.

The house looked festive. Tina's big, drafty mess of a house, of which she was so proud! The place was all hers now, and this showed in every detail. By the main door, on a rickety stand, she'd placed a mint plant and a rosemary. The light of dozens of candles flickered in the drafts. On every surface were jars of dried yarrow, cattails, and goldenrod; cider and apples; painted pinecones; and pressed leaves from the ash tree in the yard. On the walls were wreaths Tina had woven with grasses and dried flowers, as well as her artistic magazine pictures. Beautiful people draped in gauze, green pastures, leopards and goats. Set out on the kitchen table was a motley assortment of dishes and glasses in auburn, green, brown, cream, and pink.

The night was chilly, but they had banked up two big fires in the stoves. The rooms were toasty, almost too hot. Cinnamon simmering on the stove mingled with the faint livestock smell and colorful bottles of alcohol covered the countertop.

The house was still in the half-finished state it had been in since the Blocks had moved in with their brood of children and no time for renovations. Jesse and Tina hadn't touched the wallboard holes, the unpainted drywall, the wires looping down into the living room, or the frigid northwest bedroom where guests were led to leave their coats.

There were only a few guests. Annika's father arrived at eight in his black boots, a cornflower blue shirt with silver snaps and stitching, and new jeans. Annika didn't even know he'd bought them. Doug and Karlyn Johnson were there as well. Tina had run into them a few times when she was out walking on the road.

Thomas and Polly did not come rolling up at the last minute. Still, it was pleasant to parade around the colorful rooms in her dress. Annika went to the living-room window and pretended to look into the yard so she could gaze at her reflection. The red-brown dress looked even nicer with her curls.

Her father went around blinking like a bear coming out of its cave. He stared at Tina and drank everything he could get his hands on. After her hangover, Annika wasn't tempted to touch a drop, but she ate gobs of Tina's homemade pink and orange candy, which Tina passed around the party on a tray.

Doug and Karlyn were talking to Jesse in the kitchen, Tina was sitting next to Annika on the couch, and her father seized his opportunity.

He asked if they'd had any more trouble with porcupines. Tina said no, not since the one he'd come over to shoot out of their tallest jack pine this summer.

Were they still liking the house?—Oh, yes. Very much.

After a pause, Tina added that maybe Jesse wasn't as interested as she was in investing in the place. She told them that Jesse had started tossing his cigarette butts in the spot she was planning to put her garden in the spring. "'Babe, just don't, it's gonna be fine,'" she said, imitating Jesse's languid, southernish way.

Her father shook his head soberly. "That's not gonna be good for your soil."

Tina asked if he could please tell Jesse that. Jesse didn't like to think Tina knew anything, but maybe he would listen to Weston.

"It's too bad," her father said mournfully. "You've got potential here."

"I know it."

"If it was my place, I'd lay cedar partway up the walls."

"That sounds beautiful." Tina looked at Annika. "You should do that in your place."

"Wouldn't really be worth it there. What's this music you got on?"

There was the sound of someone at the front door. Then Haas's hearty, carrying voice. Tina's face stayed impassive, but Weston froze. Then his eyes darted around the room. He stood up and filled the space with his tall frame and restlessly moving hands. Finally, he asked if Tina or Annika needed anything. Tina asked for a glass of water, and he left reluctantly. When he was gone, Tina murmured something and stood up.

"What?" Annika turned to her. She tried to touch her, but Tina was already gone. Trotting up the stairs, her eyes down. Annika looked after her.

She wandered into the kitchen, where Jesse was standing near the heatstove talking to Haas. Seeing them together, she thought of hearing the two men argue on the stairs the night of the listening party.

Until Jesse went outside, leaving Haas alone in the house with his wife . . .

Jesse's face had a coarser look than it had had this summer. His deep-set eyes were nervous and further away. But he was excited, too. He didn't seem angry or jealous. Poor Tina . . .

Jesse waved Annika over. When she got there, he laid his hand on top of her head. She was surprised when Haas, too, turned to look at her. He took his hand from Jesse's shoulder and clasped hers.

Standing there with both of the men's hands on her—it was strange. Though she didn't hate it. Haas's beard was growing out, giving him a wilder appearance. Nonetheless, his face had a more peaceful expression. A man who had been on his own and hadn't liked it, who was being managed and taken care of again.

Jesse told Annika he'd fixed up the song with the fiddles. He'd recorded it with other instruments, including Haas playing his keyboard line on an upright bass someone in town found in a cellar.

With Haas, Jesse had written and recorded more new songs and sent them all to his agent, who thought he could do something with them.

Haas told Jesse he'd heard back from a woman he knew in St. Paul, a theater director. She was interested in inviting Jesse to do a show in the spring. He would need a band, of course, and first the director would have to hear something from them.

"I'll try the Sycamores first," Jesse said. "I don't know if they'll be able to handle the parts. But I hope they'll step up to it. It's a good venue. This could be big for us. I'll see if I can get them up here. Or we'll take a trip down there."

"To Iowa?" Haas said. "Now? Tina, too?"

"You don't think so?"

Haas shook his head slowly. He snapped his fingers. "I have something for her," he said before calling out Tina's name. A few minutes passed before Tina emerged from the hallway in her swinging dress. She wore a blazing, masklike smile, like the one she'd put on earlier in the attic.

Haas was pulling an oily brown package out of his coat. He waved his free hand at the party as if it had come as an inconvenient surprise. "I meant to get here early, but share if you want to," he said to Tina, coloring a little. He leaned close to her, speaking low.

"Omega-3s," he said.

Jesse turned away from the two of them. He bent down to tend the stove, burying his face in the heat.

Immediately upon hitting the air, the package's strong, smoky odor filled the room. Annika's father and the Johnsons looked over. Tenderly, Haas set the package, a rolled-up brown paper bag, on the kitchen table. He unrolled it to reveal a big blackened smoked fish.

Tina's face was now expressionless. She tucked a strand of red-brown hair behind her ear, her other hand knuckling her belly. She stared at the fish for a long moment.

"Thank you," she finally said.

Annika and Karlyn crowded in, Karlyn already holding a fork. Annika glanced up to see her father standing back and looking coldly at the fish. He took a hard swallow of his drink while Haas modestly blinked his bulbous, fishlike eyes. He said he had caught it himself in the Rainy River. Doug Johnson asked Haas where he had gotten his smoker, and even as Annika was thinking she would never buy some cheap store smoker but make her own with a hollow log and hickory chips, she got her own fork and dug in. Very salty, but tangy and delicate, delicious.

She felt a pat on her back. Karlyn. Annika gave her a guilty smile. When she hadn't heard from Karlyn about the little billy goats she mentioned on the Fourth of July, Annika should have taken the initiative. That was good business.

She heard another woman's voice in the hall. She looked to see Laura, Haas's wife, coming from Tina and Jesse's bedroom. She was patting down static in her short hair. A nice-looking woman. Even with her small size, almost as short as Annika, she was poised and stately, her large gray eyes framed by exaggerated lashes like a doll's.

Laura moved through the house with a mincing distaste, as if she were walking through mud. She frowned at Tina and her husband.

"Oh, did you really bring that stupid fish?" she said.

But Annika loved a good smoked fish, golden brown and pinkish chunks flaking tenderly off the bone. Haas's was a handsome catch. The skin divided in color, one half a charred black, the other a crisscrossed bronze, one blurred band of silver across the middle. The skin was thin like gold-leaf paper, the tail and two fins featherlike fans, the edges tapered and curled like a dying corn stalk's.

Tina was eating a piece slowly. When it was gone, she licked her fingers. A small smile grew on her lips.

"Thank you, Gordon, but I'm so thirsty now." She asked if Laura might mix her a rum and Coke.

Annika was afraid that if she watched Laura's reaction, she'd give something away. She left for the bathroom to wash her hands. When she came out, Jesse was steering Tina from behind into the bedroom. At the doorway, she dragged her feet. He gave her a discreet poke.

Annika walked slowly by on her way to the living room. She paused to pretend to study a picture hanging on a wall stud of a nearly nude shepherd petting a sheep.

She heard Jesse say, "Don't torture Laura, all right? She's worried enough as it is."

"Worried? About what? Torture Laura? Ha. She tortures *me*."

"How?"

"You don't see everything. Remember, I'm doing this for us. Not her."

Jesse murmured something. Tina said, "I know. I know. Yes, I'm grateful. You didn't have to forgive me."

"No, I didn't."

"You did it pretty easily, though . . ."

"Tina. Have you been drinking?"

"No. You don't have to ask me that."

It was quiet in the bedroom for several minutes, until Annika heard a rustling of crinoline.

"Come on, Tina, not right in the middle of the party . . . I hate it when you come on so strong like that."

"But no, you don't!"

Ten minutes later, Tina emerged from her bedroom wearing a new, bright, glittering face. Annika tried once or twice to see if she could talk to Tina, to get her alone. If she got up the nerve, she might tell Tina she had overheard her and Jesse. Then see what happened from there.

But she didn't try hard. And Tina was seeking out the biggest groups she could find at her small party. She told Jesse, Doug, Haas, Annika, and her father that Jesse was some husband when it came to this house. He didn't care about anything that mattered to her. The cigarette butts in her garden plot were just one example.

Jesse rolled his eyes. "Babe, it might not even make a difference. We might not even be here in the spring."

"Why?" Tina's theatrical look faded. "Where would we be?"

"With everything that's happening, it might be time to be in a city then."

"I like it here."

Tina's voice was high and sour. Jesse winced and her expression grew harder than ever. At its first opportunity, the group dissolved. Only Weston stuck close by Tina.

By ten, Annika was getting a little tired. She'd been up to feed the horses at six o'clock. She decided she would come back to talk to Tina tomorrow. At one point, she dozed off on the couch, even with Jesse and Doug Johnson sitting on it. When she woke, she started to wonder if maybe she could get her father to go home before it was too late for her to do a little painting, or at least to read from *All Things Bright and Beautiful* before she went to bed.

She went looking for her father, but he wasn't in the house. Outside, she heard voices in the woodshed and saw the glow of a cigarette and got a bad feeling.

The wash of stars had their prickly winter look. Annika walked as quietly as she could to the back of the lean-to, though the yard's summer mud had frozen into stiff ridges that tripped up her boots. She sat on a cold cinder block.

Things were worse than she could have imagined. Her father was saying to Tina in an astonishingly soppy, warbling voice, "I just think you're so beautiful."

As spiteful and suspicious as she'd been with Jesse, Tina was gentle and careful with Annika's father.

"Thank you, Wes," she said.

"I'd like to fix this place up for you."

"That's a nice thing to say."

"You're so beautiful."

"Thank you. I hope you understand my marriage is important to me."

Weston made a choked sound in his throat.

"Don't go to the city. It's like maggots on a corpse down there."

Tina murmured something. Her smoke trailed into the night.

"Not since my wife," Weston said, as if repeating a phrase he'd already used several times.

Annika stood up and walked back to the house. Now she really wanted to go home. At the same time, she didn't feel she could leave her father alone here; she didn't know what he would do or what would happen to him.

He came back into the house loopy and staggering. Doug Johnson, ready to leave the party in his black toque and leather Polaris jacket, stood up from the kitchen table and watched him like livestock he was about to corral. He hadn't yet moved to do it when her father wandered into the living room and found Haas and Laura sitting on the couch.

Annika followed him and hovered at the entrance to the room. A hand on her shoulder pulled her gently back.

Karlyn. "Don't worry, Annika." She nodded at her husband beside her and Doug went on into the living room.

"Wes. How about a ride home?" he said.

Annika wanted to listen to what was happening, but Karlyn kept talking to her. She was tipsy and repeating herself, her pronunciation fuzzy. A narrow face and long teeth gave Karlyn a not-unpleasant rabbity look. She was the kind of eager and friendly but uncertain person who was happy when you asked her for something and seemed to find herself at a loss when you didn't. She had graduated from high school the same year as Annika's father and worked in one of the offices at the county courthouse. No doubt she was happy there, fetching whatever records people asked her for all day long.

"I'm glad to see you here," Karlyn said. "I'm glad to see you and your father. I wish I would have kept up more with you . . . But he's made it difficult . . . Did you know your mother wrote for the paper, Annika?"

"Yes," she said impatiently.

"She wrote a column for the paper. She was very smart. You screamed for her for two weeks straight."

"What?" Annika turned to look at Karlyn, who had tears in her bright blue eyes. She was definitely drunk. "How do you know that?"

Karlyn looked surprised. "We were there. We all wanted to be there for your father."

In the living room, voices were rising. Her father was ignoring poor Doug Johnson, who was hovering near the spot in the room where her father had dropped into an armchair, cracked another beer, and picked a fight with Haas. The long fingers of his free hand were curled into a hard, ropey fist he ran up and down his leg.

Laura sat up straight and smoothed back her short cap of dark hair. "Weston. I'm glad you're here. Gordon and I wanted to talk to you about something. About our field across from you on 4."

Haas groaned. "Don't talk to him about it now. You think he'll re-member?"

"That's all right for those kids," Weston was saying, "but what does it do for the rest of them?"

"The rest of them?" Laura looked at him. "Of course it's for the rest of them. Every group needs leaders."

"You mean spies."

Haas said, "Don't try to pretend you care anything about the school, Wes. I know something about your record of involvement."

"The field, Wes," Laura said. "We've decided we're not going to do anything with it. There's no reason you shouldn't have it. We want to talk to you about a price."

Wes's mouth gaped open, showing the white ball of gum on his tongue. He looked at Laura as if she were another species, not quite human, at best as if he didn't understand the language she was speaking.

He turned from her to Haas. "I'm surprised you'd show your face here."

"Why would you say that? Weston," Laura said sharply, and he turned back to her.

"I don't want it anymore," he said. "Can't you see I don't?"

CHAPTER 3

Annika moved back into the hall and turned for support. She felt let down when Karlyn wasn't there. Probably she was out warming up her car.

It was one thing to have guessed the way her father had been thinking the last several months, another to hear it out loud. What were Annika and her father without the dream of the house? Two people living in a tin trailer?

Annika told herself not to be such a child. Things had been different for some time now and she had adjusted.

She was also feeling a terrible relief. God—did she really want to mess with all that wheat? Without a wheat field, her father could continue to manage the major parts of the farm without her.

Still, her mother's carefully colored image of the A-frame house shone in front of Annika's eyes as if it were on fire. She shut herself in the bathroom for a short time. There, she laughed and cried quietly until her stomach ached.

While she was in there, she heard a commotion. When she came out, she found that the last guest had arrived uninvited. Drawn no doubt by the cars, the noise, the flickering candlelight that gave the old frontier house the impression of a warm hearth or a Christmas tree, Sherry had slipped into the kitchen, where she was picking at the smoked fish with her grimy fingers. Jesse was headed toward her. Tina hovered behind him.

"That's my shirt," Tina said.

Sherry put the hood up on Tina's sweatshirt. She snatched one more piece of fish before Jesse herded her to the door. She wore a pair of men's corduroys, the waist cinched in with yellow baling twine.

"The door wasn't locked," she complained.

"Stay in the house," Jesse ordered Tina.

When they had gotten Sherry out, Tina turned back to Annika and smiled. She said that recently, Sherry had been regularly showing up again. Just to be a pest. Knocking on the door, throwing sticks at the window.

It seemed to Annika that Tina wasn't as scared of Sherry as she'd once been. Tina laughed, for example, when she told the story of the shock she'd gotten one morning when she'd glanced out the window to see Sherry's bare butt facing the house. She was peeing on the dead brown grass.

Sherry hadn't hurt her, Tina said. Maybe she wouldn't try to. It was kind of like having a funny little ghost.

Looking at her, Annika thought that Tina had been lonely in the house since she and her father had stopped coming over this summer. Jesse said that since Sherry had started acting crazier, he and Haas had been encouraging Tina to stay inside as much as possible.

While Karlyn and Doug were herding Annika's father into their car, Laura came up to Annika in the kitchen. She touched her and said, "I heard you had a scare with a big cat this summer." She said she'd heard about the cougars' den and the blueberry patch from Tina, but she wanted Annika's take on it. Were big cats something they should be worried about around here?

Soon, Haas joined the two of them. After they were done with cats, he wanted to discuss another of Annika's favorite topics, the history of the Lake of the Woods. In particular, the story of the French fur traders whose heads were cut off by angry Dakota Indians and found arranged in a circle on Massacre Island in 1736.

From there, Laura took the conversation back again, to a time she had worked briefly at a reservation hospital in Colorado. She spoke of the workings of tribal law she had observed there. It was all very interesting. Haas beamed as he watched his wife talk. Annika had never seen him listen so quietly.

Laura said she could give Annika a ride home later if she liked. When Karlyn came back into the house to get her, Annika smiled sheepishly and shook her head. It would be nice to be at the party by herself for a while.

Laura and Haas went to wash dishes while Annika stayed in the living room with Jesse. Jesse changed the music to something with a couple of eerie, quivering stringed instruments, a piano, another high and plinky instrument, and something else—possibly a wire mesh bag filled with broken glass?

"You'll like this, Annika." A friend of his had made him a mix tape for Halloween.

Annika had gotten a fresh surge of energy. She felt now she could stay up all night. As for Tina, she came to stand before the two of them, yawning. Her feet hurt and she was tired; she said it was time for her to go to bed. Tina was so pretty and tall, only three inches short of six feet, that often Annika saw in her a kind of glowing, supernatural quality like the big fleshy goddesses in the classical pictures Tina liked; though once tonight when Tina, holding a drink for someone over her head, had sidled carefully past the elegant Laura, Tina had somehow looked in comparison pinched, young, and small.

Tina closed her eyes and danced for a short time in the living room. There, she regained some of the magic Laura had drained away. She lifted her face and spun, singing along to somebody knocking and should they let him in and a grunting maniac moaning, I put a spell on you. In a room filled with shadows and candles, the unfinished wood floor, her stockings off now, her bare feet.

She was dancing for Jesse, but he was thumbing through his records. He selected a few and stacked them on the floor. After Tina had gone to bed, he put another mix into the tape deck, with "The Gambler," songs from a medicine show band, and Alison Krauss on "Little Liza Jane."

CHAPTER 4

Haas and his wife continued to chat with Annika on the ride home that night. The next morning, Annika found she did not like to dwell much on the situation Tina was in.

Or, for that matter, on Haas's sudden change of heart about Annika. Haas worked at her school. He was supposed to like her. He simply hadn't gotten around to it before. It was her turn now.

Perhaps the reason was as simple as the fact that she'd started dressing sharper. More like a normal person rather than a Mennonite or Daniel Boone.

At times, Haas did act like a dog . . . But now, with Laura back, maybe he would be all right.

The next morning, Annika made her father a meal Jesse said would be good for him: a greasy hamburger, black coffee, and a Coke. He didn't come out to eat it until one o'clock in the afternoon. Afterward, he went out to fix a section of fence in the cow pasture, but came back pale and sweating and lay down for another hour.

That evening, Annika made him soup and tried not to tease him too much. He sprawled on the couch watching *The Fresh Prince of Bel-Air*, which usually made him shout with laughter. Tonight, it might have been an instructional video on how to keep bees or darn a sock.

Her father was quiet that day. In the following weeks, however, that began to change. Other things were changing too.

A few days after Tina's party, Annika came into the house to find a message from Haas on the answering machine. He and the band director were organizing student teams for the Music Listening Contests. They were looking for teachers and members of the community to mentor them. It was a volunteer position with a budget for a modest stipend.

Annika was surprised at the number. More than she'd made in the entire three weeks she'd spent cleaning out and putting up Chrissy Rebarchek's garden. The sum would get her halfway to her goal of buying a decent little secondhand car and getting a job as a smoke-chaser.

In Music Listening, teams of two competed at a regional competition built around musical pieces and knowledge compiled on tapes put together by the state public radio station. Until the school had participated in the contests the year before, Annika had never heard of public radio. The signal didn't reach up here. Last year, she'd been interested in forming a team, but had been too shy to ask anyone. And the contests were in the spring, right near planting time.

As soon as she got the message this year, Annika knew she'd do it. She knew of the students Haas wanted her to work with. Two of his favorites, Nathan Peterson and Heidi Cook, a couple of years behind her in school. Smart kids, never overly friendly with her, but who had been? Not unfriendly, either. They were not animals the like of Angie Torgesen, who, on the back of Michelle Pickar, used to shove Annika's euphonium case onto the highest shelf where she couldn't reach it even with a stool.

The idea of working with the kids didn't worry her as much as it would have the year before. She had her degree; she was the teacher now. The kids didn't have to like her, and she didn't have to like them. She just had a job to do.

In the message, Haas told her she could meet with the kids anywhere she wanted. At the school, somewhere in town, even out here. He could give them a ride out if that would help.

When Annika called Haas back, he told her Heidi and Nathan were excited to know Annika had a good ear for music and had spent the summer offering feedback to a musician friend of his in Graceton.

❧

Annika wanted to go somewhere to meet her students. She wasn't going to have them come here, to the trailer, with its feeble orange light and her bedroom door busted now on the bottom. When she asked her father about borrowing the truck, he balked.

"Every week? What am I supposed to do if it turns out I'll need it? Or if you're in town and something comes up?"

"You can call Doug."

Her father sneered. "Call up the neighbor and ask him for a ride?"

He went on grumbling. Annika ignored him. When the time came, she would just take the truck. He wasn't going to try and stop her anymore.

Still, she lied about who had contacted her. She said it was the band director. Her father might put up more of a fight if he knew Haas was involved.

She organized a schedule of meeting with her charges once a week after school at the bakery. She was nervous only the first day. Even though she had been in band with them only the year before, Heidi and Nathan called her Ms. Rogers, sat upright and attentive at the bakery's sticky tables, and took notes on everything she said. On the drives home in the December darkness, Annika sat up on her stack of cushions thinking about the music and the money, of which Haas had already given her half, eating fresh Bismarcks from a white bag, swiping spilled vanilla cream from the gear shift and popping it in her mouth.

Tina called a few times in December, asking Annika to come over to make caramels. But Annika was so busy now, she couldn't find the time to make it work. Apart from her music sessions, she had all her chores besides. Heidi and Nathan would be tested not only aurally, but on the technical and historical information included to introduce the pieces. Annika studied the tapes hard. She was proud to be able to quiz the kids without even looking at the booklet. They seemed quite impressed. She felt this made them work harder. If they kept it up, they might even win.

The timeline on the tapes went from Gregorian chants to contemporary music. There was an interesting bit on medieval polyphony and an analysis of "Mack the Knife."

After her students finished the study-at-home curriculum she'd set for them, Annika moved the meetings to the band room at the school where, with access to a tape player and a nice sound system, she played excerpts from the tapes and tested them over and over. Once or twice, she stayed after the kids had gone and pulled out the school's euphonium. Thinking of the evening this summer she had watched Jesse and Haas play duets, she remembered she had learned that the succession of notes on the page did not indicate only how she should change her fingers at such and such a time. There was phrasing. There were dynamics. In the music file, she found her piece, "Allegro Spiritoso," from solo contests the year before. She had not played the euphonium for almost six months, and it hurt her lips; when she tried to play again with what she thought she knew now, it didn't sound any different.

Still, the old brick building at these late hours was pleasant, quiet and ghostly, most of the lights switched off, the wooden floors creaking behind her long after she'd passed down a hall.

One night in late January, Annika was getting into bed, having just pressed play on side two of her Music Listening tape, beginning with the transition from the classical era to the romantic, so she could listen to and absorb the music as she fell asleep.

It was Beethoven's Fourteenth Sonata, the *Moonlight*. A piece of music, the narrators said, that was difficult for many people to really hear, as they could never remember a time when it was fresh.

For Annika, it was really something. She felt it spoke to a tension she had often felt in life. That between her desire to be immersed, entangled in some wild, treacherous thing—lightning, frigid cold, a pack of wolves, the deepest water in the middle of the lake—and an equally deep longing, something she felt in her best moods, to live to see it again, as many times as she could get.

She didn't know whether or not her father had ever heard that piece of music. That night, he didn't act as if he had. The first movement had already gone by, and the second. She didn't even know he was listening. She was almost asleep when he came into her room weeping during the agitated third movement.

It was worse than hearing him moan over Tina in the woodshed. He shook her awake. "Nick. I don't know what I'm gonna do," he said.

"What is it?" Annika sat up.

She had seen her father cry before. He was not unsentimental, especially when moved by something beautiful. But this was something else again.

He was in a panic. His tears coming freely like a child's, sheeting down his face. He wiped his eyes behind his glasses until finally he took them off, laid them on Annika's nightstand, and covered his face with his long hands.

He said he was worried about Tina. He wasn't sure Jesse was taking care of her as he should. Tina was a special person and deserved better. From what he could gather, too often Jesse left her all alone in the house. Had Annika gotten that impression, too?

Annika said she didn't know. What she did know—she didn't say it—was that she wanted to get up at a decent time tomorrow to review her tapes and clean out the chicken coop.

Her father asked, did Annika think he should step in and help out? Be a bigger part of Tina's life? A better friend to her? At Tina's party and a few times since, he said he had asked Tina this. She said no. He shouldn't worry. She and Jesse were working on things. They were going to be all right. She had asked him not to call anymore, or to come uninvited to the house.

It had struck him, though, that maybe Tina just didn't want to be a bother. Would she contact him if things changed? Would she be too embarrassed or shy? She wasn't a bother. Not at all. He wanted to be there for her.

At one point, for an instant, Annika's father came out of his reverie. He seemed to see Annika in front of him. He pointed a finger at her.

"You see what can happen, Nick, if you get married young." As if he hadn't done so himself!

"I guess."

"Have you seen her, Nick?"

Annika closed her eyes. "A little bit."

But no. She hadn't seen Tina since her birthday party. She'd been having such a nice time. And Tina's life was such a mess.

"And she seems all right?"

"Sure . . ."

Her father asked her, if Tina told him to stay away so she could work on her marriage, did he have a choice? But what was he supposed to do with himself? Annika murmured a few noncommittal things. Then her father began to steer the conversation to a place she did not want to go. "Nick, I haven't felt—worried like this for someone—in a long time." He looked at her and waited.

"She'll be all right," Annika said.

CHAPTER 5

One week, Haas called Annika to invite her to do her regular weekly meeting with Nathan and Heidi at his house. He said he'd bring the kids out himself. He and Laura would make dinner and give the kids a coaching.

Annika didn't tell her father. She drove into town as usual and got the groceries. At the store, she grabbed a bag of apples before booking it through the produce aisle to avoid the attention of the middle-aged stock boy who had been watching her since she was eight or nine. Thankfully, he was bent over a box of something. She was the only girl over twelve she'd ever seen him pay attention to. It was common knowledge he was probably a pedophile.

In the freezer section, she dearly hated to pull out plastic bags of corn and peas. She left it until last and hid them shamefully under the bread.

In the check-out line, she ran into Chrissy Rebarchek. A big, wide-hipped, graceful woman with an antiquated feathery hairstyle, Chrissy was mentoring a Music Listening team as well. She asked if Annika was having a good time working with the kids.

"Yup, and the money's not bad either!" she said.

Chrissy laughed. It took Annika a second to realize Chrissy thought she was making a joke.

"Well. It's nice to give back," Chrissy said.

Annika stood with her mouth half-open and after a moment Chrissy gave her a funny look. Finally, Annika guessed at the awkwardness she had stepped into, laughed as naturally as she could, and changed the subject to the weather.

On the drive home, it started to snow. Annika squinted into the bits and streaks of white driving at her and wondered, Why was she getting paid and not Chrissy Rebarchek? At first, she had felt, wow! Haas must think a lot of her. That was really something.

As she drove, her high spirits deflated. No. Chrissy had far more experience and musical knowledge than she did. There must be another reason.

She dropped the truck and groceries off at home. She told her father she had picked up vanilla for Karlyn Johnson and was going to walk it up there. When Haas, coming from town with Heidi and Nathan, saw her on 4 and stopped, Annika got into his car quietly.

They didn't notice her mood. The three of them were in a crazy one. Nathan, in a hat with long braided ties and a reindeer knitted on the crown, was pretending to yodel, the way Annika's bus driver Harland could do. Nathan and Heidi both spoke to Haas as if they were all the same age.

"Turn here, Gordon. No, you're going to miss it. What, are you stupid, Gordon?" Nathan cried.

He swore and Heidi squealed when Haas, turning onto Jesse and Tina's corner, jerked the wheel on the snowy road so they fishtailed. Nathan wasn't buckled in and he toppled over in his seat. It was warm out, just over thirty degrees. The wet, slick snow was beginning to come down hard, heavy flakes gathering thickly in the headlights. The plows would focus on the blacktop first. They wouldn't come down the county roads until tomorrow, or whenever they could get to it.

Annika looked at Tina and Jesse's house as they passed. There was one light burning. No vehicle in the driveway. When she could no longer see the house, Annika turned to study the back of Haas's big head, encased in a bomber hat with fur flaps.

At his place, before she could organize the kids into a listening session, Haas started helping Nathan with his lines; he was in the school play. Annika hadn't been in the house since Joel Kapinsky had owned it and it looked very different. A striking hand-hewn oak table with its irregularities intact, circled by four diamond-willow chairs. In the living room, a record player, filled bookcases, and two oil paintings that looked like something from a museum or an art-history book. One an arctic landscape colored brilliantly in red, purple, and blue, the other a Puritan family seated around a table, this one realistic like a black-and-white photograph.

In the living room, where they finally settled down to work, Heidi sat cross-legged on one end of the couch, an afghan spread over her lap. Tall, blond Nathan lay sprawled on the other, his long arm dangling to the floor. Haas and Laura took charge of guiding the two of them through the Music Listening tapes while Annika sat on a kitchen chair feeling awkward. She wasn't leading the session, but of course she wasn't supposed to answer the questions either.

Not that she wouldn't have liked to, especially after Nathan and Heidi's disappointing performance. At one point, she broke in to say, "You're not concentrating."

The two children turned to her slowly, looking sufficiently guilty. "I know it, Ms. Rogers. Come on, Nathan . . ." Heidi hit him on the leg.

Haas seemed to think it was funny. Laura gave Annika a knowing look. She rattled off stylistic devices for the kids to listen for, then played some Stamitz live on her clarinet, her back erect and curved like a swan's neck in her wooden chair.

And nothing would have been easier for Annika to point out, had she the chance to compete in a round of "Mozart/Not Mozart," that, as sweet as the little Stamitz was, it didn't have the greater composer's easy, swinging grace!

Watching his wife play, Haas's face held an admiring look. It was also grateful, the way Annika had used to greet the trailer's lit windows after a long day at school.

At other times, when Laura showed she was displeased with him, Haas would practically grovel at her feet. When Haas took a drink of beer and belched, or sliced cheese off the block with his fingernail, she scolded him.

"Without me, he'd be an animal," she said.

While Haas and Laura started supper, Annika stayed in the living room with Nathan and Heidi. The two began to talk about other things, the band schedule, the independent study Heidi was doing with Haas in philosophy. From the kitchen came the fragrance of onions and celery frying in butter. Nathan and Heidi shared some kind of easy understanding that made them unguarded and sympathetic with each other. When Annika was with them, they tried to bring their teacher in on it too. Heidi was particularly good at this. Any reference that had gone over Annika's head, whether it was to a social drama at the school or a popular band even the Amish probably knew, Heidi would explain as if it were a private juvenile joke between her and Nathan, something so silly and inconsequential Annika should be glad she had never heard of it and wasn't some stupid little nerdy kid like they were.

Dinner was excellent. Haas made soup with leeks, wild rice, and sherry, and Laura pulled a crusty loaf of homemade bread out of the oven. There were also turnips mashed with milk and butter. Haas asked Heidi about *Twilight of the Idols*, Nathan about playing Hank in *A Connecticut Yankee in King Arthur's Court*.

He turned to Annika. "What do you think, Coach? Do these degenerates have any hope in May?"

Annika finished chewing and cleared her throat. She did not look up from her plate.

"If they start taking it seriously," she said.

She felt an uneasy look pass around the table. She wondered how she would know, since she hadn't done anything, when her job was done for the night. She hadn't enjoyed the work as much as usual, and it was already seven thirty. Unless her father had done it for her, she still had to feed the chickens and the cats. Some of these late evenings, her father had taken to doing Annika's chores and making all the suppers too.

Annika was bringing dishes into the kitchen and Haas was at the stove with his bowl, ladling out more soup, when Laura, at the sink rinsing cups, saw him and said in a low voice, "Save some for Tina."

"It's not too salty?"

"It can't be worse than all of that awful fish."

Laura turned and saw Annika. She blinked, then put a neutral look on her face. "Oh, thanks, Annika. That was nice of you." Nathan and Heidi hadn't bothered to help; they were listening to pop music in the living room.

Haas was watching his wife as if for a cue. They were certainly a strange couple. Haas might be a dog, but they both seemed to like it when Laura kept him on a short leash. Except that sometimes, she couldn't seem to hold him . . .

Haas put down his bowl. He turned to Annika with a look she couldn't read. Maybe he was going to change the subject, but nothing came to him fast enough. Annika tried to smile before leaving the kitchen. In the living room, she sat down again with Nathan and Heidi. They were lounging on the furniture again, their eyes closed. Nathan with one hand on his belly, the other in his hair. When Annika sat down on the arm of the couch, Heidi opened her eyes and smiled at her.

"I'm sorry we're so lazy," she said.

She could say it because of course they weren't, not really. As tired and silly as they'd been tonight, next week they'd be on top of it. Sometimes they burned out and had to relax. Annika had noted this pattern in them before. They were some of the most active and involved kids in the school. Between them, band and pop choir, Academic Triathalon, golf, speech, track, drama, yearbook, and Model United Nations.

They both had high ambitions for college. Not just to go, but to be choosy. This wasn't an easy thing to do. They were so far away from everything up here. How did you find out about a place, and what did you judge it by—how did you tell a good school from a bad one? Even when you'd made a judgment, how did you know how to approach the place? Figure out what the guards at the gates needed to hear? Annika had heard the two of them talking anxiously about things like this. Their parents hadn't gone to college. They couldn't have helped if they'd wanted to. So the kids had to figure it out, find ways. Because they weren't sheep to be dumbly herded into this boring, pointless life or that one; Nathan liked to say that. Yes, Nathan liked to say—they had a moral obligation to pursue their own deepest happiness.

Annika looked at Heidi. She was a freckly, energetic girl. At times, she didn't seem to know what to do with all that energy. She was only a junior in school, but she seemed ready to burst out of this place. Tonight, something made Annika think to ask her, "Do you know Jesse and Tina—Mr. Haas's friends—they live down the road?"

Heidi hesitated. "I know about them. I think. Have you ever met them? Nathan?" She turned to him. Nathan opened his eyes with an elaborate yawn to say yes, he thought he had met Jesse one time—in town?

"What about them?" Heidi spoke in a measured voice, and Annika looked at her foggily—in her mind, she had already moved on to something else. She moved off the couch arm onto the cushion, closer to Heidi. She asked in a low voice if it was true Mr. Haas had gotten drunk and driven recklessly and acted flirty with the girls when he'd taken several kids, Heidi included, on that trip to Minneapolis in September.

Heidi giggled. She looked nervous now. She glanced at Nathan again, faintly raising her eyebrows. She put her mouth near Annika's ear and spoke in a low voice that was equally spooky, as if she were telling a ghost story, and oddly erotic.

"Oh," she breathed, "we're not supposed to talk about that."

Annika frowned. Then she pulled away. She moved back onto the couch arm. Haas came into the room telling Nathan and Heidi he would drive them home now. While Nathan was groaning and stretching elaborately, Annika stood up.

Mr. Haas shrugged into his black and red flannel coat. "I'll drop you on the way, Annika."

"You know, it's so nice out, I think I'm going to walk."

Mr. Haas looked at her while doing up his buttons. His eyes were not hard, exactly, but they'd lost the soft look they'd had for Laura in the kitchen. "I don't think so, Annika. In the dark?"

"I've got my flashlight," she said. "I might check some traps."

"No. You're not thinking of going through the woods?"

"I'll be fine." Now Annika was really feeling she needed some of that fresh, mild air. She put on her coat and said goodbye.

The snow heading into the woods was deep, but she had on tall boots that went up over her jeans. The moon was very bright, the night dazzling, with a rich, stirring feeling rare in the coldest months. As if all the creatures that had been tucked up against the cold were stretching their limbs and venturing out for the night. Annika's light scared up a couple of deer and a small furry animal dashing from the cover of one tree to another. It dove into a drift, leaving a spattering of snow.

Annika had been bad about checking her traps, especially the ones Jesse and Tina had let her put on the Blocks' land. That was a terrible thing to do. She couldn't believe her good luck when she found that none of them had been sprung. She sprang them now and decided she wouldn't set them again until she could commit to it.

At the hunting cabin, she shined her light around. The black heaviness of the trees, drooping under pillows of snow, and the liveliness of the night, were just gorgeous. Every thin branch was rustling in the light wind, every thick one groaning under its fresh and beautiful weight. A damp yet crystalized feel was in the air. Annika's lungs and the skin of her face could be open to it. Crisp, cold, but without fear or pain. She stood listening and looking for a long while. No footprints or other signs of Sherry. Snow had drifted against the door.

Not far off, a fox barked. On the other side of the meadow, a second answered. From the west came the low, intersecting whines of two or three snowmobiles crossing the frozen bog.

North of Jesse and Tina's place, instead of going along to 4, Annika cut through their fields to stop by and say hello. Tina was in the middle of the yard up to her knees in snow, wearing a black snowmobile suit and looking at the house, her now prominent belly giving her body an unbalanced silhouette against the untouched layer of white reflecting the moon into every speck of darkness.

She said that Jesse was in Iowa. Inside, the house was still the colorful, comfortable place from the party—and yet it wasn't. It seemed smaller. Colder, too. On the kitchen table was a cardboard box full of photographs, on top of the pile a younger-looking Tina in a skimpy halter, her arm slung around the bare shoulder of another girl. When Tina peeled herself out of her snowmobile suit, Annika felt a sharp urge to either laugh or cry.

"Wow. You can't hide that anymore, can you?" she said.

Tina looked hurt. Her skin was rough, her catty eyes too small in a puffy, yellowish face, her upper arms bulging at the sleeves of her sweater. Not exactly like a fat person's, but like something filled with air, about to bust. "Well, maybe I could. I'm so fat all over, who would notice this gut? But it doesn't matter. Laura and Gordon bring me everything, anyway."

"You're not going out at all? Why didn't you go to Iowa?"

"How would I even get anywhere unless I asked them for a ride?"

"We could take you. Maybe my dad would just think you were fat."
Tina frowned. "I don't want anyone to think I'm fat."

"Aren't you going crazy cooped up in here?"

"I don't know." Tina eased herself into a chair. "I am getting sick of Laura." She lowered her voice. "And Gordon. You know what he's like." Annika looked up, but Tina didn't meet her eyes. "They're terrible people. Both of them. Really. Do you know what? I think they just want a baby so they can make it into someone awful, someone exactly like themselves . . ."

Something dawned on Annika. "You don't want to keep it now, do you?"

"No . . . but that doesn't mean I don't care what happens to it."

Annika nodded and sat down at the table, too.

"Laura," Tina said with disgust. "Who doesn't buy the food a poor pregnant woman asks for? Who gets her bitter lettuce when she wants the good kind? And the way she looks at me. Like I'm some dirty dog in the corner." Tina told Annika she had found out that during the brief period in which she'd left Haas, Laura had traveled to some Latin American countries, hoping the runaround she and her husband had gotten in the past at agencies in China wouldn't be repeated there. But what did conservative Catholic adoption agencies want with a single woman pushing fifty, estranged from her husband and contemplating divorce?

If Laura knew what was good for her, Tina said, she'd be nice.

Annika sat still and Tina glared at her. "You can't be serious. You feel bad for *her*? She gets what she signed up for. And don't think you can trust her. She's just like him, she thinks the same way. She can cover it up when she has to, that's all. Gordon's just stupider," she said, her face growing red. "He's an idiot and he can't control himself."

Annika looked at her. Tina stared back. Annika waited, then said, "He's a jerk, all right. Do you think he's dangerous?"

"Dangerous?" Tina echoed. "I don't know."

"What are you going to do?"

"It should be Jesse taking care of me." Tina added in a lower voice, "I could still lose it. That happens sometimes even at this stage. I guess that would take care of everything."

"Are your feet supposed to look like that?"

"Even if I do have it, I can give it to anybody I want."

Annika continued to point at Tina's swollen ankles propped on a chair. Tina looked at them somberly and said they weren't good, but the doctor from town who Laura brought out sometimes said she was still all right as long as she didn't move around much. Laura was taking Tina's blood pressure regularly. She worked part-time as a nurse at the clinic in town. After a moment, Tina said, "It's cold. Don't you miss it being summer and going out for blueberries?"

"It does feel cold in here." Annika went to the heatstove, stirred up the embers with the poker, and added a couple of slabs. She poured water from Tina's battered tin pitcher into the coffee can they kept on top of the stove. Tina stood up, holding her back and groaning like an old lady. She took the pitcher and watered her plants, whispering to the rosemary that stood guard by the door. She fingered its needles, her hand on her engorged belly that seemed to spread up bulging practically to her chin. Little gray Charlie, looking fat too with her winter fur, mewed at her feet.

Tina looked down at the cat. "I'll make us some cocoa." She snapped on the kitchen light, bringing her colorful dishes, lined up on shelves nailed to the wall, into view. At the refrigerator door, she turned to Annika, a carton of milk in her hand. "Would you come look at this? Honest to God, I wish you'd take some of it with you when you go."

Taking up almost an entire shelf were five, six, seven rolls of oily brown paper. In each of them, Tina said, another smoked fish. "He brings this shit twice a week. For a while, it was almost every day. I think Laura made him back off. But she can't let me starve. Even plain bread makes me nauseated five minutes after I eat it, but fuck if I can't eat goddamned smoked fish morning, noon, and night."

"You're swearing a lot," Annika said.

"You would too if you looked like this. I really wish you'd take some." Annika didn't pause before ducking under Tina's swollen arm and grabbing two, then three, of the packages. Tina laughed weakly. "Take as much as you want. It really can't be good for me, what with all the salt. I'm glad you came, Nicky," she added and hugged her from behind.

After only a second, Annika felt smothered in Tina's bulk. Gently, she pulled away.

"I've missed you," Tina said.

"I missed you, too." Annika came out of the fridge, closed it, and turned around. Tina was still standing close behind her, on her wide face a strange, blank look.

"Then why haven't you been here?" she said.

Slowly, Annika shook her head. She sat down again at the table with her rolls of fish. Something made her start, she wasn't sure what. "Did you hear something?" she said. Tina was already pressing her face to the back window. A bang against the outer wall made Annika jump. There was a crack, the shattering sound of ice breaking. In seconds, Tina was working her bloated body back into her boots and snowmobile suit.

"Aren't you supposed to stay inside?" Annika asked her. After all, if Tina ran into anything dangerous when she was in this condition, how would she get away?

But Tina was already lumbering back out into the glittering, balmy night. Annika followed her. In the backyard, Tina squinted into the shadows cast by the yellow-orange yard light.

"Oh, jeez, I think she's jealous . . . You can have him. I never wanted him!" she said.

After a minute, a thin shape rose from behind the septic tank. Sherry, in a stocking cap and trench coat, holding a snowball.

"You're jealous of *this*?" Her hands on her back, Tina shoved her mammoth belly forward. She started to laugh, sounding nearly hysterical.

In response, Sherry threw the icy snowball, hard. Tina dodged it, staggering like an elephant stabbed with a spear. "Don't leave yet. Let me get you something," she said. She was still gasping with laughter as she lurched back inside. When she came back out, she was clutching brown packages to her chest, the rest of the fish.

CHAPTER 6

When Annika came in, her father was putting on his coat. He had called Karlyn and Doug earlier but got no answer. Then Laura had called to make sure Annika got home all right.

"What were you doing over there?" he said.

Annika explained about the coaching, but her father was angry. He said he hardly even cared about her being dishonest. She could lie to him all she wanted now. How was he going to stop her? But if she wanted to be on her own that way, she'd better start using some sense. She'd seen enough of Haas to know better.

"He's my boss," Annika said.

"And who signed up for that?"

Annika didn't tell her father she'd seen Tina. If he was this worked up already!

The next week, she canceled Music Listening practice. She wanted to work on some of her neglected projects around the house and barn. When she called them, she thought Heidi and Nathan sounded relieved, the little connivers . . .

It got cold again, just below zero. That Saturday, she went into Jesse and Tina's woods to reset her traps. At the property fence they shared with the Haases, Annika stood a minute and watched one of the horses come shambling out of the barn into the attached corral to stand in the hazy winter sun rising barely over the tops of the trees.

The horse treaded for only a short time through the two or three feet of snow.

It was four and already evening was coming. The woods in long, frigid January and February were pretty in a flat, blue-shadowed way, but also they had a harsh and empty sadness that struck Annika the most at this hour. Winter could be pleasant and restful for people. Skating, woodsmoke, crafts by the fire. But for the wild animals, it was only something to bear. On a subzero day, you would never find a badger or a fox doing anything for pleasure as you might in spring or summer: sunning in a meadow, toying with a mouse. A lot of wasted deer looking for a dry branch to gnaw on got caught floundering in the deep snow and couldn't make a decent run for it, and during one of the unusual winters, cold but with no snow at all, then it was the wolves that starved.

Annika stopped again at the hunting cabin. She kicked at the ice sealing the door and wrenched it open. Sitting on the boards beneath the window, she listened to the quiet and the muffled sound of dry branches moving faintly in the cold. She dragged in a broken birch log, dusted off the dirt and snow, and took her gloves off at intervals to peel the bark in a wide strip. Later she could burn a design onto the bark with her electric pen, then bend it into a miniature canoe.

She imagined living here alone, every sound her own. Soon, she would be able to detect a difference in character between one cardinal in the bare tree and another. She could whittle and hunt all day, the birds weren't going to stop her. Only if the quiet grew too loud and she could no longer hear any birds at all, whether there were one or two or dozens. That was when one started coming up with wild ideas or looking for trouble the way Sherry did.

When she started having thoughts like these, Annika jumped up and left. By the time she came out of the woods, it was dark. Approaching Jesse and Tina's house from the back, she stopped to look at its cockeyed roofline in the glow of the yard light. As Arvid Block told it, the building was made of two houses that had been structurally combined, resulting in a draft you felt when passing through the hall as well as a bathroom that in the summertime filled up with crickets. The house on the west side had been hauled out of the peat swamp early in the century, only half a building itself, the section of a house that had survived a countywide fire started in a dry summer by sparks from a train in the grass.

Following the driveway, Annika came around the front of the house. A shadow crossed the living-room window and she paused. Thinking of Tina's anxious, engorged face, she decided to keep walking. It was getting late. She was feeling down and seeing Tina was hardly likely to make her feel better; she'd come back tomorrow.

She was almost home when she heard someone walking toward her on the road through the dark. She stopped moving. It wasn't her father's long gait, his heavy-soled work boots crunching on the snow. The steps continued to come, light and quick. She hadn't brought her flashlight. She called out but no one said a word.

She crouched in the ditch and saw emerge out of the dark a slender shape, then Sherry's face leering in the moonlight.

"Scared you, didn't I?" she said.

Annika stared at her, breathing hard, before straightening up. Sherry was still wearing a trench coat, too big for her. Combined with a peaked cap pulled over her knit hat and her purposeful stride, the coat made her look almost official, like a professional bandit. Sherry didn't look starving or frostbit. Rather, a little plumper than before. "You been over to the house?" she said.

"My house?"

"Who cares about that? I was just there looking for you. Did you see her?"

Annika shook her head.

"Well. You'd better get over there. Things aren't good," Sherry said. "And tell her to watch out. There's something out here."

"What?"

"A cat, maybe."

"A bobcat?"

"You think I'd be worrying about that?"

"Not here," Annika said slowly. "They wouldn't come this far from the woods."

Sherry turned back the way she had come, heading toward the blacktop. "How would you know? I saw it, didn't I? I gotta go." Annika watched her without moving. After a minute, Sherry paused in mid-step. She stood for a moment like a deer listening for a sound in the wind. The night was very still. Sherry turned around. The excess material of the dark, baggy coat rose with her arm like a wing. She pointed past Annika, in the direction of Jesse and Tina's.

When Annika stood where she was, Sherry swooped down on her like a bat. At the last second, Annika shut her eyes before being knocked to the ground. She felt a light kick to the bottom of her boot.

"It's your turn," Sherry said. "I'd keep doing it if I could, but I can't."

Annika's butt was cold on the hard snow. She got up and brushed herself off and after a second turned around and began walking. For a while, she heard Sherry behind her, like a dog running her off its property. Finally, Sherry's steps stopped, started again, and faded.

Annika had chores and she was hungry. She hurried forward, listening into every inch of the cold air.

When she was turning into Tina and Jesse's driveway, a horse nickered nearby. Maybe the Haases' Appaloosas had gotten out. In the east side yard, Annika clucked her tongue and peered into the dark drifts. Moonlight gleamed on bits of iron and sheet metal poking out here and there.

She couldn't see well enough to tell about the horse. She went to the front steps and knocked on the door. No one came at first and she knocked for a long time. When the door finally opened, Annika was surprised to see not Tina, but Laura. Laura wore tall, furry moccasins and held a cup of steaming tea in her hands. She didn't start in the same way, though some anxiousness did cross her face. "I think I heard one of your horses," Annika said.

"I rode her over, Annika. She's all right." Laura stood with her little bow mouth open, working over something in her head; Annika could see it in her face.

"It's getting cold."

"Do you think she should be in the barn?"

"Probably. How long are you staying here for?"

"I'll put her in the barn in a minute."

"I can do it if you want."

"No, I'll get her. Don't worry about it. You like animals, don't you, Annika?" Laura gave her a faint smile and Annika saw regret in it. She hadn't yet spent much time with Laura. Despite what Tina said, there was something about her that Annika liked. An old-fashioned, delicate manner, a shapely, matronly figure that put Annika in mind of the corseted women in her favorite childhood book, an illustrated volume on pioneers and American Indians in the Old West. It seemed for a moment Laura would have liked to ask Annika to come in. If things had been different, maybe they would have gone out to attend to the horse together.

Annika looked into Laura's gray eyes; the two of them were almost the same height. Yes, of course she did, Annika said.

"Do you?" she asked Laura.

"Yes, but I don't know much about horses. And that's too bad, because there's a lot to do to take care of them, isn't there? I guess I like wild animals best. They stay outside and take care of themselves." Laura gave her a full smile and ran her hand over her short, dark hair.

"Well, I'm already out. I don't mind. Do you have a blanket on her?"

Laura blinked her big eyes and chewed her lip, and the nice moment between them changed. Annika squinted down the length of the house. She asked if Tina was there, and Laura said, "Oh! She is."

But when Annika asked to see her, Laura said she couldn't. Tina was asleep.

Annika felt annoyed. If only she'd just walked in as soon as the door opened, as she always did. It was too late now. "I might wait for her, anyway," she said.

Laura took a sip of tea and licked a droplet off her top lip. She pulled down the waistband of her sweater. "Well, Annika, but she's not feeling real well today. She told me she'd rather not see anyone."

Did she expect her to believe that? Annika thought for an instant of telling Laura she already knew everything—if that's what this was about. Were they still trying to keep the baby a secret? She couldn't quite see why. In the backyard, the Appaloosa nickered again. "Is Tina all right?" Annika asked, and Laura's mouth tightened. She told Annika with extra patience that Tina was fine, just tired. Laura was helping her with a few things and checking in while Jesse was away. In fact, they expected him back the next morning, so—

She faltered. She smiled at Annika unhappily, certainly to cover the fact that she was afraid. She had almost forgotten. She had been going to say Annika should come tomorrow and see them both.

Annika stood a moment more. "All right. Well. Tell her my dad and I say howdy." Maybe Tina had asked Laura to keep the pregnancy secret because she didn't want anyone to see her this way. Who knew what Tina might have threatened Laura with if she messed things up? Laura closed the door. Annika considered knocking again. Instead, she turned to leave. She had the feeling Laura was watching her and resisted an urge to check around the perimeter and peer through a window or two.

All the next morning, Annika thought about Sherry coming to find her and about Tina alone with Laura in the house. In the afternoon, she did her chores and went over to Jesse and Tina's again. No vehicles or horses. When Annika knocked, no one came to the door. She tried it, but it was locked. She called Tina's name. She thought they must have left lights on by mistake until Tina called faintly from the back of the house.

Annika waited. She knocked and shouted again. Tina didn't call out or come to let her in. Annika got the keys from the woodshed, let herself in, and went to the bedroom, which was freezing cold. She felt the temperature difference from the hall as soon as she opened the door.

She halted in the doorway. If Tina had looked bloated and distorted a few days ago, now she was downright grotesque. Her body so wide, her skin so dry and tight, it was as if her body were made of attached balloons. Red scales crusted her forehead and cheeks. Annika found it difficult to find the defining features in the face she had known before, like meeting someone she'd known only as a small child but who now was as old as herself.

Tina had fallen asleep since she called Annika at the door. She roused a little when Annika said her name; she was groggy, however. She lay on her back under a pile of quilts, her thick legs spread-eagle, her hair in a tangled, greasy-looking, dark red pile on top of her head. She was bundled in mittens, a scarf, a butter-yellow sweat suit, and a robe that looked and smelled sour. Annika left her coat on. Under the covers, Charlie was curled in a crook of Tina's body, a warmish lump that mewed when Annika patted it. Annika sat in the kitchen chair beside the bed and Tina eyed her out of her puffy face.

"I feel sick," she said.

"Where's Laura? Isn't Jesse back yet?"

"They're angry with me."

When Annika asked why, Tina blinked slowly like a cow. "Are you on something?" Annika said.

Tina's head lolled back; she closed her eyes. Annika looked at her cracked lips and asked if she wanted a glass of water. She told Tina she would get her a glass if she would open her eyes. Annika asked if she should call someone. Her father? Tina's breathing slowed; her eyes stayed closed. Annika stood up.

"I'll call Haas," she said to the quiet room.

In the kitchen, she found the number by the phone. In the middle of the second ring, Annika heard something else. Had she heard it in the ear next to the receiver, or the other ear? She thought maybe someone had picked up. She stayed on the phone and said hello. It rang again.

Suddenly, for the first time, she disliked this house. She longed to escape it. She stood listening for a while in the kitchen. In the hallway, she paused and looked up at the ceiling. A raggedy white wire hung down from a hole as always.

In Tina's room, she set a glass of water on the nightstand and shook her awake. "Is someone here? Jesse?"

Tina blinked heavily. She shook her head.

"I heard something. Didn't you?"

Tina yawned and shrugged. Annika sat by her on the bed and looked up at the dark rafters, a few cobwebs hanging down. Neither of them spoke. There was a listening feeling in the house.

After a minute, a scuffling on the second floor. A small animal. In a quiet house, one mouse with its nails and teeth could sound like a bear in the woods.

Tina's eyelids drooped again. "Don't fall asleep," Annika said and patted her hand. Tina sighed and laid a hand over her face.

The animal was scratching or chewing on the wood. Annika found a pencil on the dresser and threw it up at the ceiling. When it bounced back onto the bed, Tina barely stirred. Things were quiet for a second. The boards overhead creaked, as they will do in an old house, but it made Annika uneasy. There was a loud iron ping, as if something ran into the barrel up there. It might be a rat caught in a glue trap.

Mice were all right, but Annika didn't care for weasels in a house, or rats. She wanted out of there. If Tina had been well, or if it had been bright and warm outside, she would have done it, dragged Tina's dead weight down the hall, out the door, onto the thick, fresh grass.

She thought of the big cat Sherry thought she'd seen. No. Annika couldn't bring Tina outside without a car to put her in. She thought of running home again for the truck. Should she bring Tina to the hospital?

There was a vehicle on the road. A light flashed into the house and Annika jumped; it was Jesse's truck with its crap muffler. She ran out to the hall, where the sound of a vehicle door opening startled her again. Then another car, behind Jesse. Were they going to flip out when they saw her here? She thought of hiding. Instead, she rushed into the kitchen. She was staring at the door when they all trooped in.

Jesse cried, "Jesus—Annika! How did you get in here?" He dropped a bag of groceries on the table, his deep-set eyes as wide open as they could go. "Did you break in?"

She stared at him. "What? No."

"You have keys?"

"The ones you keep outside. Tina showed me. I think you have a rat." The house was filled with the cold sweeping in, noise and color. Laura and Haas were stomping their boots, wearing heavy scarves and mittens, furry collars.

Annika looked at Haas. "I was trying to call you."

"About a rat?" Jesse said.

Haas glanced downward. Laura's doll eyes widened, and she smiled quickly. "No, Jesse. It's all right. Annika. It's all right. We were going to tell you about Tina anyway."

"It's all right," Annika repeated. "Tina already told me a long time ago."

Laura looked back with an expression Annika couldn't read. She told Laura, "Tina's sick."

"Sick how? A fever? Is she throwing up?"

"She can't stay awake," Annika said.

Jesse glanced at Laura, whose face stayed composed. Haas took off his gloves and scarf and draped them on the empty cardboard freezer box in the corner, where Annika usually liked to put her own things. Laura got out of her coat and headed for the bedroom. Annika started to follow but stopped and turned on her heel. Her head felt vacant, exposed. Instead of filling with private thoughts, only the magnified sounds of the things happening around her reverberated around in there: the creak and thunk of a snow boot, the crinkle of the grocery bag, Laura's light steps on the floor.

When Haas asked for the bootjack, Annika began to go retrieve it; she had seen it earlier by the couch, one of Jesse's cowboy boots stuck in the wedge. While heading for the hall, she stopped awkwardly. She thought of offering to make coffee, but it no longer felt like her place to do that, either.

Jesse sat at the table. His curls had gotten long, fluffing out from under the band of his hat. He wore coveralls with oil stains on the knees. Annika hadn't seen him, except passing on the road, since the party months ago. Haas stood by the stove, turning his hands over in the heat. Annika glanced his way, wavered in place a moment, then sat down with Jesse.

Haas came to sit down, too. He looked at Annika distantly, then said, "Tina's fine."

"Do you think she has a fever? Should she see a doctor?"

"No. We just gave her something to help her sleep."

"In the middle of the day?"

Haas stared at her somewhat coldly. Jesse burst out, "Annika—Tina tried to throw herself down the stairs."

"What?" Annika turned to him. "Why?"

"Laura barely got to her in time."

"Are the hormones making her crazy or something?"

"Why would you say that?" Jesse said. "Have you noticed anything? The thing is, she's been threatening to hurt the baby."

"Has Tina ever said anything like that to you?" Haas asked her.

Annika sat for a second. "She's awfully big, isn't she?"

"The swelling?" Well, that was another thing, Jesse said. The doctor had ordered her on bed rest, but she didn't want to stay put. They had to do something to keep her quiet and easy. Annika asked how much longer until she was due, and Jesse said a little under two months.

"You're going to keep her on sleeping pills for two months?" she said.

Haas had given up trying to stare her down. He dropped his eyes and folded his hands in his lap. Both men looked up when Laura came back with her report on Tina. She said Tina's blood pressure was all right. But Laura was cranky, worried the drugs couldn't be good for the baby and mad at Jesse for dumping the stuff into Tina's spaghetti sauce so he could leave her alone this afternoon and get out of the house. She said that Jesse didn't need to use the pills on Tina the way Laura did; he could calm her down in other ways.

Jesse acted resentful for being scolded. He said he was also just plain sick and tired of Tina and all of her bullshit.

Haas was mostly quiet. He kept leaning over the table, rubbing his face with his squarish hands.

Laura sat up straight in her chair. She ticked off complications as if reading them from a list. She brought up the cold bedroom, and Jesse said sure, but what did they want him to do about it now?

"You can't leave her alone anymore," Laura said.

Jesse looked indignant, almost frightened. "I can't be trapped in this house all the time. I'll go nuts."

"She's still your wife."

"I don't need you to tell me who my wife is."

"She's not *my* wife," Laura said, her voice rising, "and yet I'm the one who's had to deal with her." Haas reached out to stroke her arm, but she pulled away. "Do you think I want to be here? In a house that smells like a barnyard?"

It was Haas's turn to look worried. He said maybe he could get a short leave of absence from the school so he could tag-team with Jesse. Or he and Laura could bring Tina home with them.

Laura stiffened. Haas turned from his wife to stare at a spot on the wall, looking as if he didn't know quite what to do with his face.

"No," Laura said. "I would rather—"

"Would you?" Haas said gently.

Laura's face crumpled; she was crying a little. "*That* house—that is *my* house. My *civilized* house. I won't let it turn into—*this* one."

Haas looked at the floor. "Do you want to walk away from it, then?"

Laura sat up in her chair again. She pulled a handkerchief from her pocket and wiped her nose. "No," she said. After a minute, she went on complaining to Jesse. "I just wish you'd do some things to make it easier . . ."

"I'm sorry, Laura," Jesse said. "I can't fake it anymore."

Haas gave him a look. There was a pause, in which Annika felt they had all become aware of her again. When the silence was broken, something around the table had changed. The three of them seemed to unite in a decision to turn to pleasanter things: Tina had had a good appetite this morning, could eat anything and everything, after a few weeks of feeling sick to her stomach. They ended the discussion completely when it was determined they were all starving, and someone had to make something to eat. "Stay for dinner, Annika," Haas said offhandedly as he went out of the kitchen, and she looked after him. Laura got up and began washing a sweet potato in the sink. Jesse came and stood behind her. He kissed the top of her head, murmuring something, and Laura bowed her head and nodded.

In the living room, Haas put on music. Annika bit her thumb when she realized what it was, one of Tina's favorite old Delta blues records. The music was compelling and, as usual, it had a relaxing effect. It assured her that it didn't matter who liked her or didn't, whether she was pretty or ugly. She was only a creature doing for itself.

But hearing the music tonight also made her angry. She felt almost as if Tina were dead, and if that record had been passed to anyone, it should have gone to her.

She wandered into the living room and stood staring at the black disk moving on the turntable. Haas stayed across the room by the other heatstove, still warming his red hands. She left the room without having told him yes or no about supper. Then she made her way to the door. Quietly, she began to put on her coat and hat. As she was bent over tying her boot, she felt someone walk up.

"You're not going to stay?" Laura said.

"It's my night to cook. But thank you."

"Oh, you make dinner for your dad?" Laura was waiting for Annika to look at her. Finally, she glanced up through the yellow strands of her hair. Dark spots of water stood out on Laura's sweater, patterned with reddish blue berries. Annika caught a faintly astringent but savory smell on her, what a sprig of juniper might put off if it was cooked.

Laura kept talking to her. Did she ever play the euphonium these days? While Annika was lacing up her other boot, Haas joined them.

"You're not staying?" he said.

"She's making dinner at home. Annika," Laura added quickly, "did you know I'm a nurse?"

"Yes . . ."

"We're going to make sure Tina's all right."

Annika stood up. "All right."

Some kind of light came on in Laura's eyes. "But if you talk to Tina again, remember her blood pressure isn't good."

"I thought you said it was."

"It's borderline. So don't say anything that might upset her." Both of the Haases were looking at Annika and she stared back at them. "And remember, Tina wants this to be a secret," Laura said.

Annika was about to leave when Haas got the big whites of his eyes up close to her. He said in a calm, strangely amiable voice, "If you tell your father, Annika, I think you'll regret it."

Laura was hissing his name as Annika slipped out and shut the door. It opened again just as quickly and Laura's panicky voice rang out into the cold: "Annika . . . He didn't mean that the way it sounded." Annika kept moving forward without turning her head. She clenched her fists in her mittens. She wanted to go back in there and smack Haas's hairy insect face.

"Annika?" Laura said.

Finally, the door shut, and Annika stopped in the driveway. Why not go back and do it, let them know exactly how she felt? Haas would probably be sitting down at the table now. If she rushed in fast enough, he wouldn't have time to get up. He'd be right at her height.

She wished at least she had told him she was quitting Music Listening. And that she didn't appreciate being bought off.

Forget the rest of the money . . . She wasn't going to give back what he'd already paid her, though.

The thought of the stubbly, loosening flesh of Haas's cheek under her hand made her feel nauseated. God. What if he liked it? Or caught her wrist in midair? She kept walking. She still had the spare keys in her pocket. The whole time, she had sat waiting for Jesse to remember them, so she'd pretended to forget about them too.

Laura seemed to think that with his last comment, her husband had slipped up. Tina saw him the same way, as a man who couldn't control himself. Annika wasn't sure.

He might be able to pull this kind of thing on Heidi and Nathan—

At home that evening, Annika was quiet. She sat in the living room with her father, playing checkers. Part of her wanted to tell him everything. A year or two ago, she never would have kept something like this from him. They had talked over almost everything then. But how to begin? She thought she should at least talk to Tina first.

She also dreaded his reaction. Spending more time away from the house had helped *her* put the subject of her father's feelings for Tina out of the forefront of her mind; on him, it may have had the opposite effect.

In all the hours Annika had been leaving her father alone, she wondered if he hadn't begun to hear her mother's voice again, unsummoned this time. Something was making him jump whenever Annika walked through the door. Making him ask her questions at once to fill the house with their voices. Sometimes, Annika came home to find he had brought Mash in and was roughhousing with him, maybe just to get him to bark.

Her father would ask about Music Listening. His voice bright and keen, yet distracted. If her answers went on too long, he would start to fidget. His arms would swing. When he had waited as long as it seemed he could stand it, he would start with, "Nick, today I got to thinking—"

He'd been thinking that maybe Tina had gotten married looking to make the family she didn't have. Had she really gotten what she wanted? Or he had gotten to wondering if Jesse ever went out on "the road," and how Tina liked that. Several times, her father went over how Tina had told him, back in November, not to visit for a while. He'd gotten to thinking he didn't know how long that was supposed to hold. Did Annika think he should call her? He didn't want Tina to think he'd abandoned her. That she couldn't still count on him for anything she needed. Once he was thinking about the Blocks' old plumbing and betting that Jesse's rat's nest of long, curly hair clogged the sink.

Annika didn't think he should call her—that's what she always told him.

That night, Annika had just been kinged in checkers and her father was sitting back in his chair looking listlessly at the board. Then he sat up straight.

"You know, Nick," he said, "I've been thinking . . . We wouldn't even have to build a whole new house."

Annika looked up at him. Already, her father was bent over his checkers again, studying them as fiercely as if they were tarot cards.

"What do you mean?" she said.

Her father said they could find a house that was already standing and fix it up. Add wood accents, stonework, a cedar deck. Remodel the inside however they wanted. You could buy a house to do a thing like that—or you might rent one. Say, make a deal with the owner that you would fix up the place in exchange for not paying any rent.

"What? Rent one? But make all the changes anyway? Then you don't own them." Annika stared at him.

"That don't mean you can't live in it," her father said uneasily.

"But—you mean move? What about the farm?"

"Well, if we found something right around here . . ."

Annika sat silently, staring at the checkers. She felt any pity she'd had for her father tonight evaporate. "What about Mom's log house?" she said.

She almost never spoke of her mother directly, as a person she too had known. What did Annika know about what her mother had really wanted? Her father had kept her mother almost entirely to himself.

And yet, Annika found it wasn't difficult to trick him into thinking she *did* know. She put her hands on the table. She leaned forward, pushing her mother's features into her father's face.

"Mom wanted that house," she said.

Her father winced. For a while, the game staggered forward. After it was over, neither of them was willing to suggest they quit for the night. They started again and got nervous with one another, snappish, competitive. At the same time, they traded off threatening to end the game, claiming to be too tired to finish. Finally, it was her father, yawning hugely, who won that, the real game, the contest of who carried the burden of his or her bad feelings more heavily. He was the sour-faced winner, the loser even more sour.

As her father was heading into his bedroom, Annika said, "I didn't know Karlyn and Doug stayed with us after Mom died."

Her father paused mid-step in a strange pose, as if his long body had been electrocuted. "They didn't stay here. Jo stayed."

"But they helped Aunt Jo?"

"Yes, they would stop over. Nick, can we talk about this another time?"

"Karlyn says I cried." Where before the revelation had only shocked her, now it brought her a warm feeling. She could not feel her mother's arms around her now, but once she had acutely felt their unique absence when they'd been taken away. At least two other women available, but she'd wanted only one!

"I screamed for weeks," Annika said, hardly even noticing her father had gone out of the room.

After watering the cows the next day in the early evening, Annika walked again to Jesse and Tina's. The brown truck was there, covered in a thin layer of fresh snow. From the far backyard came the ringing of an axe. She stood for a while listening to it and wondering what to do. One second, she thought she should go tell Jesse she was here. In the next, it seemed better to see if she could talk to Tina while she was alone.

Annika got a small armload from the woodshed. When she found the house door locked, she felt she might have picked the wrong thing. At least a troublesome thing. She let herself in with the keys from her pocket. In the kitchen, she unloaded the wood, dusted dirt and bark from her coat, hung it up, and stood a minute listening to her breath in the quiet house. In the living room, one of Tina's cattail wreaths had fallen off the wall. The little cat Charlie had pulled most of it apart. Annika picked up the biggest intact piece of the wreath and laid it on the coffee table, piling it with sticks and torn pinkish blossoms.

Tina was asleep. But she woke easily and said hello, even pulled herself into a sitting position. Though Annika wouldn't have thought it possible, today the swelling looked even worse. Tina's hair had been washed, however, and her layers of pajamas were fresher looking. She groaned and complained as she hefted her body. Annika stood, shifting her weight from one foot to the other, looking out the bedroom doorway into the hall until Tina said, "What's wrong with you, Annika? Sit down."

"I should go tell Jesse I'm here."

"What? Why?"

"I let myself in."

"He's just out back, isn't he? You used the keys? That's all right—I'm here."

Annika nodded slowly.

"It's nice to have company. I'm on bed rest now, and I'm going crazy here." Tina's chin wobbled and her eyes got watery. "Look at me . . . all emotional . . . Well, it's just nice to see you. Thanks for coming, Nicky. Go ahead and sit down." Finally, Annika sat, still feeling jumpy. "You're so nervous it's making me nervous," Tina said and looked at her. "What is it? What's the matter? Is everything all right at home?" Her voice grew softer. "How's your dad?"

Annika stared at her. "You were so out of it yesterday."

"Yesterday? You were here? Was I asleep?"

"Yes."

"I'm not surprised. I've been so tired. I think I slept the whole day practically. Laura says that's not unusual."

"Okay."

"No. What is it? You look so worried. Nicky!"

"How's your heart? Do you think it's beating fast?"

Tina pressed her hand to her chest. "What? Why?"

Annika's own chest hurt. "Laura gave you sleeping pills."

"No, she didn't. I never take those." Annika sat with her mouth open. Tina leaned closer to her. "Wait a minute. Laura told you this?"

"Just to calm you down and keep you quiet."

"She's drugging me? How?" Annika shrugged and slumped in her chair. But Tina was struggling to sit up straight, her eyes suddenly bright. She looked almost happy. "I knew it!" she said. "I thought there was something off around here. And that those eggs tasted funny. Laura was here in the morning and made me breakfast. I thought something was funny, but I couldn't say for sure. And I was so hungry . . . Oh, my God. She's crazy. She's actually crazy. Wait until Jesse hears about this."

The back of Annika's mouth filled with sour water. She swallowed.

"I think it was lunch," she said, "and Jesse already knows."

For a long moment, Tina looked at her. Outside, there was still the slow, clapping rhythm of wood being split. She leaned back against her pillow. "No. I don't think so."

"You don't think what?"

"Jesse didn't say anything to me about sleeping pills."

Annika groaned and shook her head. "He used them on you. Did you try to throw yourself down the stairs?"

Tina closed her eyes, gripping the comforter in her fist.

"No. Of course not," she said.

They sat another while. Jesse stopped chopping wood. Tina sat with her hands folded; they were so swollen they looked like baseball gloves. She opened her eyes and stared at her lap. Occasionally, she would look at the wall. Once, she pushed her sleeve up to show Annika her elbow, grayish and dry as a stone.

"Look at this. I'm a hundred years old. Don't ever get pregnant, Annika."

"Do you want me to tell someone? My dad?"

"No—I don't know, Nick." Tina closed her eyes again. "Let me think."

Annika muttered, "He's going to leave you anyway." The front door opened and she turned in her chair to listen as Jesse, breathing hard, got his boots off and dropped them on the floor. He rustled out of his coveralls, ran a glass of water, set it on the table.

He must have noticed Annika's coat hanging in there. "Hey, Annika," he called.

As he was coming down the hall, Annika leaned over the bed. On an impulse, she said quickly to Tina, "It would make a difference if you told someone that Haas—made you do it. Did it to you."

Tina closed her eyes. "You mean the pills?"

"No . . ." Annika looked at her. She didn't want to say the ugly words—Tina had never said them. She called back to Jesse that she was coming out.

"No," she whispered again to Tina. "I mean. I know what Haas did to you."

A strange look rippled over Tina's face. She opened her eyes but wouldn't look at her.

"Did to me," she said.

Annika raised her eyebrows and stood, right before Jesse walked into the room. "Annika," he said, "it's nice of you to come over, but you can't just keep letting yourself into the house." One of these times she'd scare Tina, he said, and who knew what she'd do. Then she'd be sorry.

Annika and Jesse both looked at Tina, who was again staring broodingly at her swollen hands. Jesse gave Annika a studied look before asking Tina what was the matter.

"I need to talk to you," Tina said to him.

Annika made to leave, but Tina looked up, her face blank. She held her arms out. Annika bent over the bed to wrap herself into them.

In the cold room, Tina's big body felt hot. Tina turned her face away from Jesse and whispered to her.

"Tell your dad," she said. "Break in if you have to."

Annika straightened. She could feel Jesse looking at her. She stood dumbly for a moment, then patted Tina on the head.

"Feel better," she said.

She looked for Charlie under the covers, and patted her, too. She began to leave, and Jesse said, "Oh, hey, Annika?"

She glanced in his direction but avoided his face. "You're not leaving right now, are you?" he said.

"I should probably get home."

"Well. Just wait a second. I had something to ask you."

"All right." She went on to the kitchen. Jesse did not stay to talk to Tina, but followed Annika out and shut the bedroom door behind him. When the two of them were in the kitchen together, he just looked at her. Annika stood by the table, her fingers on it. Jesse's hair was flattened on the crown from his hat; idly, he began fluffing his curls. His eyes looked distant. He was standing only a couple of feet away.

Annika said, "What was it you wanted to ask me?"

Jesse sat down in a chair. "What were you and Tina talking about?"

"I don't know. How she's feeling."

"How did she say she's feeling?"

"Okay, I think."

"She seem upset about anything?"

Annika played with the hem of her sweater. "I don't think so."

"It's not good for her to get worked up, you know."

"That's what Laura said."

"It's not good for the baby."

Annika nodded and waited a moment. "Okay. Well. I think I'd better go."

"All right. Annika, listen. I'm sure you can understand this. We're a little worried about what Tina might say to people."

"What people?"

"You know . . ."

"Like the doctor? Does he know about the sleeping pills?"

"Of course he knows. He thinks they're fine. He knows we have to protect the baby when Tina starts acting like that. But your dad, for one. You know why."

"What are you afraid she's going to say?"

"Annika . . . Sometimes you have to do tough things in order to do the right thing. You can't let yourself be weak. Don't you think that's true?" Jesse waited.

"Yes. I guess so," Annika said finally.

Jesse nodded and smiled sadly. "Yeah—I'm sure it's like that on the farm. I'm sure there are a lot of things—Annika, Tina told Laura and Gordon they could have this baby."

"I know."

"You know she did. She told you that herself, right? And they've been thinking about it for a long time. Building it up, getting excited. And doing a lot to take care of her. They've been paying all our grocery bills. Most of our rent, too. I haven't made much money since we got here. I've got lots of things coming, but the money's not here yet. And most of what's coming, Gordon set me up with. If it hadn't been for this baby, I don't know what we would have done. I would have had to get a job. Laura and Gordon believe in what I'm doing. This is about the baby, but it's about that too. They wanted to help us out. They wanted me to stay focused. Tina got pregnant, and what the hell were we gonna do? The point is, Annika, they've invested a lot in us; they've spent a lot of money. If Tina changes her mind, what am I supposed to do? Pay it all back? I couldn't. I don't have it. Laura's been wanting this for a long time. You need to know that. If it doesn't work out, just think about how she's going to feel. She's tried to have a baby of her own, but it hasn't happened. And now she's forty-four. That's getting old to have a baby. She'll feel terrible, and I will too. They've done so much for me. And they're probably going to keep doing things for me. You see what I mean? You can appreciate that. You can see how shitty I'd feel about it. If Tina decided she wanted to keep the baby, that would be a different story. Of course, it would . . . But she doesn't want to keep it. So what difference does it make to her? I know Tina's got a side to this—I know that. And she's told you her side. That's fine. I'm glad she's got you for a friend. But try to see my side of it, too." He cleared his throat and lowered his voice. "You know Tina slept with Gordon. You know it as well as I do." When Annika blushed, Jesse added, "I'm sorry. I know. He was your teacher. You look up to him. I'm sorry. But that's just the way it is. And now—maybe the baby's his, anyway. Have you thought of that?"

"Yes," Annika said. "Do you think it is?"

Jesse's eyes shifted. "Annika. I don't know. How would I know? But if it is, don't you think that gives him some kind of rights?"

"What kind of rights?"

"Like the right not to see his baby get thrown down the goddamn stairs?"

After a moment, Annika said, "You don't seem very mad at him about what happened."

"Annika . . ."

"It might be yours."

"Don't you think I know that?"

"Are you going to stay with her?"

Jesse didn't blink. "Yes. We'll work it out."

"Tina was pretty drunk when this happened," Annika said.

Jesse shook his head. His face took on a hard, vacant look. "You think that makes it all right? You've never been drunk. You don't know what it's like."

"I mean she was too drunk," Annika said.

Annika watched Jesse sit back in his chair. Then he stood up. Probably he was just going to run himself another glass of water. Annika kept her eyes on him. He picked up his glass from the table and drained it.

"Tina doesn't see it that way," he said, "so I don't, either."

"Tina—" Annika shook her head and stopped.

"What?"

"I bet Laura doesn't know about any of this."

"No," Jesse said. "She doesn't."

"But I bet it wouldn't take much for her to believe it."

Jesse widened his eyes. "You'd do that, Annika? You'd break Laura's heart like that? For what? Gordon's not going to run around on her anymore. This last time, when she actually left him—he got scared. She'd never done that before. He's not going to do it anymore. He's all in."

Annika held her breath a moment. "When did you know about him and Tina?"

Jesse still had his hand on his water glass. When the cup rattled on the table, he pulled his fingers away. "What do you mean, when? You were there. You saw me. The same time you knew."

Annika nodded slowly.

"When we heard it," Jesse said. The look on his face was like a rabbit's caught in a fence. He gave her a weak smile. "Do you want to listen to what we recorded in Iowa?"

"What?"

"With Thomas and Polly. It came out pretty good. They said to say hi." He tried to smile again. Annika said sure. As soon as he had turned, she moved closer to the door. She glanced at her coat draped on the freezer box. When Jesse started to walk down the hallway, Annika stood still, and he turned around and looked at her.

"Aren't you coming?" he said.

"I do want to hear it. But I've got chores."

"Come on. It'll only take a minute."

"It's getting late."

"Aw, Annika . . . I really want to know what you think." Jesse came forward and took her hand, lacing his fingers through her own. It was such a strange and unexpected sensation, at first Annika only watched him do it. She hardly felt what it meant. By the time she thought about it, she was already letting him pull her, and the hair was standing up on the back of her neck.

Oh, God, she was such a child!

To follow Jesse was like tracking a wolf through the woods. She had a recurring dream of walking down County 66 in line with a pack of timbers. In the dream, she was still a mile from home. She could hold herself back from starting to run, a move that would certainly bring disaster, as long as she walked slowly enough that not even one or two ever got behind her. But what if they simply stopped in their tracks? What would she do then? One was already taking his time. Dropping his heavy head, angling out his front leg. Keeping his small black pupils zeroed in on her. She backtracked to get behind him, but he waited. She couldn't stop moving completely. Then they would, too. All of them, not just this one. And one was enough.

Right before she woke up, Annika had always come to the understanding that a bloodbath was inevitable. With no way out, she was poised to leap forward and get the animal's slashing snout between her teeth, wrap his shaggy body in her arms and legs, roll him in the dirt, take what was hers and what was coming.

As she followed Jesse, she was looking at his big halo of hair, the back of his slender neck. They approached the door behind which Tina lay. Annika imagined that despite the drafts, she could smell seeping out of the lit crack beneath it the staleness and despair of a sickroom.

Annika wasn't sick. No. She and Jesse were vital, strong, slim, limber, carefree, and reckless, too. Tina had already lost him. Given him up, even. For God's sake, Annika was already eighteen years old . . .

As they passed the bedroom door, Jesse pulled his hand slightly from hers to tickle the center of her palm with his finger.

In the studio, Annika sat next to him on the piano bench. Jesse let go of her hand and busied himself with setting up the recording. When he was done, Annika grabbed for him again. She laced her fingers through his calloused ones, then rested their intertwined hands on her leg.

The music played. Annika was too keyed up to listen. Jesse stared straight ahead at the changing lights while she squeezed and toyed with his fingers. His hand was stiff now. He had on an intense, critical expression, some red-faced emotion beneath it straining to break out on his face. She tried to get him to look at her. At one point, she turned toward him and brought one leg up on the bench. She went all the way and straddled it. He let her take his hand again. But when she placed it on her small breast, he shuddered and pulled away.

Jesse murmured her name. His face flushed above his beard. Annika put her hand on his leg.

"What's the matter?" she said.

Jesse stood up and walked off. Annika sat for a second. Then she got up too, staring right at him. She didn't feel embarrassed, as she had with Tina; she was mad. She started heading for the door. Jesse only watched. Then he moved to block her. "Where are you going?" he said.

"Get out of my way."

"Annika." Jesse sounded worried. "Are you going to tell your dad?"

"About what?" she said provocatively. Jesse took her by the shoulders and started to guide her back into the room. Annika planted herself. She went up on tiptoe to try to kiss him and he pushed her away. When she yanked him to her again, he slapped her lightly across the face. Annika let out something halfway between a hiss and a scream and struggled to disentangle herself as Jesse worked to get a hold on her again.

"I'm sorry," he said, "I'm sorry! Annika. I shouldn't have done that. What's wrong with me? Don't look at me like that, Annika. I just feel crazy. I've been holed up in this house all day . . ."

She tried to knee him in the crotch, but Jesse caught her leg and shoved it away. He pushed her to the floor. He looked down at her, breathing hard. Then his face changed.

"We know you used to break into this house, Annika. Did you know that? You want your father to know? Sherry told Haas about it. It's one of the first things he told us about you. But we trusted you anyway."

Downstairs, Tina called out. Annika started to yell, but Jesse yanked her up by her elbow and clapped his rough hand over her mouth. Then Annika did get him in the balls. He doubled over swearing and she shoved past him.

Running past the bedroom, Annika could hear Tina talking, trying to get out of bed. Already Jesse was coming down the stairs groaning.

"Annika, stop," he said.

She took off, opened the door without stopping for her coat, and flung herself out into the dark. She was halfway up the driveway before she realized Jesse wasn't following. She paused a minute, took a breath. Until there were steps on the snow, coming from the house.

She started to jog again. Jesse didn't say anything at first. Then, "Annika, come on. Your goddamn coat."

When he came pounding up on her, she went all out. He chased her the length of the driveway and about twenty yards down the road before he stopped.

He had a longer stride, but all the cigarettes must have made it difficult for him to run. As she took off, her boots clomping over the packed snow, she heard Jesse behind her coughing. She ran hard the whole way home on a night lit up with a big yellow moon. On either side of the road, the great flat fields, tips of dead grasses poking from drifts, spread far and glittering and white.

CHAPTER 7

She sprinted at least a quarter mile. Her fingers were red and stiff, her ears burning. About fifty yards from home, she saw the trailer was dark. When she was close, she heard the dogs barking with muffled voices.

Only Tippy came trotting haltingly out to meet her. Annika patted her cold fur. In the driveway, she stopped to look around the place. Her father's truck was gone. For some reason, Mash didn't want to come out of the barn.

The chicken coop was shut up tight, but inside the hens were fretting. Annika peered at the ground. There might have been something here, circling the coop; the snow was too packed to tell.

She called Mash, at first coaxingly. In the cold, she lost patience and screamed at him. Finally, he came out of the barn whining, and she brought both dogs with her into the house. Typically, she and her father kept them outside at all times, even on the coldest winter nights, to protect the place. She locked the front and back doors, too. There was a note on the kitchen table. Her father had gone into town for groceries. In the refrigerator was a plate of supper.

Annika checked the locks again, then went to the heatstove and threw in some wood. A few pieces fumbled out of her numb hands and tumbled to the floor. It was twelve degrees below outside. When her fingers began to thaw out and burn, she sucked on them, stomped her feet, and howled. Her own voice sounded frightening in the empty house. Tippy jumped up barking to scold her.

Soon, the dog was whining at the door to be let out. Annika watched her and sat down at the table. Her mind was skipping from one thing to another. She looked out the windows, paced the house, pulled tight cracks in the drapes. She imagined that her face still stung from where Jesse had hit her, but it was probably just cold. Sitting down with her plate of pork and buttered noodles, she found herself crying, her face low over the table, shoving the food in quickly and eating some of her tears with the vanquished satisfaction of a boxer swallowing her own blood after a match.

When she was finished, she scraped the gristle and congealed butter into the cottage cheese container they kept on the counter. It already held bits of hamburger, vegetables, tomato sauce, bacon grease, cereal milk, and soggy bread. Annika looked at it. She peeked out the frosty window. Finally, she threw on a work coat, nudged the dogs back at the door, and ran outside to call the cats.

They were slow to come. She yelled at them and swore. They were probably all piled in a heap in the crawl space under the house, just below the stove. Finally, one slunk out crying and walking spitefully over the snow. Then two more, and Annika dumped the food on the ground, then onto the head of the first cat, who would not get out of the way. She didn't stay to see if the rest of them would come out, or to watch the two cats eat off the first one until everything but a scrap of lettuce and some colored liquid that had frozen almost instantly was gone.

As she was headed inside, she saw something on the south side of the house. A small dark spot in the snow. What was left of something one of the cats had caught, maybe. Good. Maybe that's why they weren't hungry.

But no—it was what was left of one of the barn cats themselves. One of the big brown toms, poor thing . . . Most of its belly eaten up, the rest of it left maybe when she arrived and scared whatever it was away. Farther into the backyard, where the snow was softer, Annika thought she could see where the trail of a big animal began, heading across the pasture and into the trees. So that's what had scared the dogs.

She turned away grimacing, hurried back into the trailer, and hung up her coat. Still her father hadn't arrived. She thought about calling the grocery store. She might have heard of people doing that. How did you go about it? Would they send a message over the store intercom?

A minute later, she heard a vehicle slow down near the driveway. Tippy rose from where she had finally settled by Mash at the stove and both dogs began to growl. The chewed part of Tippy's black ear flopped softly when the rest of it flattened tight to the top of her head.

Annika stood, too. The dogs barked and she didn't calm them. She looked out the front window to see not her father's truck, but Jesse's.

She pulled on the work coat again, then grabbed her .22 from the bedroom and went out the back door, closing it quietly. She let Tippy and Mash out with her and they streaked around to the front. They barked harder as Annika tried to make a dash to get behind the well house.

About five yards out, she went off the packed path and floundered in the soft snow. It came up nearly to her waist. She was making as much noise as a herd of cows, and now Jesse would be able to see right where she had gone.

Annika pulled herself back onto the path with the butt of her gun. She got behind the well house and leaned her head against the aluminum siding. She was breathing hard and shivering. She yanked the collar of her jacket up over her chin; she hadn't had enough time inside to warm up all the way.

From in front came the creak of a vehicle door. Then the murmur of a low voice. Annika's heart fell as Tippy and Mash quieted down.

Now they would lead Jesse right to where she was hiding around the back of the house.

She waited for the truck door to slam. It didn't. From her coat pocket, she pulled out a bullet for the .22 and peered at it in the dark. She shifted to let some of the yard light gleam on it and opened the chamber and dropped it in. She closed it and sat there.

Boots creaking on the snow. Then the rattle of the doorknob. The sounds didn't resonate but were swallowed in the absorbing cold of the night.

Now here came the dogs. When Mash rounded the side of the house, Annika yanked off her gloves. Hard balls of snow that had caught on them when she was struggling in the drift fell up one of her sleeves.

Jesse was coming up the north wall, trying to keep his feet quiet. When Annika saw him creeping like that, she really hated him . . .

She cocked the gun and aimed it far over Jesse's head at a cluster of fat icicles hanging off a corner of the trailer roof. She moved the barrel a shade to the left so she wouldn't put a bullet in the wall. Mash was almost upon her, his eyes glowing green, his tail wagging.

At the last second, Annika's eyes skipped down to the dogs. Then she looked back up at Jesse and her hands shook with fear or anger. When she took the shot, she accidentally hit him instead.

Jesse cried out and went down. Annika gasped but didn't lower the gun. Now the dogs went completely crazy. Tippy ran to the front, Mash stopped coming toward Annika and slunk low to the ground. He was barking and Annika watched his shape in the dark.

Jesse staggered to his feet. Favoring one of his legs, he moved into the shadows alongside the house and managed to get himself into the front yard; the truck door slammed shut. Annika called to Mash but he wouldn't come and Jesse started up the engine and with a groan muffled by the closed cab drove away.

CHAPTER 8

Annika backed around the well house so she wouldn't be caught in Jesse's yellow beams. She watched the truck until she couldn't see his taillights in the dark.

She headed for the house again, leaving the dogs. In the dim light, she saw a flash of Mash's teeth. She wanted to pat and reassure him, even to throw her arms around him. He was still snarling softly as they passed one another at a wide berth.

In the house, she sat at the kitchen table, the gun across her lap. It did not feel good in her hands. Its weight was a burden. But if she flung it away from her as if it were a bomb, then what had happened would really have happened. To occupy her mind, she sang "The Battle Hymn of the Republic" half a dozen times. Until the phone rang, maybe half an hour later.

Annika looked away from the phone until it was silent. When it started up again, she stood, carrying the gun, and answered it.

Haas's voice was not without warmth; he sounded almost excited. "Annika. Listen to me. You need my help." Annika sat silently. He said her name a few more times. When he spoke again, his voice was cooler.

"Stay where you are," he said.

Ten or fifteen minutes later, the door opened. It was her father. Annika stopped singing and had the oddest feeling. She was no longer tethered to her own body and could see clearly how she must look sitting in that chair, the gun across her lap. A funny look in her eyes. Beginning to hum her song again. She tried to say something, but couldn't.

Her father was sizing her up. He looked at her hands. Annika put them on the table; she could do that much.

"Nick. What are you doing with the gun?" He was still halted in the doorway.

"I was scared."

"Scared of what?" He came in and shut the door. "Did you hear something?"

"Yes."

"What do you think it was?"

"It was Jesse." Upon saying his name, she saw the spasm in his body before he went down into the snow.

"What?"

"One minute. Just one minute." Annika pushed back from the table, got up handling the gun with exaggerated care, and stowed it in her room. She caught a glimpse of her thin, haunted face in the mirror over her dresser. Why, look at her—she was just a child! Anybody would be able to see that.

When she came back, her father was sitting at the table watching her. He took off his gloves, laid them in front of him. Annika wished she had just crawled under her covers. She sat down not at the table but on the couch and stared at the blank television.

Too late, she remembered the dead barn cat. Oh, God—if she'd only thought to mention that instead . . .

Her father asked what had happened. She told the television that Jesse had driven over and scared her. So she'd gotten the gun out—scared him back.

"You mean—he was playing around trying to scare you?"

"Well—"

"Nick. You're talking crazy here." Her father sounded desperate. "A gun isn't for playing around. You know that."

"He wasn't playing around."

"What are you saying?" He could smell it on her; he knew she had done something. She glanced over at him. She didn't know how to start. Her father got up to check the fire.

Annika stretched out her toe and rubbed a dark stain on the carpet with her sock. They'd never gotten it completely clean since they'd had the dogs in here this summer. Now, again, the animals had littered it with crusts of melting snow. "I shot it. I shot the gun," she said.

"For cripes' sake, Nick!" Her father shut the stove's iron door sharply. "You knew it was just Jesse—didn't you?"

"He was trying to get in the house. He tried the knob."

"So what?"

"He didn't knock."

"Don't you think he might have just seen the light on and figured you were here? Nick? So you went out with the gun? Why?"

"I went out the back. He started to come around."

"Did he say anything?"

"No."

"Was he acting like he was on drugs or something?"

"No . . ."

"What did you do—you shot in the air?"

Annika began to whimper. She wrapped her arms around herself. "At the icicles," she said, panting slightly.

"What icicles?"

She pointed to the northern wall.

"You shot at the goddamn house?"

"No one was in it." She was still whining like an animal.

"Stop that, Nick. No one that you knew of—what if Tina had been along?"

She stared at him. "She was at home."

"And how did you know that?"

"I saw her there."

"You didn't think she could have come over here with Jesse?"

"No," Annika said. "She couldn't have."

"Why not, for cripes' sake?"

"He wouldn't have let her."

"Nick." Her father came to stand before her, both hands on his head. He was wearing a tan canvas coat like Jesse's and he pulled it off. Annika wanted so badly to have said the thing about the cat instead of what she had said, that she groaned and buried her face in her lap.

Outside, there would be Jesse's blood on the snow!

A minute passed. Annika could feel her father trying to speak more calmly. She couldn't pay attention. She thought she might throw up. She wasn't going to be able to do this. She should have crawled into bed and shoved her head under the pillow.

Tippy was whining outside. When her father opened the door, the dog cowered and barked. She wouldn't come in, but she wouldn't leave the doorway either, so that he could shut the door.

"Goddamn dog," her father said.

Annika stood up and snapped her fingers. She talked sweetly to the dog and Tippy trotted in, steering clear of her father. Annika sat at the kitchen table, where she bent down to scratch Tippy's black-and-white head with both hands. Outside, Mash, who hadn't wanted to come, was still barking and trotting uneasily around the yard.

Annika started to cry. She gulped the air in sharp bursts that hurt her chest. Tippy slinked by her father to get to the stove. Her father came to sit down with Annika at the table. She could feel his leg jiggling. He was trying to sit patiently.

Finally, Annika looked up at her father and said through her tears, "Tina wanted me to tell you something."

His brown eyes brightened. He pulled his chair closer to Annika's.

"Tell me," he said.

Annika smothered her face, mumbling into her hands until her father told her to speak up. She moved her hands slightly away from her lips and told him Tina was pregnant. Laura and Jesse were supposed to be taking care of her. But the way they were doing it—especially the sleeping pills—

"Pregnant?" her father said unhappily. "What's this about sleeping pills? Tina's afraid they'll hurt the baby?"

"No . . ."

"These are pills Laura's getting from the clinic?"

"I don't know. I guess so."

"Tina's having trouble sleeping, though?"

"She didn't ask for them," Annika said. "She doesn't want them."

"They're making her take them," her father said after a pause.

"Yes."

"Why? They don't think she's sleeping enough?"

"No."

"Then why?"

"To keep her—from getting up."

"Why? Because she's—what? Doing too much?"

"No," Annika said slowly. "She's—I don't know. Acting up."

Her father sat thinking about this for a while. "Is she trying to run away?" he said. Annika didn't answer. She didn't have to. Her father was already putting his coat back on.

CHAPTER 9

Annika didn't want to go along. But what else could she do? Stay at home alone with her stupid shaking hands and her terror of what was going to happen to her? In her head, she had been protesting, "It was an accident," as if she were already being hauled away.

It was not the kind of accident that counted. She would not get off because her aim was bad.

Why hadn't she just called out to warn Jesse she had the gun?

She hadn't wanted to warn him; that's why. She'd wanted to see shock jolt his body amidst a shower of falling ice daggers. Surprise was a key ingredient in teaching him the lesson of what he'd done.

She rode in the truck with her father through the cold night. They were halfway down Tina and Jesse's driveway when Haas appeared in the headlights. He wore a big coat and his furry bomber hat, his light-colored mustache and beard glittering with ice. Her father slowed down, then stopped. Haas kept striding toward them down the middle of the drive. He raised his arm to point at Annika. His icy, hairy face growing bigger in the yellow light.

She didn't turn her head when he came up and rapped on her window.

"I told you to stay put," he said.

"You what?" her father said. "Take it easy, there. We're here to check on Tina."

"Tina? Tina's fine. Jesse, on the other hand . . ."

"We're going up to the house." Her father drove forward, leaving Haas standing behind them. After a moment, he started running after the truck. In the rearview mirror, his head covered in fur, he looked like a Viking or a caveman, and yet Annika could feel in his superior, spiteful gaze exactly what finely tuned theory he had developed for each of them, her father the pathetic, small-minded bumpkin, Annika the unaspiring, unimaginative, miserable weak little worm who didn't know an opportunity when she saw one, the baby who'd gone crying to her papa.

While her father was parking behind the Haases' car, blocking them in, Haas huffed it past the truck. He ran into the house and shut the door. When Annika and her father got up onto the steps, no one answered their knocking. The door was locked. Annika dug into her jeans pocket for the spare keys. She couldn't find them. Had she left them in Tina's room? She had just found them in her back pocket when they heard a commotion. Scuffling feet, chairs scraping across the floor.

The door swung open. Haas and Laura, carrying Tina between them. Her long body wrapped in a blanket, part of her face covered as if she were already in the morgue. Laura had hold of her feet; it was the big curve of Laura's behind they saw first. Her knees were bent under the great weight, and she took small steps backward on the ice and snow.

Annika backed away. Her father tried halfheartedly to block them, until Haas said, "You want us to drop her, Wes?"

Once Haas and Laura had gotten Tina down the steps, Annika's father came forward again. This time they did stop, Haas breathing hoarsely in the cold. He shifted to get a better grip on Tina's shoulders. He watched as Weston got a closer look at her.

"She's asleep," Laura said.

Annika's father took a step away. He appealed to Laura. "It don't look like it."

"Well," Laura said.

"You need some help with her? Annika said you might."

"No," Haas said.

"Bring her back into the house. We'll help you out with her."

Haas stared at him for a moment. "It's too cold for her in the house. Could you move your truck, please?"

"Where are you bringing her?"

"To our place."

"And she's all right with that?"

"Wes. We have to move. We can't lay her down on the snow."

Her father came forward again, to support Tina with an arm under her midsection. With a signal between them, Laura and Haas started moving again toward the car. Her father walked with them. He touched the blanket with his free hand, then moved it to get a look at Tina's face. He pulled aside a strand of her red hair that had gotten tucked into the corner of her mouth. The way he looked at her, if he thought she was bloated and ugly, he didn't show it. When Tina groaned, he covered her back up.

For some reason, her father's careful touch made Annika want to scream. She found herself imagining him suddenly wringing Tina's limp neck instead.

Oh God, what was wrong with her? Was she going crazy in the head?

Poor Tina . . . But if only Annika weren't the only one with blood on her hands!

Poor flopping, lumpy, lifeless Tina, passed from one hand to another, fondled and dragged like a doll.

After a few steps, her father stopped, forcing Laura and Haas to do so as well. "Maybe you could just take her back into the house for now," he said.

"Maybe you could move your truck," said Haas.

"It's too cold," Laura said.

"It's too cold out here to talk about it," her father said.

Haas nodded to Laura. For a second time, they began to walk, Tina's heavy bulk swaying between them. Haas shoved past her father, who stepped back, his arms swinging.

"You can tell me what's going on," he said. "You can do that."

"You must know by now about us taking the baby," said Haas.

"What do you mean, taking it?"

"We're taking care of Tina because we're adopting the baby."

"I'd like to hear that from her."

"I don't know what you're going to do about that right now."

"Well. I'll tell you what. I don't feel good about this."

"Well. How do you think you're going to stop us?" Haas said. "Are you going to shoot us?"

Her father looked surprised; Laura hissed at her husband to be quiet.

"You barbarians," Haas snapped. "You think we'd leave Tina in this house with you two nutjobs running around?"

"Gordon!" Laura said.

"It's not gonna come to anything like that." Her father looked taken aback. "I guess you wouldn't have any problem talking to the sheriff about it, though."

"The sheriff? You want to call the sheriff?" Haas was half-sitting in the back of his car now, arranging Tina's limbs on the seat. He put his head out of the car to point at Annika. She had gone back to the truck and was crouched on the running board.

"Go ahead," Haas said. "You call the sheriff. I bet he'd be interested to know about her running around taking shots at people."

Her father looked at Annika uneasily. "It was just a warning shot."

"A warning shot? Wes, she nearly killed him."

Her father went white; Annika hardly heard his protests over the long, low wail that escaped her.

No. It wasn't possible! "It's just a .22," she said, "and I hit him in the foot or the leg." Her father was staring at her. "It was an accident. And he got up. He got up and drove away!"

Her father looked back at Haas. Unfortunately, Haas said, Annika was mistaken. Her warning bullet had ripped into Jesse's liver. He was at the hospital now, holding on by a thread. "But Annika," Laura put in quickly, from the other side of the car, "Jesse wanted to protect you. He made up a story about cleaning a gun."

Laura's tone sounded funny. Annika looked at her and relaxed a little. Now she knew they had to be lying. As if Jesse cared about her or anybody else. Jesse cared about himself and getting what he wanted. He would do anything. Play any trick. Tell any lie. "I don't believe it," she said and sighed. "I think I only nicked him."

"You think that wouldn't be enough to get you into big trouble?" Haas said. "Especially with your history. Breaking into this house. Stealing gas from Tina and Jesse."

Annika shook her head at her father. "It was Sherry."

"What would she be stealing gas for?" her father said. "I've got twenty thousand dollars in the bank."

Annika was thinking—remembering now, or meaning to learn to remember—that on impact, Jesse's hand had gone down almost to the ground. Grasping his shin or his ankle, as if a small animal had bitten him. A .22 bullet was quite small! She watched Laura tuck Tina's long feet into the car and shut the door. Her father was looking at Laura, too.

"Jesse's at the hospital now? It wasn't something small you could take care of here?" he said.

Laura glanced up at him and shook her head.

"Which hospital? In Baudette? So if I call the hospital, they'll tell me that he's there?"

Laura hesitated. "Somewhere else where they have the resources to treat him."

"Where?"

"You think we'd tell you?" Haas answered for his wife.

"Did he drive himself?" her father said.

"Weston," Haas said.

"Laura. He was dying, but he drove himself?"

Laura opened the driver's-side door of the car. "We've got to turn on the car. Do you want her to freeze to death?"

Annika was watching her father and Laura and she didn't even notice Haas had moved until he spoke quietly beside her and she jumped. Out of the corner of her eye, she saw him lean down toward her, his hands in big furry mittens on his legs.

"Do you want your father to call the sheriff?" he said.

Annika stared ahead at the snow.

Haas added, sounding almost kind, "No one has to call if we can agree on what to do."

"Where's his truck?" Weston started to walk toward Laura. She got in the car and shut the door.

"Do you want us to take care of this for you or not?" Haas said.

CHAPTER 10

The next morning, the school bus coming up 4 to Highway 11 woke her. For a reason Annika couldn't remember right away, she'd slept on the couch.

Under an afghan, her arms were crossed over her chest, her knees tucked up. Pausing at the corner with 66, the bus wheezed like an old monster from a half-forgotten dream. Annika pulled the blanket over her face and breathed into the woolly darkness. Then she got up and watched out the window until she saw the high orange beams of the bus, that sickly color. It was frigid, thirty-one below, the sky clear of clouds, the light beginning to show dim and powerless on the flat eastern horizon.

That bus. She was free of all of that forever. Relief and freedom— that's what she'd celebrate and exercise today!

Annika pulled on another sweater and tended to the stove. That's why she'd slept out here; she'd been keeping an eye on the fire. When they'd gotten home last night, her father had gone into his bedroom and shut the door without glancing in the stove's direction.

Annika thought she'd go back to sleep, but she only lay on the couch shivering, her eyes open. Looking at the room through the blurred colors of the afghan over her face. Hidden at this pivotal moment, she was pulsing with pure potential energy. Through the soft holes of the blanket, she could see everything outside of her in the room of the trailer, every little thing.

And everything beyond it, she could imagine. The world was so close. Ready to receive her, to be attacked. She could pull aside her veil at any moment. Until then, she felt drowsy with a sumptuous, anticipatory pleasure.

She got up and made peanut-butter toast. The sun began to rise sharp and dazzling on the crystalized expanse of snow.

She'd forgotten to leave the faucets trickling last night and the pipes had frozen. She dragged the portable propane to the house and for a half hour hauled buckets of water from the well. In case they needed it today, she tried to start the truck. They hadn't plugged it in last night. It didn't even cough. She plugged it in and for good measure pulled the other heater out of the garage and tucked it under the engine.

The sun was blinding. Annika's eyes ached, the pain distracting her some from the cold that needled into her face. She peered at the world through her gloves. Suffocating in the moist yarn of her scarf, she pulled it away from her mouth to take in a harsh pull of air. The tips of her fingers were numb. Snot froze and crackled in her nose.

The dogs were curled up together in the barn, close to the horses. On the south side of the house, Annika walked out from the frozen remains of the dead barn cat until she picked up the predator's trail in the deeper snow. Even in the frigid air, her stomach grew hot. A round cat track. Yes. It could just be because the snow was soft—it could just be that—but it looked to her that the track had been made by an animal two, three times the size of a bob.

Sherry had been right. Annika could hardly wait for tomorrow. It was too cold to track the animal today. She didn't go to look at the blood on the other side of the house.

After a warming break by the stove, Annika exchanged her coat for her coveralls, bought in the boys' section at Hardware Hank's. She went out and fed the horses and cows. She fed the chickens, huddled together and quiet now, checked the heat lamps and got the eggs, slipping her hand under their warm, velvety bodies, getting in return a feeble peck or two.

At eleven, she got the truck started. She drove it down the road a ways just for the heck of it. Slowly, the truck groaned forward in a dirty white cloud of pungent exhaust, the tires spinning, then crunching like teeth on a bone on the slick, hard pack of snow. The ditches had been filled by the plow. In the spots where the tallest brush was buried and there were no trees, the only marker for the edge of the road was a faint difference in the quality and texture of the snow.

When she got back inside this last time, her throat and chest were aching. She made a tuna-fish sandwich and heated a can of soup. At lunch, she played her Music Listening tape quietly—her father was still in bed—and whispered aloud a list of all the chores she would do today. She wrote them all down in her most careful script with her favorite marker pen. At the thought of her list, her mind going to the ins and outs of each job as she pronounced it, she thought of how satisfying it would be to do them all and have them done. She didn't even mind the thought of going out in the cold again. In a way, that would make it even better.

Not until dusk did she feel Tina's dry lips on her ear again.

"Tell your dad," Tina had said. Well. Annika had fulfilled that promise. What else could be expected of her?

Yes—Tina would be all right if she kept her head down and pretended she'd had a change of heart. If she said she was ready to be good. That she'd decided she loved the Haases and they would be wonderful parents. That she believed Jesse still loved her, too.

Or at least if she stopped fighting. What choice did she have?

What choice! There were always plenty of choices, if you included the bad ones.

Even if she were willing to pretend, would they believe her? What would they do to keep Tina still if Laura decided drugs were too dangerous for the baby?

How low and hopeless Tina must have felt when finally she gave up and asked for help. Tina. Who had given her the keys to her house, even when she knew Annika was a sneak.

As night came on, Jesse's liver, which in Annika's imagination in the cold, blinding light of noon had been merrily intact, was now lacerated, spilling out in pieces on a white hospital sheet. As she started to drift off to sleep, the bloody image dissolved into Jesse's finger touching her palm. His hand on her breast. Annika groaned and writhed in her bed. Pulled the blankets between her legs.

Jesse wouldn't tell a lie about cleaning a gun to protect Annika. But what wouldn't he do if Haas told him it was for the best and that there was something in it for him?

Silence for silence. That's how Haas had put it to them.

Annika unloaded her gun and stowed it in her closet, smothering it with blankets and old clothes. In her defense fantasies, plugging a bullet into any wandering derelict who wanted to steal her horse or rape her had always felt somewhat akin to pulling a stubborn weed out of her garden. That cruelly satisfying death pop. The real thing had felt flat. A dull, creeping horror.

That night, she didn't fall asleep until two. She woke again at four and thought, "No. I wish I could. But I can't tell. How could I?" It was too late. She had made an enormous mistake. She was in it with them for good. She couldn't go back and not shoot Jesse now.

She began replaying in her mind the early days of last summer, before Jesse and Tina arrived. When, soon after her graduation, she'd made the alarming discovery that solitude, however pleasant it was at first, could drag out into a bottomless anxiousness.

Of course, in jail, she might also be surrounded by more people than she cared to think about. Annika began thinking about one more walk beneath the pines. One more cup of sweetened coffee, one more brown owl swooping low across the road.

❧

It *was* her choice. Her father had made that clear.

The day after they'd abandoned Tina, when Annika had accomplished so many things, her father started and finished only one job, rubbing out splatters on the exterior wall and carrying a cardboard box spotted with bloody snow into the woods. He stayed less than an hour and came back with his hands empty.

First, he'd had a talk with her. Did she really want to hide from what she had done? Was she sure?

She'd stared at him, shocked, from the duck chair in the living room.

"You shot him, Nick." Her father's hands were on his head. "You shot at him in the dark like he was a goddamn raccoon."

He didn't know everything that had happened. So Annika told him how Jesse had meant to trap her in the house. Her father groaned and came across the room to lay his big hand on top of her head. "Jesus Christ, Nick. You were scared. I know it. But you got away. Why didn't you just lock the door? You were the one with a gun in your hand. Jesse didn't have a gun."

Under the weight of his hand, Annika slumped in her chair. "Do you think Haas is telling the truth? That Jesse might die?"

"No. But it doesn't matter." When her father asked again if she was sure she didn't want to go to the police, get it off her conscience, Annika fell apart.

"You decide." She started crying. "Please! Do it for me."

"No, Nick. Just think about what you're asking me," he said.

❧

All night, she was racked with guilt. Late the next morning, her feelings turned yet again. She began to look coldly at her father.

Her bad mood started when she woke up and saw the sky had clouded over. It had warmed up overnight, but it had also snowed. The tracks of the big cat, leading out of the yard and into the woods, were gone.

All day, her father was gentle with her, but very quiet. Their deal with Haas stipulated that Annika and her father weren't only to shut their mouths about Tina; they also had to stay away from her. If her father was upset, Annika felt that most likely it was only about that.

By the following afternoon, her father had begun to respond to Annika's iciness in a like-minded way. Then she knew she was right. It was not her he cared about at all.

They spoke little to one another, finally only when it was necessary to run the place. This went on for several days. The coldness became a habit, until all of Annika's suspicions were realized: her father was numb to her, as unconscious of her presence as if she were a tree that had long been growing in the middle of his house. Maybe one day, she needed some extra water, or dropped a few leaves; he swept them up and moved on.

One morning, her father was out shoveling and Tippy's circle around the woodshed led her straight into him. Unthinkingly, he had strayed into her path and, surprised, Tippy bit him in the leg.

Her teeth didn't even get through his coveralls. But this was one thing he and Annika had to discuss. Tippy couldn't stay on the place anymore. Last fall, her father had talked to the Johnsons about them taking her if things didn't get better. Tippy might be soft in the head, but she was familiar with Doug and Karlyn. She only hated Weston and she was a good guard dog. They'd agreed to give her a try. All winter, her father had continued to hope things might change.

Annika walked the dog down to Karlyn. She felt that in some way, her heart must be broken. But during the transaction, she could tell she was coming off as cold and stony. She thought that Karlyn was even a little afraid of her. Annika couldn't help it, and she didn't care.

At one point, her father started giving her requests and instructions in notes written in his back-slanted, wide-looped script. As if they were two lightkeepers on different shifts in the same tower, a suitable occupation for two old, solitary bachelors like themselves.

On one of the days after this turn of events, Karlyn, in a long quilted tan coat that fit her like a sleeping bag, stopped over to tell them one of their heifers had gotten out. Her husband had seen the animal making her way onto the bog.

At the first sign Karlyn's car was threatening to pull in, Annika's father went galloping across the yard. He dove into the machine shed and slammed the door. Annika avoided glancing in that direction while she was talking to her in the driveway.

"Tippy's doing great," Karlyn ventured. "She likes the goats, all right."

Annika looked at her. Even if she had thought, after her revelation with Karlyn at Tina's birthday party, that she might consider striking up a relationship with her, it wasn't going to happen when she was feeling like this.

"Thanks for letting us know," she said, as if Karlyn were a county official come to deliver information about construction on the road.

It didn't take long for her father's silence to take a toll on Annika's state of mind. It didn't matter that she was the one who had started this. He was the adult here.

She felt so bad, she got into town one day to do a little surreptitious research at the public library. Reckless endangerment with a deadly weapon, a felony charge. At least. And not a minor anymore. No. She couldn't turn herself in. It was simply impossible.

With winter not even over yet, Annika skipped ahead to worrying about how she'd feel in the spring. What would happen to her when the snow melted, the ditches went down, the deep spread of water in the backyard dried up, the new green came, and piece by piece the county was lit on fire? Would she feel her usual thrill when the burns that got away from farmers smoldered in the peat bogs, putting off the dark, musky and sweet, stirring and pungent spring smoke that filled her eyes with water? When the land that had been a soft, bright green a day before one morning looked, as far as she could see out of either side of the bus windows, as if it had been rubbed with charcoal? It had always been a satisfying challenge to her imagination and heart to look at the charred potato fields and feel they were ready for her now.

Her father was the one thing that had always been available to her. So. Perhaps none of her joys could be separated from her father, had in fact never been separate from him.

In a series of March storms, they got dumped on, another two feet of snow. One day when her father was in town, Annika sat in the house letting the stoves go out. She pulled a charred piece of wood out of the fire and let it cool until she could handle it. It worked pretty well to mark up her face. She rubbed it under her eyes, across her forehead, cheeks, and neck. She looked at herself in the mirror. She had the idea to put on the torn leather vest from the hobo costume she'd put together one Halloween. She took off the vest, tore it up some more, and put it on again. Around her wrists, she tied rags from the garage, stained with paint and varnish.

By the time her father's truck pulled into the driveway, Annika had added more things. She wanted to show him. She crouched by the stove, her head buried in her chest. When her father came in, she raised her face.

He rolled his eyes and walked away. Later that morning, Annika left the house for the barn, where she sat atop the dwindling pile of hay bales, still in her costume, and cried. The horses' stalls needed to be mucked out. They were starting to smell. If her father wanted her to do it, he could say so. Otherwise, she was done. She wasn't going to respond to a stupid note, either. Her mad, feverish feeling doubled when she sat long enough to intentionally miss lunch.

She ducked beneath the barn window when she saw her father walking around the yard. He was calling her name. She slipped out the door and took off past him at high speed, heading toward the cow pasture.

She slogged through the drifted snow. At one of the warming sheds, she felt weak and ducked inside. Shocked by her sudden appearance, two of the cows almost fell over on their buckling legs to get away from her, one rearing halfway up on the other, then pushing her with a moan out the doorway.

An oozing patty steamed and slowly froze before her. Annika sat dizzily in the shadows looking at it and breathing in the fresh stink. Finally, she went back outside, blinking. There was a lot of snow. Several yards out, breaking through the frozen top layer, she fell to her knees and began digging a hole; when she had gotten far enough, she began to dig horizontally, beneath the crust that was as thick as a frosted glass plate.

Putting her head into the hole, Annika dug a tunnel the length of her body. When it was done, she crawled inside and lay there. Then the cows were not afraid, and she felt them begin to come around and look. She lay on her back, a tremor in her stomach. Even through the ice, the glare of the white sun was too bright. She closed her eyes. She listened for the cows' breath, for their cumbersome bodies like leather sacks of metal tools, for their sharp hooves, for the moist splat of their piss on the soft snow.

In time, the possibility of one collapsing with a great suffocating bellow into her hole filled her with a sweet terror. That was something. It felt good to not want to be crushed. She waited. One of the herd got close.

Annika was just about to crawl out when there was bawling and a rush of hooves away from her. Something lightweight broke the brilliant crystal sheet. Not only crumbles of ice, but Mash's warm tongue was down her collar.

Poor old lonely Mash . . . who had started trembling when he went into the barn at night. They would have to get another dog. He did not have Tippy's stoutness of heart. He wouldn't be able to stand it.

There was fur in Annika's eyes and mouth. She pushed Mash's soggy mouth from her lips. A few yards away, her father was standing in the early-afternoon light. Annika sat up patting the dog. Her father squinted at her and pulled out a fresh stick of Doublemint. Annika scraped fur from her tongue and stood.

"I know you hate me," she said. "Do you at least still love me, too?"

Her father's long body sagged to one side. "Nick. You know I do."

For a minute, he stood there chewing. He sat down cross-legged in the snow, and Annika came to cuddle up beside him. He held her and asked what were they going to do? Not this kind of thing. They had to stick together.

Annika felt like sobbing. She sat quietly and shook her head into her father's coat.

After a while, he said that he had gotten to thinking about something. He waited quietly until Annika asked what.

"When do you think Tina's due?" he said. And what was going to happen to her after she had the baby?

"Do you think they'd hurt her?" Annika said.

"I don't know enough about the whole thing to know if they would or wouldn't."

Walking back to the house, all at once Annika felt something new: she was going to do something. Yes. She didn't know exactly what. Tina was due in less than a month.

In a few days, she had decided. She was going to sneak over to the Haases' sometime after dark. Peep through the window to check on Tina, the way Sherry used to do.

CHAPTER 11

Before Annika had picked a night to go, part of their question was answered for them. A few weeks later, after being dark all this time, there were lights on at Tina and Jesse's house. Smoke rose from the chimney. The brown truck was still gone. It hadn't been there since the night Annika had fired her shot.

A day or two later, Annika and her father saw Haas and Laura in the parking lot of the grocery store in Baudette and Haas was carrying a car seat. How strange for the child to be so suddenly real! For Annika, Tina's pregnancy had been so much about her being pregnant that she'd hardly considered the baby at all.

When she stepped away from the truck to get a closer look, her father put his hand out to stop her. But even from this far, she could see it: undoubtedly a real, live, tiny baby, slumped in its seat. Mostly covered with a blanket, that was all she could see. Possibly a shock of dark hair, maybe only a shadow on a bald head.

She wondered if it looked like Jesse or Haas. Maybe just like Tina. That would be a cute baby, with little red-brown cat eyes.

The Haases looked tired and unkempt. Haas's beard was downright wild. You could hardly see his neck. His curls getting more gray than blond now, growing into a cloud like Jesse's. Haas had once made Annika think of a man who made his living out of doors, a lumberjack or a voyageur, one who kept a neat cabin, a mat to clean your feet on, carving boards hanging on the walls made from slices of raw tree rounds, well sanded and oiled. A good friendly dog in there or a cat. But what did the drawings of voyageurs that hung in the county museum know? The men going over a waterfall in their Montreal canoe were shaggy, but still they looked clean. Haas wasn't clean. A white dribble ran down his coat. His bug eyes were tired and hooded. He looked like a sloppy old drunk.

There were circles under Laura's big doll eyes too. She walked several steps behind her husband, looking irritated and trying to catch up, hauling two sacks of groceries, trudging in the direction of their car.

"Gordon," she brayed at him across the parking lot.

If either she or her husband saw Annika and her father, they pretended not to. After getting their groceries, Annika and her father went to the bait store. On the drive over, Annika mentioned with contempt that if she ever decided to have babies of her own, she wasn't going to wait until she was old enough to be somebody's grandmother.

Her father wasn't listening; he seemed to be thinking about something else.

While Annika was waiting in the truck for her father, someone pushed the shop door open. It was Sherry. She stalked out muttering to herself. Annika hadn't seen her since the night Sherry had come to find her in the dark on County 4.

Annika sat up straight and watched out the truck window to see where Sherry would go. She got out of the truck and found her father in the bait store. She told him she had something else to do in town and to wait for her.

She found Sherry having a smoke on the sidewalk. Huddled under the awning of the brown-brick Rex Hotel in her baggy black trench coat. It was strange to see her wrecked tennis shoes on pavement instead of sinking into mud or snow. With the addition of a duster hat and a neckerchief, she would have looked as out of place here in civilization as Calamity Jane.

Sherry was watching a neatly dressed woman come out of the bank across the street. When the woman got a look at Sherry, she turned around and walked the other way.

Annika stepped in front of her. Sherry kept her eyes fixed across the road. She looked tired and subdued. And sober. That was unnerving. "Hi," Annika said.

Sherry didn't look at her. She let out a stream of smoke.

"Well," she said finally. "You been keeping yourself busy?"

"I guess so. How about you?"

"Oh, yeah."

"What are you doing in town?"

"What are *you* doing in town?"

"Are you living here now?"

"Living in town?" Sherry said. "Not this stuck-up town."

"You're not staying at the Rex?"

Sherry shrugged.

"Well. It was getting cold." Sherry was quiet. "Do you have family in town?" Annika asked her.

"No. I wasn't born here. Thank God."

"Where are you from?" It was hard to imagine Sherry being born or coming from anywhere; it was easier to imagine her springing fully formed from a tree or rising out of the ground.

"Cold—it wasn't even that cold. I can build a fire. This is the South to me."

"You're from Canada?"

Sherry shrugged and finished her cigarette. She flicked it to the sidewalk and ground it under her shoe. She put her arms around herself and shivered. She stared at Annika as if to avoid turning to look at the door to the Rex. "Well. I'm done with my smoke," she said.

"Do you still have family there? Did you come to the States to work for the DNR?"

"What's with all the questions?"

"I'm just curious." Annika smiled bravely. "We're friends, aren't we?" Sherry softened and grinned back at her. Then she moved up close, smelling of tobacco and shampoo. No alcohol. In her low, throaty voice, she said she hadn't left Graceton because it was winter. No. She hadn't wanted to go. She'd been cozy in another shack she'd found deep in the woods on Haas's place. This place was deluxe. Kapinsky had insulated it and put in a stone fireplace with a roasting spit. Flashlights and batteries, a metal trunk filled with books. A rocking chair. Sherry stayed until the day Haas figured out she was in it.

"He didn't want me near her," Sherry said.

"Laura?"

"It didn't matter anymore about Laura."

"Tina? What did he think you were going to do to her?"

"Do to her? He didn't want me to help her escape," Sherry said.

"You were going to?"

"Why not?"

"Did she want to?"

"Of course she did."

"You asked her?"

"Did *you*?"

"Did you think he was going to hurt her?" Annika said.

"I saw he got the baby," Sherry said.

"She didn't want the baby . . ."

"He said that if I didn't clear out, he'd make me disappear. He would've done it, too." Sherry added that once, Haas had knocked her out cold. Of course, he would say that had been part of their game. But that blow, for Sherry, marked the end of anything she was playing. She should have known from the start they were an ill-suited match. Neither of them liked to play the role of the prisoner. That was a big problem. Both of them preferred blocking the door. They were terrible for one another. They traded off grudgingly, until they didn't. By the end, playing had become a real battle for both of them. That day, Haas started knocking Sherry around as if he were going to kill her. Not that Sherry didn't get in a few good ones, too. But she was in over her head. Running away, she got as far as the stairs.

When she woke up in the dark of the attic, the back of her head was killing her. She figured the coward had whacked her from behind. He had stripped her too. "I wouldn't have done that to him. Taken his clothes? It would have been funny. But I wouldn't have done it," Sherry said.

Annika listened squeamishly, looking down at the sidewalk. Sherry was lighting another cigarette. "She didn't want *him* to get the baby," she said. "But you knew that."

"Well," Annika said.

"How's Tina now? I saw the baby," Sherry said again.

Annika noticed her father's truck coming slowly down the street. She looked back at Sherry. Sherry shook her head.

"You didn't check on Tina," she said. "You didn't check your traps."

"What?"

Sherry laughed and after a moment, Annika did too. A roasting spit! Had she fed Sherry through the winter? That was all right. "Are you going to say anything?" she asked Sherry after a while.

Sherry stopped laughing.

"About what?" she said.

Annika spoke in a low voice. "About the Haases. Tina and the baby."

"Why?" Sherry said slowly. "You think I should? Are you?"

"I don't know."

Sherry looked at her for a second. She gave her a hard smile.

"Maybe," Annika said.

"I doubt it." Sherry took a step back toward the building. "Did he send you to check on me?"

"No." Annika felt a guilty-looking flush rise to her cheeks. She shook her head. Her father was parking next to them on the street. She glanced at the truck as Sherry drew away from her, getting closer to the door.

"I'm not making trouble for him," she said. "Tell him that. I haven't been out there in months."

"I don't talk to him," Annika said.

"I'm not even drinking. I'm not going to get drunk and say nothing. Why's he asking about my family?"

"He's not. He didn't send me," Annika said as Sherry turned and went into the crumbling old hotel and reached back and slammed the door.

On the way home, Annika read aloud from the Baudette paper that Haas would be leaving his job at the school when his contract was up at the end of this year.

Her father didn't respond. After seeing the baby, he was probably thinking only of Tina. Where was she now? he wondered aloud. Was it Tina who was at the house?

Now it was time, if Annika was going to do it, to find out. To check in on her. Yes. Sherry was right. It was rotten not to do it. She could do it quietly.

Why hadn't she gone yet? Many evenings, she'd watched her father stand outside in the chilly air, looking at the gray-pink sky to the north. One morning, she found him in Sparky's stall, his face pressed into the gelding's neck, the horse's mane caught up in his fist. What was worse, what was hurting him more? That he'd betrayed her mother? Or that he'd done it for nothing?

Her father's quiet melancholy began to wear Annika down. She thought after a while that as awful as it had been, she preferred his iciness. She began to wonder if the bad feelings that had developed between her and her father this past summer had ever gone away, and if the two of them would always swing back and forth like this as long as they lived here together.

On a Saturday afternoon in late April, Annika planned her first reconnaissance mission, a stroll past Tina and Jesse's house. As she was
leaving the driveway, she had an idea and stopped. She went back to
the trailer and packed a bag. Clothes and food, matches and a flashlight, a small handsaw, a few other tools.

She went up 4 instead of turning at 66. At Karlyn and Doug's driveway, after a few minutes of looking around, she began to call softly
for Tippy.

She raised her voice a little. The dog rounded the corner of the
house. But at first, she didn't come. When Annika stepped into the
driveway, the dog began to bark. Another call and whistle finally
brought her slobbering into Annika's arms.

Continuing to call the dog, while looking back every once and a
while to see that she was following, Annika ran back south on the
road.

Spring was on its way. The temperature was fifty-five degrees, the
remaining snow soft, even in the heavy shade of the pine trees. Dirt
and dead grass were everywhere. In the ditches, nearly five feet of water was running as hard and fast as in the river. The level kept rising
as old snow and new from spring storms went on melting in the sun.
The water inched up toward the road, threatening to lap over. Soon
the crappies would be running. Annika threw in sticks and watched
them be borne off on the noisy current until they caught in the fence
or brush or swirled into a culvert. She felt just a glimmer of the pleasant springtime anxiety this activity had always brought her.

Sloshing through the icy puddles, the thick wet dirt and gravel, she
started thinking that with a clean-up job Frank Gamache had hired
her to do in May, she could soon have her car. If she still wanted it.

With her own vehicle, she would be able to go wherever, whenever.
Into the state forest as much as she wanted. For mushrooms, wild onions. Photographs, too, for her wildlife paintings. She had gone back
to a more conventional, fully representational style. Ben Svitok, the

only professional painter in the county, who had the market cornered on every duck, stag, walleye, or moose commissioned by a resort or restaurant, had to be seventy by now. His hand wouldn't stay steady forever.

She could also put in her application for a smokechaser. Probably smokechasers didn't make a fortune. But who could save money the way she could? She and her father might build that house someday after all. A big cabin, with plenty of room to stretch their legs.

Annika could even put on a dress and lipstick once in a while, drive over to some of those wild Canadian town-hall dances she'd heard about, held on Saturday nights in Stratton and Berglund after curling tournaments and softball games.

Maybe she'd even drag her lonely old dad along, why not?

Ontario had a lower drinking age, nineteen. She'd be nineteen in July. She'd have to be careful not to get too drunk. Or to get very close to anyone. What if she spilled the beans about how she'd once shot a man? That kind of thing could happen when your guard was down. What if someone turned her in? Even if she got out of jail one day, she was sure you couldn't have that kind of criminal history if you wanted to work for the DNR.

The thought was depressing. Annika reverted to her initial plan of disappearing with the dog into the woods.

She turned onto 66. Sherry wasn't using Tina and Jesse's cabin anymore. Why shouldn't she?

She had meant to avoid pausing at Jesse and Tina's driveway. But a blue car was parked by the house. While she was standing on the road looking at it, a girl with short blond hair, not Tina, came out of the house with a cardboard box and packed it in the trunk.

Fiddling with a branch in her hand, Annika stared at the car and the girl. Then, carrying a length of orange cord, Tina came around the corner of the house.

Annika felt a current of emotion jolt through her. Tina looked so different from the last time Annika had seen her, when she'd been so sluggish and uncomfortable. At least from this distance, she was now the sleek, lively girl she'd been when Annika had first seen her last summer.

She wore a pale green coat, a jaunty beret. Her red hair swinging. Just as it had been with Tina's baby, it was somehow a shock to see her alive at all.

The other girl went back into the house. Tina tossed the rope into the open trunk and started to follow her. Something made her turn around—did she feel Annika's eyes on her? For a moment, they looked at each other.

Annika raised a hand and waved. She tossed the branch, took a few steps forward.

Tina turned without waving back. She went into the house, shutting the door firmly behind her.

The sound stuck in Annika's chest. For several minutes, she stood and looked at the quiet yard. The girls didn't come back out. A killdeer looping the sodden fields made its disquieting, cantering song. Finally, Annika started walking again, continuing east, her legs shaking.

At the pasture turn-off, she tossed her bag over the fence. She crossed it and walked through the field, up into Tina's woods, where she knew every single ditch, copse, leaf, tree, log, and stone. The waterlogged mush of mud and grasses was putting off its sharp, melancholy, decomposing smell.

Tina was free, it appeared, to go wherever and whenever she chose. So things had turned out all right?

But why hadn't she gone to the police about the Haases and Jesse? Told them what she'd gone through? Told the police that when the time came, she was all alone. That she hadn't had any real choice about what she did with the baby.

Maybe Tina was protecting herself. Maybe she was afraid of the Haases and wanted to get far away first. That would make sense.

Or maybe, if the Haases had told Tina about Annika shooting Jesse, Tina's silence was to protect *her*.

And Annika had done nothing—nothing—as brave and selfless as that!

She felt vomit rise halfway up her throat. She stopped walking in the sopping field to bend over and gag.

She came up on a pond of opaque water twenty feet across which had collected in a depression. In the middle of the water rose a stubborn, moldy-looking lump of snow like an iceberg. Swallows skittered over the surface and the sun glinted off it. Tippy started to wade in. She dipped in only her front paws before backing out and shaking herself.

Annika threw a rock at a jay. Then she bent a young sapling in half with her boot until it broke tenderly into white and green splinters. It made her feel rotten and she didn't do it again.

She felt course through her another charge of feeling. She ran her hands hard up through her hair, went down on her knees into the chilly muck. Her bag fell off her shoulder and her matches and peanut-butter crackers spilled onto the wet ground, but it didn't matter anymore.

She was going back home. She was going to get in the truck and drive and she was going to find out what the inside of the police station looked like.

Terror, relief. A vicious gladness. Oh, the hour was coming . . . Oh, God, it was now . . . Yes, she was going to go ahead and get it over with, quickly, before Tina left today. Annika got up and stumbled and began to run. Tippy barked and dashed ahead of her to the road.

Until the last moment, she hadn't even known it was happening . . . that she was getting up the nerve to tell!

NOTES

"Rosalita" on page 72 is an original song by Matt Pudas. Recorded by the White Iron Band on *Live @ Cabooze* (2006) and *3rd Rate Country Stars* (2010), produced by the White Iron Band (Matt Pudas, Eddie Juntunen, Samher Weyandt, Jeff Underhill, Matt Walvatne, & Greg Hall).

"No Meat on the Bone" on page 72 is an original song by Doug Otto. Recorded by Doug Otto & The Getaways (Doug Otto, Albert Perez, Chris Gray, Eric Struve, Shane Akers, & Kari Shaw Akers) on *Waltz of Pain*, by Doug Otto & The Getaways, 2017.

The quotation on page 78 is from Elinor Wylie's poem "Sea Lullaby." Quoted from *The Premiere Book of Major Poets*, Ed. Anita Dore. New York: Fawcett Books, 1970.

Lyrics on page 131 are excerpted from the author's free translation of "Margoton va-t-á l'eau" (Margoton goes for water), a French Canadian folk song, found in *The Voyageurs and Their Songs*, Ed. Theodore C. Blegen. Minnesota Historical Society: St. Paul, 1966. Pp. 17–18.

BIOGRAPHICAL NOTE

Cheri Johnson has won grants and residencies from organizations such as the McKnight Foundation, the Bush Foundation, Yaddo, and the Fine Arts Work Center in Provincetown. She studied writing at the University of Minnesota, Hollins University, and Augsburg University. Her chapbook of poems, *Fun & Games*, was published by Finishing Line Press in 2009 and she's written two series of nonfiction books for young readers for Full Tilt Press. *Crocus Hill: A Ghost Story*, a literary performance project she created with the composer Julie Johnson, the filmmaker D.J. Mendel, and the new-music ensemble Zeitgeist, was supported by the Knight Foundation. She's published fiction and other work in magazines such as *Pleiades*, *Glimmer Train Stories*, *Puerto del Sol*, and *New South*, and her novel *The Girl in Duluth*, which she published under the name Sigrid Brown, won a 2023 Midwest Book Award. She lives in Minneapolis, Minnesota, where she critiques manuscripts as an editor at the Loft Literary Center and writes about books and the performing arts on Instagram @CheriJohnsonArt.